Saving Texas

Nancy Stancill

To Erin –
Fellow IRE
enthusiast and
reporter. I thank
you for your
support.
all the best,
Nancy Stancill
4/6/15

Black Rose Writing
www.blackrosewriting.com

ISBN: 978-1-61296-257-3

PUBLISHED BY BLACK ROSE WRITING

www.blackrosewriting.com

Printed in the United States of America

Saving Texas is printed in Adobe Caslon Pro

To my parents,
Phyllis Harrill Pruden and the late Godfrey Wells Stancill
with gratitude for educating me and believing in me.

Saving Texas

CHAPTER 1

Annie wondered if there was something about Texas that unleashed the worst in its people. Was the state she loved unraveling, its golden age receding, an era of chaos looming? Her deadline approached, so she wrote quickly. She tapped out a story and posted it on the *Houston Times* website.

Her story detailed a bizarre crime along the Texas border. Four armed Hispanic men had attacked about 20 elderly parishioners shuffling out of early mass at a Laredo church. The sheriff had told her the assailants beat them and stole their cash and jewelry. One victim had died and two were hospitalized with serious injuries. He blamed it on the Zetas, the notorious drug ring based across the Rio Grande, but Annie was skeptical since he had no evidence. Annie wondered if he was letting border-city paranoia color his judgment.

The story pulled at her heart and lingered as she scrambled toward the end of her early-morning shift as a fill-in reporter for the website. Would such casual cruelty put border cities off-limits for travelers? Could something like that happen to her parents? Would her headache go away if she poked out her throbbing eye? She had drunk too much last night, again. As she fretted, her cell phone rang, showing a name she knew. She straightened up, feeling the tension in her shoulders. It was a call she'd hoped for, but didn't know how she'd handle.

"*Houston Times*, Annie Price speaking."

"Is this the lady with the loveliest legs in Houston?"

"Hello, Jake," Annie said in a low voice, whirling around to see if anyone was listening. Reporters sat in pods of four desks with no privacy for personal calls. Luckily, it was still early enough that the newsroom was sparsely occupied.

"Are you mad at me?" He said in a plaintive tone.

She let him hang while she decided how to answer. To her chagrin, just hearing Jake Satterfield's voice made her body tingle. Tall and nicely built, the state senator from Kerrville had curly hair, twinkly blue eyes and a slight, Elvis-like swagger when he walked. But she was hurt and angry that he hadn't called for two weeks.

"Why would I be mad?"

"I've meant to be in touch before now," Jake said. "I'll explain later. What are you working on?"

"I just posted a story about an attack on some old folks in Laredo."

"I saw it on your website, so I took the chance that you'd be in. Do you have a moment to talk about a really big story?"

"How big?"

"Do you know who Tom Marr is?"

"Isn't he a legislator from somewhere in West Texas?"

"That's right," Jake said. "He's a friend of mine and quite an impressive guy. He's a great politician who wants to be our next governor."

"Yeah? He's not exactly alone in that ambition," Annie said. "I can think of a dozen possible candidates and the election's two years away. What makes him so special?"

"One word. Secession."

"Oh no, not that crazy idea again. This had better be good."

"It's better than good, it's fantastic. His deal is to make Texas more like a nation than a state."

"I guess he's taking that bumper sticker seriously," Annie said. "You know, the one that says, 'Texas: It's like a whole other country.' Is he a wacko?"

"Not at all," Jake said. "He's from a good old Texas family of ranchers. He owns lots of land in West Texas and people love him out there. He's done really well for someone who's only forty-eight, but he lives a pretty quiet life on his ranch near Marfa."

"Marfa? Where the heck is that?"

"It's the sweetest little town in Presidio County."

"Down near the border?"

"Yep, midway between Alpine and Valentine."

"Gosh, that helps a lot. Keep going."

"Tom got a history degree with honors from UT a few years before I did," Jake said. "He could have stayed in Austin or gone somewhere bigger, teaching and writing books. But he went back to West Texas and took over the family business when his dad got sick."

"Tell me more," said Annie, jotting notes on a legal pad she kept beside her phone.

"His wife died about six years ago from breast cancer and he stayed close to home after that, raising his little girl. But now that Betsy's older, he's had time to get involved in politics."

"In what way?"

"Four years ago, he ran for the Legislature from his district and rolled over his opponent without breaking a sweat," Jake said. "He spent his first term learning and now he's like a man who's just discovered his purpose in life."

"And that would be?"

"Governing Texas in a whole new way. Saving Texas from the corruption and stupidity in Washington. Making Texas great again."

He paused briefly. "He could be the leader we've been waiting for since the Alamo."

Annie shifted in her seat, irritated by the awe in his voice. "Is this a man-crush?"

He laughed. "I'm not that easy. He's a once-in-a-lifetime candidate."

"Where do I fit in?"

"You're not only bewitchingly beautiful, you're the best reporter in Houston," Jake said. "I thought you could spend time with him and write one of those long stories you do so well. What do you call them?"

"Sunday profiles?"

"That's it," he said. "You know if it's in the *Houston Times*, AP will pick it up and every paper in the state'll run it. I'll make sure you get exclusive access. I'm going to be heavily involved in his campaign because Texas needs him now."

"So you're a secessionist now, Jake?"

He ignored her question and said, "I'll be in Houston Wednesday. Can I meet you for a drink to tell you more?"

"I'll meet you somewhere, but I won't be drinking anything but coffee," Annie said.

"Aw, Annie. Don't be sore at me. I think you're terrific. And you know I'm trying to get my personal life in order. I'll explain when I see you."

"Yeah, yeah, yeah," Annie said. "Let's keep this on a business level. What time on Wednesday and where?"

"Can you meet me at Chuy's on Westheimer at 5? I'll buy you some Tex-Mex. I need my fix before I drive back to Kerrville."

She scribbled the appointment on her big, month-at-a-glance desk calendar, which she preferred to digital scheduling. "Okay, see you then."

"Did you get the roses?" Jake added.

"Yes, they were beautiful." Her tone softened. "Thank you."

"Bye, Annie."

Annie smiled as she hung up the phone. She found Jake's rakish charm endearing, but knew she should steer clear of him. She was a 36-year-old journalist who was serious about her work and he'd be, at best, a distraction. She didn't want her heart broken by a man who had split with his wife and could easily find his way back home. At her age, many of the men she dated were divorced or divorcing. But that made for complicated relationships that often ended disastrously. In one short-lived romance, the guy she was smitten with suddenly picked up and moved 2,000 miles away to be with his kids. In another fiasco, the man's estranged wife threatened to hunt her down, shoot her and dump her body in the Houston Ship Channel.

Also, Jake was an up-and-coming politician, someone she probably would have to deal with on future stories. Sleeping with a source happened now and then in the high-pressure craziness of the journalism world, but it wasn't exactly a smart thing to do.

Annie had worked at the *Houston Times* for six years as a general-assignment reporter. As a GA, she reported on just about any kind of big story that cropped up, ranging from Friday night killings to coastal oil spills. But she had made a name for herself writing in-depth profiles of politicians and people in the news. She hoped the increasing sophistication of her work would convince her editors to promote her. The best reporting jobs in the newsroom were reserved for the veterans on the investigative team. She wanted to be like them, to spend months on big projects and produce important stories that led to meaningful change. She worried that she was running out of time in her professional – and personal – life.

Two months previously, her assignment to cover a three-day state budget retreat in Austin had spilled over to the weekend. After she filed her final daily story and the weekender that wrapped it all up for the Sunday paper, she went to an informal drinks session at the Intercontinental Hotel, which old-timers still called the Stephen F. Austin. Politicians filled the second-floor bar and terrace that jutted out on Congress Avenue, downtown Austin's main street. The late afternoon light shimmered down the long, sloping thoroughfare and metamorphosed into a brilliant orange January sunset. She felt exhilarated to be in that room, listening to the high-level political talk and relaxing after three days of tense reporting on the budget.

She found herself standing next to Jake with her glass of Chardonnay. Annie, five feet eleven and three-quarters inches, liked men to be at least as tall as she was. Being a tall woman wasn't easy, even in Texas where men and women often seemed larger than life. Shorter men either resented her height or flocked to her like the seven dwarves around Snow White. She'd had her share of dates that reminded her of what the mother-in-law of the late Alabama Gov. George Wallace had said about him, "He ain't titty high." Taller men often seemed to prefer short women, which she viewed as a tragic waste.

Annie thought she looked okay. Her long, dark hair, green eyes and a face she thought resembled the black-and-white photographs of her Scots-Irish great-grandparents, weren't bad. But her height seemed to jinx her luck with men. She didn't lack attention, but she felt it usually was the wrong kind. Why was it that she always got more propositions than dinner dates? The pattern seemed to continue at the Austin bar that night. Jake, whom she had met a few times on stories, took charge of the evening. After a long night punctuated by his funny political tales and many glasses of Chardonnay, she ended up in his hotel room.

When she woke the next morning in the four-poster bed at the Driskill, she slid out from under the covers, intending to escape. But Jake was awake and put his arm around her, pulling her back.

"Not so fast, Sweet Annie," he said. "I haven't had enough of you yet."

He made love to her carefully and slowly, as if making up for the night before when they rushed into the room, threw off their clothes and grabbed each other. Annie didn't usually enjoy morning-after sex, thinking most men seemed better when she was drunk than when she experienced them in the sober light of day. It was different with Jake. Afterwards, she nestled in his arms for a few minutes.

"Hey, don't look at your watch," Jake said. "You're spoiling the vibe."

"Sorry. I've got to work a Sunday night reporting shift starting at 3. I can't hang around here, much as I might like to."

He laughed as she sat up and swung her legs to the floor beside the bed.

"What are you laughing at?"

"I've never been with a woman whose limbs are as long as mine."

"Is that a bad thing?"

"No, it's a wonderful thing. We fit together well."

"Consider it my leg-acy."

"Oh no," he groaned. "Not a punster!"

"Only when I'm happy," she smiled. "I can't help being a word geek."

Jake came to Houston the next Sunday to see her. A week after that, he asked her to spend a Saturday with him in Austin. Their relationship seemed to hold promise – until her phone had gone silent two weeks ago.

However, red roses had arrived last week at the office, drawing whistles and comments from her raucous colleagues. But he hadn't followed up with a call until today.

She didn't know where things were heading with him, but she had a bad feeling about it. His cryptic words about needing to explain something added to her pessimism. She vowed again to cut down on alcohol – and the men who usually came with it. But as a journalist, she wasn't going to pass up a great tip for a story, just because it came from a source with whom she had the bad judgment to sleep.

She'd focus on his tip about Tom Marr and think about the relationship later. She lived by the journalist's maxim that men came and went, but a great story lasted forever. Marr sounded interesting and secession was a sexy topic. Could he be the big story she was looking for?

CHAPTER 2

Annie knocked on the door to the small glass office where her editor, Priscilla Gage, was talking on the phone. Cilla, as everyone called her, motioned to her to wait, so she stood outside. Assigning editors like Cilla had the smallest of the fishbowl-type offices that ringed the newsroom. Higher-level editors had the larger spaces with window views and nicer furniture. Annie knew some of her fellow reporters watched their bosses' visitors and interactions obsessively and sent gossipy emails speculating about who was in favor – or in trouble.

She looked at the short, stubby figure inside and wondered what kind of mood her mercurial boss would be in today. Would Cilla allow her to work on a profile of Tom Marr? Annie was doubtful, because she knew Cilla wasn't keen on assigning her to stories on politicians. She just might refer it to the political desk. She'd be a hard sell, so Annie would step carefully and chat her up before broaching the request.

Cilla was a 45-year-old assistant city editor who had joined the *Times* staff ten years before. She had done her time on small-town Texas papers before making it to the big-city newspaper she had grown up reading. Annie knew Cilla had worked her way out of redneck poverty in Pasadena, a gritty town near Houston nicknamed Stinkadena for the noxious odors rising from its oil refineries.

She could be demanding and temperamental, but Annie loved her big heart and passion for good stories. She knew Cilla cared about her and the five other reporters she supervised and tried to look out for their interests in an increasingly difficult newsroom environment. She noticed that Cilla had cut her difficult-to-tame, red-gold hair into a bouncy bob.

"Hey, Cilla, your hair looks great," she said, walking into the office.

"Yeah, it's better, isn't it?" But Annie noticed she looked shaken.

"Damn it," Cilla burst out. "We're losing another good reporter. Bob Tolliver is taking a PR job with the University of Houston."

"Another traitor? The nerve of him!" Annie said.

"He says he's given up on the industry and wants to jump ship before it sinks."

"Rotten coward. Of course he does have to support a wife who can't work..."

"And two kids," Cilla finished. "I suppose I shouldn't blame him."

"Will you be able to replace him?"

"I seriously doubt it," she said. "It stinks. We used to have three reporters covering cops twenty-four hours, four education reporters to cover all the bigger school districts and ten reporters covering most of the smaller towns around Houston. Now we just patch and fill."

"You're right about that," Annie said. "Is the paper ever going to hire another reporter to cover border issues? Things are getting ugly there."

"Probably not in our lifetime."

She continued ranting for a few minutes. Annie had heard most of it before. She sank into a chair beside Cilla's desk and let her mind wander.

A year ago, feeling confident of her future at the *Times*, she had bought a small house in the old Heights neighborhood near downtown. She adored the two-bedroom bungalow and didn't regret the purchase. But she stretched to pay the mortgage, and real estate values had fallen since then. What would she do if she were laid off? Her neck stiffened with tension and she tried to push back those thoughts.

"We can't put enough reporters in the newsroom on weekends any more. What happens if we have another hurricane?" Cilla was saying.

"I know. It's depressing. Are you hearing any fresh rumors?"

"No, they're keeping low-level editors like me in the dark. But everyone seems to think it's just a matter of time before the paper changes hands."

"God, what would that mean for us?"

"You know the two small layoffs we had last year? They'd be nothing compared to the slashing that a new owner might do."

"Why did I ever think it would be smart to buy a house?" Annie moaned.

"Annie, you're not the only one with a mortgage under water. We're all screwed right now. Of course, I may be wrong."

"The Carters have always cared about this paper. Didn't they put money into it to keep it going during the Depression?"

"Yeah, but we've got to face reality," Cilla said. "Family-owned publications are dying off because the younger generation thinks newspapers will be toast in five years. They'd rather Twitter their time away."

"But Old Man Carter still loves the paper, doesn't he? I still see him coming to work."

"Yeah, but his days are numbered, in more ways than one. I'll bet that if the family gets a halfway decent offer, the younger Carters would take the money and run quicker than you could say so long, partner."

"You're probably right," Annie said. "But maybe one of the grandchildren will discover an urgent calling to be a journalist."

"Yeah, and I'm going to be crowned the queen of Dallas," Cilla said. She abruptly changed the subject. "What do you want, Annie? I've got to get to the news meeting."

Annie took a deep breath and forced herself to sound composed.

"I got a great tip about a politician who's going to announce for governor soon."

"Yeah, who?"

"Tom Marr, a West Texas House member from Marfa. Of course, our Austin bureau can handle his announcement, but I'd like to profile him," Annie said.

"Why should we care about a West Texas nobody at this stage of the game?"

"He supposedly supports secession and has the money for a big secessionist campaign. Remember the big flap when Governor Perry shot off his mouth about Texas leaving the union if it didn't like what the feds were doing?" Annie said.

"Yeah, the Guv made Texas the laughingstock of the country," Cilla recalled. "But that was 2009 and he was just showing off."

"Well, Marr's different. He's a history scholar who's looking at secession in a serious and practical way."

"Jesus Christ. Why does Texas keep producing these lunatics?" Cilla said. "We'll embarrass ourselves so much, other states will want to throw US out."

"Yeah, we've got more than our share of nutty politicians," Annie said. "But he doesn't seem to be one of them. Senator Jake Satterfield says he'll get us exclusive access. I'd like to be the first to pin down Marr in a Sunday profile. It could be political dynamite."

"Not a bad idea," Cilla admitted. "But we don't have much money for travel, you know."

"I'll do the background work from here and drive myself to West Texas for interviews," Annie said.

"Come on, Cilla," she urged. "We're still a statewide newspaper. We can't stop doing big stories because they break beyond the Houston borders."

"Okay. But you've got to finish up two other stories. And where's the profile you promised me last week about the murdered hooker in the bayou?"

"I'm all over it."

CHAPTER 3

Alicia Perez woke up at dawn in a room that smelled like jasmine flowers. For a few seconds, she panicked, not recalling where she was, but then she relaxed and stretched lazily. She remembered that she had slept with Carmen, whose long dark hair splayed across the pillow next to her. Carmen was a potter who lived in a small frame house in a tattered barrio in San Antonio. She was one of a few dozen artists recruited by Alicia to make high-quality goods for her sales business at the Mexican Market.

Alicia had been staying with Carmen during the last few months when she came to San Antonio on business. Last night, the two of them had gone to a Peruvian restaurant to celebrate a great Christmas season at El Mercado. The market was popular with tourists who came to San Antonio to celebrate the season and its festive lights on the River Walk. El Mercado, near the river, drew throngs of visitors for its popular, south-of-the-border wares and a large Mexican cafe serving everything from early-morning breakfast tacos to late-night margaritas. Alicia never ate where the tourists ate. She preferred the smaller South American restaurants in the anonymous maze of barrio neighborhoods. She and Carmen had gone to a nearby cafe where they enjoyed roasted goat meat and a beautiful bottle of Chilean Carmenere before coming back and smoking marijuana in bed.

Alicia had her man, a devoted, longtime lover who visited her fairly often at her West Texas home. But when she traveled to San Antonio, as she frequently did, she did whatever she liked. When she returned to West Texas, she mostly kept to herself and didn't seek out the company of men -- or women.

As Carmen slept beside her, Alicia thought about the day

ahead. Besides the lucrative booth she maintained at El Mercado, she had a second business. Alicia knew it was more dangerous, but in some ways it suited her talents and inclinations better. She was what Anglos called an assassin, so good that she could find full-time work if she wanted. However, she accepted missions only from a few people she trusted. Today's assignment in Brownsville, a long drive to the south, would probably not be difficult, she thought. Her target was considered a loner, she knew where he worked and she doubted he'd be expecting trouble. Alicia had overheard some talk, so she had some idea why he was being dispatched, but no particular interest. She didn't pass judgment on her victims. Someone had already done that.

She padded softly to Carmen's hall bathroom, which also bore the scent of the jasmine perfume the potter used. The smell was beginning to feel cloying, probably because her instincts were telling her to hurry and leave. Alicia knew she was as smart as the next person, but she paid more attention to what her body told her because it had kept her alive. In Peru, where her life had been fraught with danger and hardship, she'd learned to trust no one.

She thought about her man as she showered in the tiny bathroom with the 1950s black and green linoleum. She suspected that he knew about her female lovers, but she doubted that he cared. He was gone most of the time anyway, so he shouldn't have the right to complain. It was sex and boredom, not love, that drew her to the women, mostly craftswomen she did business with in the barrio. She stepped out of the shower and dried herself with a worn yellow towel, pausing a moment to inspect her naked body for any evidence of fat. Though she was not young – she had just turned 50 – she prided herself on maintaining her slender, supple shape. She was disciplined, ate just enough to keep her weight stable and exercised diligently. She hated fat men or women. When she saw them on the street, she looked away in disgust. She touched the crescent-shaped scar on her forehead and wondered whether she needed to disguise herself. Probably not for this job, she thought. She knew that the white streak in the front of her long black hair was memorable, but she'd pile it all into a cap so it wouldn't be seen.

"Mi Cara Alicia," Carmen called from her small but spotlessly clean kitchen.

Alicia smelled good Colombian coffee and could see Carmen standing over the stove with a mauve robe tied over her slightly thick but shapely body. Good, Alicia thought, she could eat quickly, make her goodbyes and be on the road to Brownsville before 8 a.m.

She sat down at the small table for two beside the kitchen window and smiled as Carmen slid steaming scrambled eggs with green chilies and hot tortillas onto her plate. Alicia ate quickly without talking, eager to leave.

"Can you stay with me today?" Carmen said. "I could fix a picnic for us and we could ride out into the country in my pickup. I know a beautiful part of the river where we could swim naked."

Alicia could hear the pleading in Carmen's voice and knew she should snip that neediness in the bud.

"No, mi chica," she smiled. "Last night was fantastico, but you know I don't stay in San Antonio long. I have business in the Valley."

"When will you be back?"

This was too much to let pass. Alicia stared at her with unsmiling eyes in a cold, measuring gaze that usually stopped questions. Carmen looked away quickly.

"I'll be back in a few weeks, as usual," Alicia said. "You must stay busy making your beautiful turquoise bowls. You know we will make even more money with the new design."

"Si," said Carmen. They finished eating silently and Carmen carried Alicia's bag to the car like the obedient servant she was. Alicia made sure her goodbye was cool, just to keep Carmen at bay.

Soon Alicia was heading down U.S. 77 toward the Rio Grande Valley in her black Suburban, feeling lighter now that she was alone. Except for her man, who was in a special category, she couldn't tolerate the company of other people for much longer than the essential transactions, like sex, eating or killing, required to complete.

She arrived at a small farm outside of Brownsville in less than five hours, checking the address and other instructions to make sure she had turned down the right dusty road. She knew from the photograph supplied to her that her target was a middle-aged Hispanic man who was a worker on this farm. She drove slowly until she spotted the right pickup truck parked beside a field of vegetables. She could see the man walking between rows of tomatoes. She took her pistol with its silencer from underneath the driver's seat and tucked it into her jacket pocket.

She got out of the car, walked briskly and waved to the man in the field. He stopped working and smiled at her, looking confused but welcoming a visit from a beautiful woman. She approached him, smiling in return, and asked directions to a restaurant in Brownsville, as a tourist would. She waited until he put down his shovel, took the map she offered and bent over it to explain the route she should take. Then she looked around cautiously, pulled out her pistol and shot him in the back of the neck. He went down quickly. She picked up his shovel and used it to bash his face repeatedly until it bore no recognizable features. Good, she thought, that might disguise his identity for a few hours. She wiped the shovel's handle carefully to remove her fingerprints and let it fall beside him. Now she could go into town and find a nice, late lunch.

CHAPTER 4

Now that she had her editor's consent, Annie was determined to carve out time quickly to research the secession movement in Texas.

She had finished her profile of the city's latest sensational murder victim, a teen-age prostitute found floating in Buffalo Bayou, and it was slated to run on Sunday's front page. It was good, she thought dispassionately, and Cilla and two other editors above her who read it had loved it. But Annie felt more of a sense of letdown than usual. Birthing a big story often gave her that feeling. She put her heart and mind into the reporting and writing and wanted desperately to do justice to the subject. But what had she really accomplished? She had illuminated the young woman's life, but hadn't found her killer or done anything to change the conditions that had led her to the streets. Annie was beginning to worry about being typecast as a general assignment reporter who did one kind of story extremely well. Was she becoming a sort of agony aunt, writing high-profile tearjerkers that were a bit predictable, instead of the harder-edged investigative reporting she really wanted to do?

She needed to do something to damp down her anxiety before she met Jake for an early dinner. So she called Ted Rouse, a professor at the University of Houston who often provided her with perspective on Texas history. Interviewing a good source always made her feel productive.

"Hi, Ted," she said. "Got time for a few questions on the secessionist movement?"

"For you, Annie, I always have time," he said. "What do you need?"

"Were you living here in April 1997 when the Republic of Texas took some people hostage in West Texas?"

"Sure," he said. "Even for West Texas, that one was a head-scratcher. Three members of the Republic of Texas, led by a guy named Richard McLaren, took a middle-aged couple hostage in Fort Davis. The whole thing lasted about a week and got huge public attention."

"Who was this McLaren?"

"A very odd character, by all accounts. As I recall, he was a Missouri native who apparently became obsessed with Texas in the third grade after doing a book report on the Alamo. He moved to West Texas in the 1970s and started making trouble."

"What kind of trouble?"

"He spent all of his time filing crazy lawsuits against landowners in the Fort Davis Mountains. He'd tie up property by claiming deeds weren't recorded right or that land surveys weren't accurate. This went on for about 14 years."

"Did he have a purpose?"

"He wanted land, and he actually got some in court settlements from people who got tired of fighting him."

"Incredible," Annie said. "He must have become public enemy number one in West Texas."

"Yeah, he practically lived at the Jeff Davis County Courthouse. People referred to him as a paper terrorist. When he and his band of crazies took Joe and Margaret Ann Rowe hostage at their home in the Fort Davis Resort, he became an actual terrorist."

"Why'd he pick on them?"

"Joe led the homeowners association and he and McLaren had crossed swords about the secessionists' activities in the neighborhood. The Rowes' retirement home in the Davis Mountains Resort happened to be in the path of what McLaren called the Texas Republic embassy. The embassy was a rather grand name for an old trailer with a wooden lean-to attached."

"Interesting. What did the Republic of Texas want?"

"The group claimed that the annexation of Texas by the United States was illegal – and that Texas remains an independent nation under occupation. McLaren based his argument partly on the fact that Texas voted four-to-one in 1861 to leave the union. But that was because Texas supported the South in the Civil War, not because people were philosophically opposed to statehood."

"I wasn't living in Texas in 1997," Annie said. "Did the kidnapping get much national publicity?"

"Yeah, the front page of the *New York Times*, for one. And Jay Leno cracked a bunch of jokes about them on TV. He said the Tonight Show is now seen in many foreign countries, including Spain, Taiwan and the Republic of Texas."

Annie giggled. "What happened next?"

"After a week-long stand-off with the Texas DPS, McLaren and his gang surrendered. Rowe recovered from a minor gunshot wound and one Republic of Texas member was killed by cops after he pointed a gun at them."

"Hmmm. Did McLaren and his helpers go to prison?"

"Yeah, for a long time. I believe McLaren's release date from a prison in the Panhandle is 2090. We don't have to worry about him being a threat."

"So the stand-off was relatively harmless?"

"Well, yes, and no," Ted said thoughtfully. "It ended peacefully, but as I recall, the police found tons of weapons at the so-called embassy, including dozens of pipe bombs, booby traps and a propane tank filled with explosives."

"The potential for violence was there?"

"Absolutely, and who knows how many more self-styled separatists are out there."

"Do you?" Annie asked Ted.

"No, at one time the Republic of Texas claimed 40,000 supporters in its different branches, but you'll have to find a source inside the Texas Rangers to get a professional opinion. They keep a close watch on domestic threats."

"Okay," said Annie. "One more question. Did the first Republic of Texas do anything unique or particularly great? I know that after the Texans defeated Santa Anna at the Battle of San Jacinto, Texas became a republic for ten years before it entered the United States."

"That's right," Ted said. "But no, the Texas republic was a disappointment. It was too large for an effective government, it didn't have much leadership and it almost got into a second war with Mexico."

"So why does the idea of a new Texas republic keep coming up, like the petitions for secession that appeared when Obama was re-elected?"

"Texans love their land and they tend to romanticize their past," Ted said. "I'm a native Texan myself and I don't think I could ever leave this country, uh, state."

Annie laughed appreciatively. "Thanks for the help, Ted."

"No problem, Annie," he said. "The Austin paper, the American-Statesman, ran a feature story sometime in the last few weeks on the Texas ethos. Maybe you can find it."

"Good idea. Adios."

Annie went to the Statesman's website and started looking for the story. She didn't find it right away, but she found something that twisted a knife in her gut. In a story about the opening of a new museum in the Hill Country was a big color photo of a grinning Senator Jake Satterfield and his lovely wife, Jeannie, who were attending the Austin museum society's gala.

She studied the picture with a sinking heart. Jeannie, a shapely blonde (so petite, barely five feet tall, Annie thought!) wore a pink designer suit, lots of jewelry and what looked like very expensive Manolo Blahnik stilettos. Annie's spirits plunged into gloom. She'd bet her size-10 cowboy boots that the reason Jake hadn't called had something to do with that glamorous woman. Were they getting back together? She'd find out exactly what was going on.

Late afternoon lunch hadn't fully morphed into happy hour, so Chuy's on Westheimer wasn't too crowded yet. After last-minute primping in the car, Annie walked into the restaurant looking for Jake.

He waved at her from a bar table with two tall chairs. As she approached, he stood up, embraced her a bit too tightly and kissed her lightly on the lips. Her heart thumped painfully as he grinned at her.

"Whoa, Jake," she said. "Let's sit."

She was taken aback by what she considered an overly familiar public greeting. She was intensely aware of his body, from his neat, tucked-back ears to his long, slim feet encased in cowboy boots. And he seemed hypersensitive to her physical presence as well.

"You are gorgeous, you know," he said. She saw him looking at her bare, tanned legs crossed at the ankle on her bar stool. She had worn a short black-and-white wrap dress that emphasized her narrow waist and slender torso. She thought now it was probably a little too short.

"I appreciate the compliment, Jake," she said. "But if I hadn't gotten drunk, I wouldn't have slept with you that night in Austin. You're not divorced, or even legally separated."

"I hear you, Annie, but things've been difficult."

"Well, let's give it a rest," she said. "You're in no condition for a relationship right now and I'm not good at casual sex."

"Okay, I'm backing off for now," he smiled. "What can I get you, a large Chardonnay?"

She laughed. "You're hopeless. No thanks. I'm still on the time clock."

They ordered light beers and chicken quesadillas, but when the steaming food came, she found that she was too tense to eat much. She covered the cheesy quesadilla with the spicy green tomatillo sauce she enjoyed, but only sampled it. He ate his quesadilla hungrily as he filled in more blanks about Tom Marr.

"He's a few years older than I am, but we ran into each other at UT a lot. He was a champion debater and hasn't lost those skills. He's got the kind of charisma that Jack Kennedy and Bill Clinton had in their heyday."

"Hmmm. The women of Texas should run the other way. What motivates him?"

"He's really worried about Texas. As you know, the last decade or so hasn't been easy. So many things have gone haywire – Katrina victims bringing their problems to Houston, the devastation of Hurricane Ike, the wild swings of the economy.

"But the biggest concern is the borders. People are beginning to think the drug violence in Mexico will keep spilling over and ruin

Texas," Jake said. "Like that crazy incident in Laredo you wrote about the other day."

"Well, I agree that Texas is volatile right now," Annie said. "But what does Marr think he can do about it?"

"He thinks it's high time to secede from the United States. He says he's got the support to start the process."

"Good Heavens. Isn't that akin to treason?"

"Not at all. After getting legal advice, he's convinced that nothing in either the Texas constitution or the constitution of the United States makes secession impossible."

"I don't know, Jake. That seems kind of crazy and scary."

"That's why you need to meet Tom and sit down and talk with him. I wasn't convinced either until I talked to him for a long time."

"I definitely want to do that. My editor has signed off on the profile and I want to get started soon. Remember, you promised me an exclusive."

"And you shall have it. Tom reads the Houston papers online and he thinks you're the best writer they've got. He just asks that you go to West Texas with an open mind and give him time to make his case."

"Does he have a campaign organization yet?"

"He has me and two fairly influential friends from his days at UT. One is Ed Gonzales, chancellor of Middle Texas College in Kinston. The other is Dan Riggins, who's about to return to Texas after a Washington career in national security. Rumor has it that Riggins spent time in the CIA, but he won't talk about that."

"Intriguing. I'll have to finish up some other stories before I can get out to Marfa. Can you set it up?"

"Of course. But promise me that you won't fall in love with him."

"Don't worry about me. You're the one who's infatuated."

"Not with him," he said, looking into her eyes. "With you."

She ignored that and looked at her watch. "Oops, I've got another appointment. Better run."

They stood up and he put his arms around her. She sidestepped his embrace, but he managed to plant a kiss on her ear.

"How about going back to your place?" He whispered.

"Jake, you're officially a source now. And I saw the picture of you and your wife in the paper. You need to level with me. Are you going back to her?"

He looked down for a moment before he met her eyes.

"You know I separated from her months ago. Now she says she's not sure she wants the divorce."

Annie kept her face neutral and chose her words carefully before she spoke.

"Maybe you should give your marriage another try. You have two kids."

"She had an affair with one of my former law partners in Kerrville," Jake burst out. "I'm not sure I can ever trust her – or really love her -- again."

She tried to keep it light. "I sense that I'm not exactly the first woman you've slept with outside your marriage."

"I've been a saint compared to most guys in the legislature."

Annie laughed. "Now there's a high standard to follow."

"I'd agree some legislators do more skirt-chasing than lawmaking," Jake smiled. "It's hard to resist the free-for-all atmosphere in Austin, but I've tried to be a good husband and father."

"Well, I don't want to be just the woman you take to bed when you happen to be in Houston."

"Annie, please. It's not like that with you."

"It doesn't matter, Jake. I can't be involved with you if you're thinking about going back to your wife. I won't do that."

"Somehow, I didn't think you would."

"Just be a good source right now, okay?" she said. "Let's see where things stand after the profile."

His grin was a little forced, trying to hide defeat, and of course, like an idiot, she felt sorry for him.

CHAPTER 5

Saturday morning dawned clear and cold in the small college town of Blacksburg, Virginia, a suitable backdrop for Jeffrey Price's cat-and-mouse game with his wife Joan. He hovered near the old-fashioned wall phone in their bright red kitchen with the knotty pine cabinets waiting for his younger daughter to call. Annie had sent him an email saying she wanted to talk to him about a work issue. Unfortunately, Joan's unerring nose for family intrigue could smell something afoot that didn't involve her and she couldn't tolerate being on the periphery.

So Jeffrey watched in fury as she slowly and noisily emptied the dishwasher, clanking the silverware into the plastic drawer dividers, poised to race him to the phone. He had fallen for Joan, a short, curvy redhead from Rochester, N.Y., when they were students at the College of William and Mary, and they had married soon after graduation. She had loved him too, but he sensed that her feelings had eroded in a slow-simmered stew of disappointment and disdain. She was Jewish, politically liberal and disdained living in the rural South, while he was a conservative Baptist who loved small towns, soul food and college football. They didn't agree on much, but Jeffrey knew she doted on their three children, four grandchildren and two Chihuahuas as much as he did. Luckily, Joan worked as a guidance counselor at the local high school, where her assertiveness in getting so-so students admitted to excellent colleges was harnessed in a positive way. Jeffrey appreciated her ferocious energy most of the time, but today he felt impelled to express his anger.

"When Annie calls this morning, I don't want to hear you asking if she's met anyone new," he said. "She's worried about her job and she doesn't need that kind of pressure."

"Don't tell me what to talk about with my own daughter," Joan snapped. "I'll say anything I feel like."

"Your constant references to the fact that she's not married just make her feel bad."

"That's a big, fat lie," Joan said, squaring her shoulders. "I'm just showing that I'm interested in her life."

"Would you listen to me, for once?"

"You don't understand, Jeffrey. She's thirty-six, and she's ignoring the fact that her childbearing days soon will be over."

"Annie will make herself a good life, whether she's married with children or not."

"I hate the thought of her growing old alone."

"She's hardly old. And we've met some serious boyfriends."

"That reporter from the Bronx with the terrible manners, ratty clothes and the disgusting tattoos? That was four years ago. We haven't met anybody since then."

"She probably stopped bringing anyone here because you didn't make them feel welcome."

"That's ridiculous," Joan said. "She should take my advice and go out with Vernon Threadgill. His mother would love to get them together when Annie's in town, but she won't cooperate."

"Vernon Threadgill's a pansy ass. She'd be miserable with that boy, not to mention his insufferable mother!"

"Jeffrey, really. I'm not going to listen to your ugly language."

The kitchen phone rang and Joan easily grabbed it with a look of triumph in her eyes. He retreated to the den and slumped on the couch. He balanced the morning paper on his big belly, vowing again to lose twenty-five pounds from his barrel-chested frame.

"Hi, Annie," she said. "How are you, darling?"

He heard Joan ask some of the usual questions. Was Annie well? Had she gotten her flu shot yet? Was she going out tonight?

Damn it, he fumed. She didn't ask Annie if she'd met anyone – just if she had a date tonight. Big difference.

Jeffrey felt a special kinship with Annie. She was the only one who had followed him into the journalism business and the one who most shared his offbeat sense of humor, love of writing and passion for making the world better.

He had spent his career editing and publishing small newspapers in the South that were owned by a greedy chain determined to suck their small but reliable profits dry. He had once written prize-winning editorials ranging from condemning local Ku Klux Klan marches to championing anti-pollution efforts to improve Virginia's rivers. He had retired a few years ago at 65. Now instead of reflecting on his genuine successes, Jeffrey often brooded over the dark side of his career: kowtowing to corrupting local business interests, trying to placate increasingly cheapskate owners and slaving nights and weekends to fill the never-ending gaps in a skeletal staff. He didn't want Annie to end up as disillusioned as he sometimes felt.

He thought about his gangly 12-year-old delivering the paper by bicycle on her daily route. A few years later, he encouraged her to start reporting. She protested that she was too shy. But once she tried it, she enjoyed it. Soon she was interviewing police and city councilmen along with the best of his veteran reporters. He shared her excitement when she got accepted at the University of North Carolina's journalism school in Chapel Hill and started working for the student newspaper.

After she graduated, he loved being her sounding board as she moved from a small newspaper in North Carolina to a bigger one in Georgia and finally to the *Houston Times* six years ago. He admired her drive to move up in the newspaper world and her ambition to correct injustices through investigative reporting.

But as he watched the newspaper industry he had known slide toward extinction, Jeffrey worried about the future for his intense daughter. She was so attached to her identity as a newspaper reporter. He found it hard to imagine how she would find fulfillment writing trivia for a gossip Web site, for instance. Would there be a place for her when the industry finished remaking itself?

Joan told him to pick up the phone – finally. She made a show of hanging up and going to the bedroom, but he thought she had picked up the extension in there. He heard his daughter's warm voice.

"Hi, Dad. What're you up to this morning?"

"Just hanging out, waiting for your call. I got your email saying you wanted to talk about something. What's the latest with the paper?"

"We haven't heard any more about layoffs since the one three months ago. The big rumor is that the Carter family is searching for a buyer."

"I'm not surprised," he said. "Newspaper families are terrified about the hits the industry is taking."

"Well, it's scaring everybody, given the vultures out there scooping up papers and getting rid of people. We're dying by inches."

"Are the editors talking about the situation?"

"Not to us. And we've lost some really good reporters who've gone to the dark side."

"Now, Annie," he chided. "Public relations isn't necessarily the dark side. You'd make a good PR person. You might need to think about that, if newspapers keep biting the dust."

"Ugh, ugh and boring," she said. "I can't think of any worse way to spend my life."

"Okay, sweetheart," he laughed. "What did you want to talk about?"

"I think I'm on to a really big story."

"Is it as big as Texas?"

"That's what you always say, Dad," she giggled. "Actually, it might be. I've got a big interview with a candidate for governor who wants Texas to secede from the United States."

"Is he a crackpot?" Jeffrey asked.

"No, he's a pretty respectable state legislator. That's why I'm worried."

"What do you mean?"

"He's a big story. I need time to investigate him and his ideas. I'm afraid I won't get it."

"You're pretty good at persuading people to do what you want," Jeffrey said. "You'll just have to fight for the time."

"You don't know what the newsroom's like these days. We're spread so thin it's ridiculous. It's like a sweatshop."

"I know you're discouraged, honey," Jeffrey said. "But you've got to be true to your instincts as a reporter. Go after the truth, be fair and don't stop reporting until you get to the bottom of it."

"That's the same advice you give me about everything," she said, sounding disappointed.

"She's right, Jeffrey," said Joan, her voice popping up from the bedroom extension. "You don't know anything about newspapers these days."

"Mom, could you please get off the phone?" Annie said with exasperation. "You know I like talking to each of you separately."

"All right," Joan said, slamming the phone down.

"I'm sorry," Jeffrey said. "She's right. I'm just an old coot who's been out of the business too long. My advice isn't worth a damn."

"I didn't really mean that," Annie said. "What do you think about the idea of secession?"

"I think it's really unpatriotic. I fought with a lot of brave Texans in Vietnam and some of them died horrible deaths in that hellhole. They believed they were doing the right thing."

"I didn't realize you fought with Texans," Annie said.

"Is the man you're interviewing part of that loony group that kidnapped a couple of people in West Texas in the 1990s?" Jeffrey asked. "We put that crazy stuff on our front page one day when it looked like it might turn violent."

"No, I think he's got a plan that might actually make sense."

"I'd be very suspicious. What does he really want? Who's behind him?"

"I don't know yet, but I'll find out."

"How did this country get so screwed up?" Jeffrey mused. "I know that Americans don't seem to agree on anything big these days, but secession to me is treason."

"Dad, I'm not going to pass judgment until I have all the facts. Isn't that what you always taught me?"

"Yeah. But people who have a separatist agenda are usually dangerous. Don't trust anyone -- and be careful when you're out working on this story."

"Of course I will, but this is 21st century America. I can't foresee any personal danger."

"Believe me, you don't always know the danger you're in."

"I know you're thinking about what happened with the Klan when you and Mom were young. I'll be careful."

"Call me back when you begin working on the story," Jeffrey said. "Not that you need my help, but I'd love to hear about it."

He hung up the phone, thinking about his daughter's innocence. She believed so passionately in fairness and justice and she still possessed a core of unblemished optimism. He hoped that her life wouldn't turn as dark and complicated as his own. Joan joined him in the den to rehash Annie's call.

"Annie still thinks she's got to save the world," she said. "I'm afraid it makes her drink too much. I watched her fill her wine glass too many times at Christmas."

"What's the matter with you?" Jeffrey looked at her incredulously. "Annie's working on a dangerous story, her paper's circling the drain and you're worried about her drinking and dates?"

"Those things are important, too," she said.

Surprisingly, as she sat with him on the worn den sofa, he could feel her looking past his flabby body in sweatpants and the graying beard she hated to his vulnerable inner core. It was one of those moments of understanding that kept them fused. Her face seemed softer as she put a hand on his arm.

" Jeffrey, you're trying to relive your career through Annie. But that's a burden you don't need to put on yourself or Annie. Things weren't perfect, but whose life ever is? You had a decent career and we raised three good children. Now, would you like some lunch?"

He nodded, and as she walked briskly to the kitchen, for the first time that day, he relaxed.

CHAPTER 6

Annie got up early on a mild, sunny Sunday. She ran two miles through the deserted streets of the Houston Heights, a historic neighborhood developed in the 1890s. She cherished the Heights, a tree-lined, mostly gentrified neighborhood slightly north of Houston's buzzing downtown.

Perhaps because she had grown up in a sleepy college town, Annie loved the clangorous bustle of Houston. She enjoyed working downtown with its eclectic buildings, offbeat sculptures and underground maze of air-conditioned tunnels. Even during the worst of the ultra-humid months, she could shrug off the steamy days and look ahead to lush tropical nights. There was always somewhere new to go, a trendy club or ballyhooed restaurant to try, an amazing party to check out. After a few years, she could even handle the worst of the scary traffic. Feeling at home quickly, she wanted to buy a house as soon as she could save enough for a down payment.

She couldn't afford the restored Victorians anchoring the wide Heights Boulevard or the large Craftsman-style homes on its choicest streets. But she was able to stretch her reporter's salary to buy the one-story frame house on a street where some houses were neatly renovated and others were waiting for loving care and an infusion of cash. It was a mixed area, where Hispanic families coexisted peacefully with elderly white widows and young professionals like Annie.

As her legs pumped the pavement, she felt calmer. Last night, she had lain awake for hours, thinking about Jake. Her heart had lurched when she walked into Chuy's and saw him smiling. She had forgotten how handsome and funny he was. Even his over-the-top flattery, which would normally sow seeds of distrust in her slightly cynical core, had charmed the pants off her. Well, almost charmed the pants off her. She had wanted to kiss him, invite him home and wrap herself around his sexy backside. Then she'd cuddle with him, make him coffee and put him on the road to Kerrville.

But she would have been sorry the next day. Annie believed in the ethics of her profession, so Jake would be off limits while he guided her through the Marr story. Not to mention the complications in the new wrinkle with his marriage. If he was considering reconciling with his wife, she needed to stay out of his life. But she felt sad and regretful about the relationship.

She had her standards – unfortunately, she thought wryly, she didn't always live up to them. As she moved into her thirties, she found herself drinking more wine, and drinking more had occasionally landed her in uncomfortable situations. Sometimes she thought she should probably swear off alcohol altogether, but her newspaper career and personal life always felt rife with tension. She had the kind of mind that hummed with anxiety most of the time. But after a few glasses of wine, she could laugh, crack jokes and feel as close to carefree as she ever got.

She ran back to her house, showered, put on skinny jeans and drove to the Empire Café to meet Maddy Daniels. The café, a laidback restaurant in the raffish part of Montrose near Houston's downtown, offered a coveted outdoor seating area shaded by hibiscus and other tall flowering plants in bucket-style pots, and cheery yellow umbrellas launched above wooden tables. January in Houston was often balmy and warm, a perfect time to enjoy dining alfresco.

Annie thought how lucky she was to have Madeleine Daniels as a best friend. Maddy had worked for the *Houston Times* for 17 years, for a long time as a political reporter and more recently, as an investigative reporter. She had come to the *Times* right out of Southern Methodist University after growing up in a wealthy, eccentric Dallas family. Maddy was a born storyteller and most people found her irreverent and funny unless they were being skewered by her stories. At 39, she considered herself much more experienced in the ways of love and journalism than Annie, and took the role of mentor. Her pretty heart-shaped face and cap of blonde curls topped a chunky body carrying 20 more pounds than she wanted, but men responded to her flirty nature.

Annie spotted her friend and they rushed to grab the last of the

Empire's outdoor tables. Annie went to the counter inside and ordered coffee and gingerbread waffles with bananas and strawberries for two. Both women loved to eat and struggled to keep from succumbing too frequently to Houston's fabulous foodie culture.

Although she wasn't overweight like Maddy, she worried about her hips, which she felt were overly generous for her slim frame. A few years ago, a boyfriend with more moxie than finesse slapped her rear end one morning, saying, "Nice childbearing hips." Annie was horrified and started running the next day. But her efforts at self-improvement backfired. The boyfriend broke up with her a few weeks later for a police dispatcher with a posterior much larger than Annie's.

Annie smiled as she remembered telling Maddy about the latest disaster in her love life.

"I guess he's just an ass-man," Annie had said.

"No, he's just an ass."

Annie sat down across the table from her, eager to catch up since Maddy had been out of the city on vacation. Also, she wanted to pick her brain, because Maddy stayed plugged into the gossip about the state's political elite. She would have the scoop on Tom Marr.

"How're you doing, hon?" Maddy said in her dulcet Dallas accent. "What's the latest on your love life?"

"Not much. I'm swearing off men."

"Forget that! You're too young – and too cute."

"I'm too unlucky. Why on earth did I get involved with Jake Satterfield?"

"Have you seen him?" Maddy said.

"Yeah, we had dinner at Chuy's the other night."

"The plot thickens. Did you take him to your place for a little rumpy-pumpy?"

"Rumpy-pumpy?" Annie laughed. "Where did you get that one?"

"It's my latest Brit-slang. But back to Jake the hunk. What happened?"

"I told him we needed to cool things for a while. I'm not sure he's serious about getting a divorce."

"I've heard he's been separated from Jeannie for months," Maddy said. "She's very big into the Hill Country social scene and he isn't. The gossips say they haven't been happy for a while."

"I know he's separated," Annie said. "But I saw a newspaper picture of him and his wife together recently that really threw me. He says she's not sure she wants a divorce. I don't want to be a home wrecker – or the woman who's waiting in the wings forever."

"Well, I wouldn't write him off yet."

"I'm not going to be with someone who's having second thoughts about his marriage."

"You might be the swing vote for divorce."

"I'm not going to play that game. Either he's free to commit, or he's not. But he told me something else that really complicates things."

"What's that?"

"He wants to get me an exclusive interview with his friend, Tom Marr. Marr's a West Texas legislator who's planning to run for governor – as a secessionist."

"Wow," Maddy said. "That could be a great story."

"What do you know about Marr?"

"I've only met him once, but he struck me as charismatic and intelligent," said Maddy. "I don't know much about his politics, but it's fascinating that he's positioning himself as a secessionist. You weren't around in the late 1990s when those Republic of Texas bozos took some people hostage."

"No, I wasn't, but I gather they didn't win any popularity contests with most Texans."

"Hardly. He's not allied with those idiots, I hope?"

"I don't think so. Jake says Marr's serious about changing the government lawfully. When I go to West Texas to interview him, I need to know as much as I can about the secessionist movement. Got any sources?"

"Easy peasy. I can get you one-stop shopping with Mark Ingram," Maddy said.

"Isn't he your Texas Ranger friend?"

"Yes. Part of his job is to track fringe political movements. He knows everything there is to know about the secessionists."

"In fact," Maddy smiled, "I spent last weekend in Austin with him."

"Oh my gosh. Details. I want details, Mad."

"I've known Mark for years as a good source. But I had no idea he was interested in me until we ran into each other at a party recently. Last weekend, I found out he's really fun, and pretty good in the sack, too."

"That's really great," Annie said. She knew Maddy hadn't dated anyone for a while and she worried about her friend's restless propensity for one-night stands.

"Girlfriend, have you got fun waiting for you!" Maddy smiled. "Tom Marr is drop-dead gorgeous. He's about six-feet-five with hair so blond it's nearly white, and sexy blue eyes. One of those strong, inscrutable West Texas types!"

"Great, just what I need – another hookup with a news source," Annie said. "I'm not looking for a relationship out of this. It's serious stuff."

"Well, loosen up, honey. Oh, I forgot, you already did, with Jake Satterfield, ha! Annie, seize the day. Have some fun with life. It's not all deadly serious."

Annie smiled at Maddy and they high-fived across the table.

"I know, I know," Annie said. "One more thing that's interesting. One of Tom Marr's campaign heads is Ed Gonzales, president of Middle Texas College. That's the place you've been investigating, right?"

"No kidding! Yeah, Gonzales has developed a very strange empire. That dinky college in Kinston teaches classes on military bases all over the world."

"That's unusual for a community college, isn't it?"

"Yes. The state doesn't like it, but doesn't have the authority to monitor federal contracting."

"What've you found out?"

"Gonzales and his really nasty vice-president, Will Ward, have done everything they could to keep us from getting access to their records. But we're getting close."

"What's Gonzales like?"

"He's from Mexico, but got all three of his degrees at UT. He went to work right away at Middle Texas and rose through the ranks fast. About fifteen years ago, he started the college's military contracting business at Fort Kinston."

"What kind of contracts does the military need from a community college?"

"Middle Texas puts instructors on military bases and on ships, as far away as the Indian Ocean," Maddy said. "They teach ordinary courses like math, science and English to military folks. Sometimes they even teach sensitive courses like electronic warfare."

"Is it lucrative for Middle Texas?"

"Apparently so. The community college board rewarded Gonzales by making him president ten years ago."

"That's pretty intriguing," Annie said. "When you get the records, it'll be interesting to look at the money from that."

"Yeah, the state'll be interested too."

"Tom Marr and Ed Gonzales were at UT together. That's what Jake told me," Annie said. "There's a third guy, Dan Riggins, who also went to UT with them. He's going to retire from the CIA, move to Texas and run Marr's gubernatorial campaign."

"Hmmm. That makes sense," Maddy said. "I'll bet Riggins has greased the wheels in Washington to help Middle Texas get contracts."

"Is Gonzales married?"

"My sources say that he abruptly divorced his first wife a couple of years ago to marry a preggo student. And sure enough, he's got a two-year-old and a young-looking Hispanic wife."

She paused to finish her coffee.

"Any other college would've gotten rid of him after a stunt like that. But because he brings home the bacon, whatever scandal there was disappeared. It's all very strange."

Annie got up and walked with Maddy to the parking lot. They hugged.

"It's really interesting that Marr is connected with Gonzales and Riggins. Let's touch base this week when you find out more," Maddy said.

"Absolutely. And I hope I can set up an interview with Mark Ingram right away. Can I use your name?"

Maddy laughed. "Only if you tell him a ravishing blonde babe was talking about him!"

CHAPTER 7

Ed Gonzales wondered if he was having a panic attack. His heart raced like a revved-up engine and his stomach churned like a washing machine as he paced up and down his patio on a quiet Sunday morning. The horrid sensations swamped him as he brooded on his troubles at work and at home. He knew that his shaky empire at Middle Texas College wouldn't hold together much longer. He had been able to keep his secrets for a while, but he could sense that even a minor misstep could send everything tumbling in a humiliating cascade. Then what? Disgrace? Prison? Death?

He walked inside his Spanish-style house through a back hall to the kitchen, passing a long ornamental mirror. The image he saw made him shudder. The forty pounds he had packed on in the last few years made him look like a paunchy old man. He was only forty-eight, but his protruding middle, slicked-back hair and graying moustache disgusted him.

His son, a two-year-old named Manuel, had waked early as usual, demanding food and attention. Consequently, Gonzales and his 22-year-old wife Cecilia didn't get any more sleep either.

He looked with distaste at the kitchen table, where sticky plates were strewn with the remains of eggs, waffles and syrup. Cecilia walked in wearing a pink chenille robe, with Manuel fastened to one mammoth breast. Since the baby was born, she had put on fifteen pounds and her once-voluptuous figure now just looked unpleasantly large.

"Cecilia, how many times have I told you that we need to wean Manuel? He's two and should be drinking milk from a glass," Gonzales said.

"Eddie, that is not how we do it in Mexico," she said, caressing her son's head.

He restrained himself from telling her once again she wasn't in

Mexico. He knew that would lead to a fight, something he needed to avoid. Despite his irritation, he felt aroused at the sight of her large breast.

"Mi chica," he said in what he hoped was his best seductive tone. "How about putting Manuel down for a nap and coming to me in our room?"

"Eddie, it's not time for Manuel's nap yet. He won't like it."

"I will make you feel so good," Gonzales pleaded.

"Will you take us to the park later?"

"Of course, mi querida."

"And ice cream after that? Manuel loves going to the shopping center for a chocolate cone."

"Si. Hurry, mi chica. I want to caress those beautiful breasts."

She put Manuel down in his bedroom. The baby wasn't too happy, but they shut the door so that his indignant cries were less audible.

In the big bedroom, they stripped quickly. But despite his earlier stirrings of passion, he felt curiously half-hearted. Perhaps it was the jiggling of the post-pregnancy fat that still enveloped Cecilia's body. Making love to her felt akin to plunging into a vat of Jell-O. Still, he tried his best to please her before yielding to his own mediocre orgasm. His penis was perilously close to flaccid and he feared that he wouldn't be able to perform if he labored much longer.

He thought as he showered that the problem wasn't Cecilia's out-of-shape body. It lay in the blankness of her mind and spirit. He never knew what was going on behind the dull mask of her young face. Most of their conversation centered on the baby, since she seemed mostly uninterested in his career or the wider world around her. He struggled to love the mother of his youngest son.

He had married in his twenties for the first time, producing four children. All but the oldest still lived in Kinston with their mother, Marla, but she didn't allow Gonzales to visit the three school-age children more than twice a month. He particularly missed Kenny, his middle-school soccer player. He had valued Marla for her beautiful face, lively mind and shrewd contributions to his career. Now it appeared that a high-ranking officer at Fort Kinston was courting her for the same reasons.

He cursed his stupidity, as he had done many times before. Three years ago, his orderly life had fallen off the track and never regained its stability. The abyss opened up after a shapely student assistant named Cecilia Lopez started working in his office. Cecilia at nineteen had the kind of figure he loved – large breasts and hips that shook sinuously on her frequent trips to the copy machine. He told himself he was just showing a fatherly interest when they chatted about her hometown of Matamoros, Mexico, just over the border from Brownsville in south Texas. He had grown up there too, but had left to go to college and rarely returned. She told him she lived with cousins in Kinston while she took classes in office management.

She didn't tell him she was the youngest daughter of Manny Lopez, one of Mexico's top marijuana kingpins. Just the mention of Lopez's name elicited terror throughout the Mexican state of Tamaulipas, but Gonzales remained unaware of the connection as he grew friendlier with Cecilia. One day while his secretary left for lunch, he and the seductive young woman ended up enjoying their own noon break on the big wooden conference table in his office.

Of course, it didn't end there. Within a few months, she tearfully announced her pregnancy and asked what he would do about it. While he thought that over, two of her father's lieutenants showed up and relayed a few facts about how Manny Lopez did business. They showed him gruesome photos of mutilated bodies just before burial in open desert graves. Gonzales was sufficiently moved to get a quickie divorce from Marla and marry Cecilia as soon as he decently could.

He kept quiet about the identity of his new father-in-law, and the scandal of his hasty marriage to a young, knocked-up student ended quickly. Since the contracts program brought big business to the college, his local board routinely overlooked his shortcomings.

But he wondered just how much Cecilia and her father had played him for a fool. He shuddered to think of his father-in-law, a scary man with a retinue of thugs who surrounded him with submachine guns. Gonzales, Cecilia and the baby went to see him every couple of months in Matamoros and each visit filled Gonzales with fear. Manny's ranch on the outskirts of the city was opulent in its own gangster-type fashion, but included macabre touches such as a makeshift graveyard where enemies were buried.

How had Manny learned about the college's military education contracts? Was it from Cecilia? Gonzales didn't know, but evidently Manny knew a lucrative opportunity when he saw one. Now Gonzales and his future were even more closely tied to his monstrous father-in-law.

Once they were married, Cecilia seemed much less interested in sex – and in Gonzales. The lusty romps on the conference table, inside his supply closet and under blankets in a secluded park seemed so far in the past, he wondered whether he had imagined them. And she insisted naming their son Manuel after her horrible father.

His cell phone rang, interrupting his thoughts. He gratefully picked it up.

"Ed, it's Dan. We need to talk about money and training."

"Sure, amigo. Let me go to my study for privacy."

Ed Gonzales and Dan Riggins had met their freshman year at UT. Both politically minded, they had bonded quickly with a third student, Tom Marr, whom they believed was ideally suited to be governor. Immersing themselves in political science, history and generous quantities of marijuana and beer, the three UT students had dreamed of some day leading the state to what they believed was its ultimate destiny: secession. Marr, easily the handsomest and most compelling of their trio, would be elected as its first president and they would serve as his right-hand men. That day was coming – thirty years after their first meeting. He got back on the phone.

"Everything's going great here," he told Riggins, a shade too heartily. "When do you move to Texas?"

"Just a few weeks from now, in time for Tom's first big media interview. Jake Satterfield has lined up a reporter named Annie Price from the *Houston Times*."

"What's her reputation?"

"She's single and fairly young, " Riggins said. "We're betting Tom will dazzle her and she'll write a story that'll make him a star."

"I bet she'll fall for him," Gonzales said. "He's so handsome and makes such a great impression. Is that a good idea?"

"Jake says she's the best writer, and the *Times* is the most influential paper."

"Can we trust Jake Satterfield?" Gonzales said. "He's a key senator in the legislature and Tom likes him, but we don't know him very well. We shouldn't tell him much until we figure him out."

"I agree. There are things you and I shouldn't tell anybody, even Tom," Riggins said. "And speaking of secrets, is that *Times* investigative reporter still sniffing around the college?"

"Maddy Daniels? Yeah, but I've got it under control. She won't find out anything important."

"Well, see that you do, Ed," Riggins said. "We can't afford any more bad publicity. We'll be moving soon into a critical phase of the campaign."

He let the message sink in before changing the subject.

"Tell me about the classes. Didn't you tell me you're advertising in the Kinston paper for soldiers?"

"We've got two classes going for the latest round of recruits – about seventy men."

"What're they like?"

"Good guys, mostly young, patriotic Texans from around here. They're perfect for the army, uh, I mean your security business."

"Sounds good. When'll they be ready to go to West Texas for training?"

"Probably in a month."

"Okay, I'll let Alicia know."

"When will I see you, Dan?"

"We'll meet at Tom's ranch in a few weeks. Remember, no money talk around him. You know Tom's a purist."

"And we'll keep him that way," Gonzales agreed.

CHAPTER 8

It was still early in the evening when Dan Riggins finished a steak and salad dinner with his wife Karen. They ate quietly in the cheerful apple-green kitchen at their colonial-style home in a Virginia suburb not far from CIA headquarters in Langley. Karen Riggins was a great cook who usually made buttery mashed potatoes, homemade bread and deep-dish cherry pie to go with their steak and salad. But lately she had started worrying about the thickening of her torso and legs, so she skipped the carbs and served Dan more protein. He didn't really care because he mostly regarded food as fuel for his lean, tightly coiled, six-foot frame. Although he enjoyed a rare steak and good red wine, he considered high-calorie treats too self-indulgent, though he didn't express that opinion to his wife. Generally they co-existed in separate worlds, and Riggins tried to give her little reason to complain or pry. He valued her efforts in raising their twin sons (mostly alone) while he traveled for the CIA, but now that the boys were away at college, he felt even more removed from her world. He kept such thoughts to himself.

"Excellent dinner, dear," he said warmly.

"Was it enough for you?" she said.

"More than enough. You worry too much."

"I'd just like to be 10 pounds thinner by the time we move to San Antonio," she said.

"Think you'll run into your old boyfriends, Miss Bexar County?" He smiled.

She looked pleased. "I can't believe that I ever won a beauty contest."

"I remember the night you won," he said. "We had just become engaged, your hair was long and shiny and you wore a blue strapless dress. Do you still have it?"

"Oh no, it'd be much too tight," she said. "Could you take a few minutes to look at wallpaper samples for the dining room of the new house?"

"You know I don't care about wallpaper," he said, trying not to show irritation. "I told you to pick out whatever you like."

"How about looking at tile samples for the kitchen?" She persisted. "It's expensive and I don't want to make the wrong choice."

"Karen, really," he said, getting up from the table to pour himself a cup of decaf coffee. "I gave you a budget. Surely you can make these decisions."

"Of course, dear," she said. "But since the San Antonio house will be our retirement home, I thought you'd be interested."

"It's not that I'm uninterested. I need to go into the study to make some important phone calls."

"I understand," she said, mustering a smile. "Don't stay up too late."

Decades of work with the CIA had dictated this longstanding pattern in their home life. He mostly spent his nights behind closed doors, mapping out his secretive missions with others involved in covert work. Karen knitted sweaters and scarves for a favorite charity and watched television quiz shows by herself. She didn't complain about spending evenings alone because she knew the nature – though never the specifics – of his job.

Riggins shut the door to his maroon-and-brown study with relief. Why was his wife always trying to involve him in trivial household decisions? He gave her a free hand with money and in return, he believed, she shouldn't bother him with mundane details. He stood at the study's front-facing window, coffee cup in hand, looking at the large houses and snow-covered lawns along the curving street of his subdivision. He sipped his coffee, giving himself time to reflect on the upcoming changes in his life.

His intelligence, sense of purpose and unshakeable belief in himself and his capabilities had taken him a long way in the CIA, but he'd done enough time in gritty countries with dirty problems. He'd always intended to take early retirement and return to Texas. Riggins didn't care about much, but he cared greatly about Texas and his vision for the magnificent country it could become. He had known early, after meeting Tom Marr in college, that Tom had the winning personality that he would never possess. Riggins knew he could get Tom elected to office some day in the future. Marr and Gonzales both shared his strong sense that Texas could be the perfect nation – the country the United States could – and should – have become. He worried about Gonzales, whom he considered the weak link of their triumvirate, but he'd watch him carefully.

He thought about his impending return to San Antonio, where he'd grown up with two older brothers and a younger sister. His brothers had followed their middle-class parents into their grocery business, but he and his sister found grocery stores unbearably humdrum. Amelia had married an alcoholic lawyer, who had died and left her struggling with her own alcoholism and a son. A few years ago, she'd died, too, leaving Riggins to take care of her son. Riggins had joined the CIA, traveled the world's hot spots, and met the love of his life.

Tonight, in the privacy of his study, he used his cell phone to call a familiar unlisted number in West Texas. Alicia Perez, his mistress for eighteen years, picked up on the third ring. As usual, they spoke only in Spanish, which they long ago decided was at least some insurance against detection.

"Hola, Dan. Que pasa?"

"How was your trip to Brownsville?"

"Muy bueno. As you say, mission accomplished."

"Excelente."

"I want to make love to you," she said. "I have new herbs from Peru to help you last all night."

"All night? I'm getting a little old for that."

"Nonsense, you are my bull."

"I want to be your bull, then sleep in your arms."

"Sexy hombre. Are you in your study?"

"Yes, thinking about your beautiful body."

"Should I undress?"

"No phone sex tonight. Karen's in the next room."

"Oh. When are you moving?"

"In a few weeks. We'll close on the San Antonio house and drive down soon after. She's excited, and of course, the move will benefit you and me, darling."

"I look forward to seeing you more often," she said. "But do you really think it is possible to keep Karen from finding out about us when you are living in Texas?"

"She only sees what she wants to see. She'll be so busy with the new house and her people in San Antonio, she won't notice a thing."

"And with Tom's campaign, it will be natural that you come to West Texas more often, no?"

"Yes. How's the training going?"

"Very well. The fifty-two new men are strong and eager. They will be ready in a few weeks."

"Great. I wish I could watch you teaching them how to fight, mi amor."

"You will see us soon. And they will be ready to begin excellent work for your security company."

"Have you seen Tom recently?"

"I haven't seen him much. But then, I never do."

His mind flew over the terrain of the place he loved so well, where his lover and best friend lived only 20 miles apart. Their paths seldom crossed and he preferred to keep it that way.

"How's your business this week?"

"As you know, El Mercado is slow now, but it will pick up in the spring."

"Well, I'll probably have a few more special jobs for you soon, which'll be good money. I'll let you know when the time comes."

"What kind of jobs?" Alicia said. He could hear the excitement in her tone.

"The usual kind. We'll talk in person."

"I look forward to that."

"So do I, querida."

"Adios, Dan."

"Adios, my darling."

He hung up the phone and poured some brandy into a rounded, pewter Jefferson Cup, modeled from a design by Thomas Jefferson, one of his heroes. After eighteen years, he still desired the lithe, shapely body of his 50-year-old mistress more than anything else in his life. But he didn't completely understand her and she intimidated him in some ways.

Alicia loved to kill, which disturbed him sometimes if he let himself think about it. He had often used her to track down CIA enemies and dispatch them with reliable, untraceable ease. She was an inventive assassin. Once given a target, she spent considerable time and creativity planning a death that usually appeared accidental.

Riggins regarded killing as a necessity in carefully calibrated circumstances. His CIA training had left him with the skills, but not, like Alicia, with the predilection that made dispatching enemies enjoyable. He liked hearing about her cunning in plotting killings, but not the gory details. He gave the orders and she carried them out with relish.

Her expertise with weapons and fighting tactics was another reason she was so valuable to him. Two years ago, he had founded a company he called Republic Security and it had grown to more than 700 agents. Mostly the business provided security for well-heeled corporate clients in San Antonio and Houston. But Riggins had set up his business to serve three purposes – to bring together Texans who believed in secession, to generate money for the cause and to provide the base of the future secessionist army. An army would be necessary to protect the Texas borders and to keep key secessionists safe from political enemies. Alicia trained all the men in special tactics before they started work. She was perfect in that role.

Alicia's early life in Peru had given her proficiency in paramilitary skills, but also left her psychologically damaged, Riggins knew. Her parents, high-level government officials, were kidnapped and murdered by Shining Path revolutionaries. They raped the teenaged Alicia and she joined her captors to survive, but had secretly hated the organization. She rarely spoke about her past, but he knew it haunted her.

Early in his career, Riggins had spent time in Peru for the CIA, assessing the government's troubles with the Shining Path. The militant Maoist organization surfaced in Peru in 1980 and for years, wreaked sickening violence on Peru's civilian population. The Peruvian government's inability to control the insurrectionists worried the CIA and his bosses ordered Riggins to infiltrate the Shining Path by posing as a radical U.S. convert.

Tanned and attractive in his late twenties and fluent in Spanish, Riggins had relished this assignment, especially when the opportunity came to infiltrate the bed of Alicia Perez. By the early 1990s, she had become one of the group's mid-level leaders. He found her beautiful, commanding and thrillingly sexy. With help from counter-revolutionaries like Riggins, the Peruvian government finally had success capturing key leaders and the Shining Path began to fall apart.

Alicia realized that her future lay with the handsome CIA agent instead of with the flailing revolutionary organization. Riggins managed, with the help of Marr and his South American cattle contacts, to get her out of Peru.

Riggins marveled at how easily she had settled into the quiet, anonymous world of West Texas, how quickly she had caught the spirit of capitalism. She became self-sufficient as her crafts business spread from West Texas to San Antonio. He had found he couldn't function without her, but his long marriage to Karen remained unscathed. Riggins, adept at living a double life as a CIA agent, experienced little trouble maintaining a dual personal life in Washington and West Texas. Since he traveled a lot and kept up his friendship with Marr, his layovers in West Texas didn't seem suspect.

Twenty years ago, Marr's father died and he left the vast family landholdings to his only son. Marr presented his lifelong friends, Riggins and Gonzales, each with 150 acres of land near his home between Marfa and the Davis Mountains. He hoped his friends would build West Texas vacation homes near him, so they and their loved ones could enjoy hunting, hiking and horseback riding in seasons other than the oppressively hot summer.

Riggins accepted Marr's gift of land with excitement. In the last two years, anticipating his return, he had built a two-story house on a scenic piece of the property. The adobe and wooden structure had large windows to catch the desert light and was located just miles from Marr's family home.

At the other end of Riggins' acreage was a second home. The smaller adobe house, built eighteen years ago, featured an iron fence around its front yard and a private courtyard in the middle of the dwelling for privacy.

Living there was Alicia, his beloved mistress and perfect contract killer.

CHAPTER 9

The next week, Annie drove to Austin to work on a story Cilla had assigned analyzing the capital city's perpetual growth. She never minded the three-hour trip to Austin, watching the flatlands of Houston disappear into rolling countryside, its distant suburbs melting into ranch land. If she looked long enough at the cattle grazing behind the fences, she would spot a longhorn or two. She loved Texas Longhorns, those striking, sleepy-eyed steers some Texans jokingly referred to as pasture furniture. The trip also offered her the chance to sneak in an hour or two with Mark Ingram, Maddy's new boyfriend and expert on secession. She had arranged to get together with him for a long lunch.

Ingram had told her to meet him at the County Line on Bee Cave Road, a classic Austin barbecue spot on a hilltop not far from downtown. Annie considered Austin the most appealing city in Texas, with its lively mix of politicians, musicians, university students, state employees and high-tech workers. Known for its inventive music, green politics and wacky locals, the city relished its self-proclaimed motto, "Keep Austin Weird."

To prepare for the meeting, she had looked up Ingram's official bio on the Texas Rangers website. He had joined the Rangers twenty-one years ago, right out of college. She knew he had majored in history at UT and wanted a challenging career that would allow him to stay in his beloved Texas Hill Country. Maddy had told her Ingram enjoyed chasing sophisticated villains and breaking up criminal conspiracies, so the job of investigator suited him perfectly. He often led the Rangers' high-profile investigations, which ranged from political corruption to murder.

When she delved into the history of the Texas Rangers, she was surprised she hadn't learned about them in high school. They were a uniquely American institution. In 1823, frontier leader Stephen F.

Austin had hired the first ten Rangers to protect 600 families who had settled in Texas. Later, the Rangers hunted down Bonnie and Clyde and other notorious criminals. On a less glamorous note, they were now part of the state's Department of Public Safety and legally protected against disbandment.

A short, solidly built man with a shock of red hair, freckles and tortoise-shell glasses walked into the restaurant and Annie knew he must be Ingram. He wore a conservative gray suit rather than a uniform, and she was drawn to his green eyes, welcoming grin and pleasing Texas accent. He shook her hand firmly and led her outside to the County Line's pretty, buzzing deck. She admired the view of hills that dropped off to valleys of houses and tranquil streets below.

A lanky waiter with long black hair and multiple tattoos came to their table. Ingram stood up quickly and gave him the half-hug-with-shoulder-pat Annie often saw men bestow on good buddies.

"Hey, man," Ingram grinned. "I didn't know you worked here. Annie, this is Hector Manning, one of my old college roommates."

Annie stood up and shook the waiter's hand. "Hi, Hector."

"Yeah, I just got back in town. I'm trying to get my band back together," Manning told them. "Austin's a better place for us than southern California."

"Great," Ingram said. "I'd love to hear you guys play again. Here's my card. Can you let me know about your upcoming gigs?"

"Sure thing, dude," Manning said. "You still with the Rangers?"

"Yeah," said Ingram. "Let me know when you're settled in. We can grab a few beers."

He ordered for himself and Annie and soon Manning delivered heaping plates of beef brisket, coleslaw and sweet, spicy barbecue sauce.

"One of the things I love about Austin is that people never leave for good," Ingram said. "They're always drawn back because this place gets embedded into your soul."

"I agree. I've always thought it would be great to live in a college town like this."

"Yeah, the only thing is that the students look so young and you feel old really fast."

"Thanks for taking the time to meet," Annie said. "Maddy said you were the state's expert on secession, past and present."

"As you probably know, I'm very fond of Maddy," Ingram smiled. "She and I have traded deep background information for years. I'm happy to do the same for you, as long as you don't get me into trouble."

"Agreed," said Annie. "I know you can't be quoted unless I go through the public information office."

"Probably they'd send you to my boss."

"How did you get interested in the secessionists?"

"The Rangers assigned me years ago to track the Republic of Texas movement, as the secessionists like to call it. Now it's become a specialty for me – and probably a bit of an obsession."

"Why an obsession?"

"I think it's because I'm a native Texan, and I recognize there's a bit of a crazy streak among some of us who love the state. We have a go-it-alone, we-can-do-anything mentality you don't usually find in other states. Are you a native Texan?"

"No, I'm from Virginia. I've only lived in the state for six years, in Houston."

"Let me give you some background," Ingram said. "You know that Texas fought and won its independence from Mexico in 1836, right?"

"Yeah, I've visited the Alamo and San Jacinto, where the key battles were fought. I really love the way Texans pay homage to the Alamo, by removing their cowboy hats."

"It's very moving, isn't it?" said Ingram. "For nearly ten years after it won independence from Mexico, Texas was a republic – an independent nation. It wasn't annexed by the United States until 1845."

"Then, in 1861, Texas seceded from the union and joined the Confederate states. Texans voted four-to-one to leave the union, which secessionists always say represented their true feelings."

"Okay," said Annie. "But it became part of the United States again after the Civil War, right?"

"Yeah, but the Republic of Texas folks contend that the state's annexation by the United States was illegal. They argue that Texas remains an independent nation under occupation."

"Is there any legal basis for that?"

"Most scholars don't think so. The U.S. Supreme Court ruled in 1868 in a landmark case that Texas continued to be a state, despite seceding in 1861. It characterized the Civil War as a short-lived rebellion against the country's established government."

"So why do the secessionists think they can leave the union?"

"They argue that there's nothing in either the U.S. constitution or the state's constitution that would conclusively prevent it. In fact, there's a phrase in the Texas constitution that specifically provides for people to abolish or alter their government, if they so choose. The secessionists have got lawyers and legal scholars working on this full-time. They feel confident they can win a legal fight."

Ingram paused to speak to Manning again, ordering coffee and apple crisp with ice cream for them to share.

"Since the Civil War days, there have always been some Texans who have argued that Texas is still a republic," he said. "But a real movement grew in the mid-1990s. The Republic of Texas became a militia-like organization, similar to the Ruby Ridge militants and other groups out west that refused to recognize the legitimacy of the U.S. government."

Annie listened intently and took notes as he talked. She used a tape recorder as well, but she had always found that writing it down made her remember things. She trusted Ingram and instinctively knew he'd be a great ally.

"One of the Republic of Texas branches took it to the extreme," he said. "A few of their members took a man and his wife hostage in West Texas in 1997."

"Yeah, I talked to a history professor recently about the notorious stand-off," Annie said. "It only lasted a week, right?"

"Yeah, but it's become part of the state's separatist lore. Some people made fun of it, but it could have been disastrous."

"What happens in Texas never stays in Texas, does it?" Annie said. "It becomes the butt of a thousand jokes. What's happened since then?"

"It's been quiet, but it always flares up again," Ingram said. "A few Republic of Texas groups or their imitators have websites filled with rhetoric, some selling Texas memorabilia to raise money.

"But some of us Rangers think there's serious, significant activity behind the scenes. My job is to monitor it and make sure that there's no threat of violence or political instability.

"Of course, this is all strictly off the record for now," Ingram reminded Annie.

"I understand," said Annie. "What do you think is really going on?"

"I'm not sure," said Ingram. "But I sense that it could be a powder keg."

"Really? In what way?"

Ingram thought for a moment.

"The factions that were active in the mid-1990s have gone underground," he said. "They were very much fringe groups with little power or money. Now, current, respectable politicians spout the same kind of stuff that we were seeing then. You may remember those infamous comments by Governor Perry a few years ago?"

"Yeah, my editor and I were just talking about that," Annie said.

"In April 2009, Perry told a reporter at a tax protest event that the United States better watch out," Ingram said.

"He said, 'We've got a great union. There's absolutely no reason to dissolve it. But if Washington continues to thumb their nose at the American people, who knows what may come of that?'

Ingram paused, looking at Annie.

"Now you and I know that the governor was basically preening for the cameras. But there are other people out there who take that kind of talk seriously."

"Are you talking about Tom Marr, the state representative from Marfa?" Annie said. "I've been assigned to profile him."

"He's one who's come to our attention recently. We'll be watching his run for governor to see what kind of following he attracts. But we don't think he's the only powerful Texan who feels that way."

"Is secession inherently a bad thing?" Annie asked.

"Depends upon who you ask, I guess. Personally, I would never support it. The United States has its faults, but I would never abandon it."

"I really appreciate your candor," Annie said. "Can we touch base on this from time to time – off the record, of course?"

"Of course, Annie. I'd be happy to see you again in Austin, or talk to you on the phone. Do you have enough to go on?"

"I think so. Thanks for bringing me here for lunch. This apple crisp is fabulous."

"It's killer, isn't it? Guess who turned me on to it?"

"Maddy, of course."

"Absolutely. Will you put in a good word for me when you get back? Tell her I'm debonair and sophisticated and would be an excellent catch for her."

Annie laughed. "I'll tell her that, and I'll be telling the truth."

"Thanks, Annie. I'll look forward to hearing what you find out about the secessionists."

CHAPTER 10

"Annie, can't you go a little faster? We're poking along, and it's nearly time for the big show," Maddy complained.

"Calm down, girlfriend," Annie said. "We're almost there."

She thought she had picked up Maddy early enough to make it to Kinston well ahead of Tom Marr's 1 p.m. speech at Middle Texas College. But the drive from Houston took longer than she thought and they would barely get there on time.

Marr had announced his candidacy for governor the week before in a low-key, West Texas event largely ignored by the news media. That wasn't surprising, since he had virtually no statewide visibility and the next election was two years away. He had made no mention of secession.

But Maddy's political sources had tipped her that Marr would make a "revolutionary" speech to business leaders at the Kinston community college. College president Ed Gonzales's pull in his community would guarantee a good turnout, and Marr would use the speech to test the waters on secession. Cilla decreed that both of them should cover it, since Annie had started researching the Marr profile and Maddy was still investigating the college.

Maddy had made substantial progress on her investigative project. Her latest story, based on records a source had given her, revealed that the college had used a secret subsidiary to buy a gold mine near Las Vegas. Some top college officials had hoped to make a clandestine fortune using a new mining process they'd paid a fly-by-night chemist to develop. But the process had failed miserably and the mine sat idle in the desert. Maddy had located the property and secretly visited, finding college equipment and personnel in the mine's office. When the story appeared, startled Texas officials announced their own investigation of the bizarre business venture, which Maddy notched as a victory.

"How did Gonzales and his pals react to your gold mine story?" Annie asked. They'd had no time to catch up.

"I hear that they're furious," Maddy smiled. "Of course, they wouldn't answer my questions for the story, but they had the nerve to complain to the Kinston paper how unfair it was."

"Typical tactic," Annie said. "But you'd better watch your step. The college would probably love to sue a big-city paper for libel."

"Do you think so?" Maddy said. "They seem more devious than that. I'd expect them to plot a nastier kind of revenge. Maybe they'll booby-trap my house – or let the air out of your tires today."

Annie laughed. "I have a lousy spare tire, so they'd get their revenge. We'd be doomed to spend the night."

Maddy had visited Middle Texas College several times, but Annie had never seen it. She had no trouble picking out the motley collection of Spanish-style buildings set back along a major highway near Kinston. The campus featured large oak trees, a small lake filled with ducks, and students hurrying between the open spaces.

"I hate the architecture," said Maddy. "It's the cheesy-looking, faux-Mexican garbage Texans built so much of in the 1960s."

"Well, it's a community college," Annie said. "It's not Hah-vaaaad. You could hardly expect 18th century buildings and ivy-covered walls."

"Right, folks here wouldn't take to anything that looked like Yankee Land," Maddy said.

Annie parked in a packed visitors' lot and the two hurried to the auditorium. It was about half full, maybe 120 people, Annie estimated, mostly conservative-looking business types with a generous sprinkling of students. She and Maddy walked to the front row, which was reserved for the media. A few local reporters and photographers had already settled in.

She looked at the stage and immediately spotted Marr from photographs she had seen. Tall, with an outdoorsy tan, his white-blond hair gleamed against a blue shirt, burgundy tie and well-tailored navy suit. He noticed her gaze and for a moment, his luminous blue eyes rested thoughtfully on her face. He had a regal look about him, as if he could be a descendant of a Viking king, she thought. He gave her a tentative smile, but she looked away quickly, embarrassed to be caught staring.

"Isn't he divine?" Maddy whispered. "Even handsomer in person than I remembered."

"He has the telegenic looks of a governor, for sure," Annie agreed. "But can he talk like one?"

"You see the short, fat Hispanic with the moustache? That's Ed Gonzales. The tall, balding guy with the look of a hungry wolf is Dan Riggins," Maddy said. "I hate that guy."

"Marr's brain trust, right?"

"Yep. The three of them met at UT and have been best buddies ever since. They call themselves the triumvirate."

"Isn't that Latin? A reference to Julius Caesar and his pals?" Annie said.

"Yeah, their little joke was that they'd rather be Latin than Greek. They apparently weren't interested in the oh-so-crude Animal House atmosphere of the UT frats. They fancied themselves intellectuals."

"Maddy, Riggins is looking at you. The wolf looks like he'd enjoy killing and eating you for dinner," Annie whispered.

"That's the CIA intimidation stare," said Maddy. She glared back at Riggins with equal ferocity.

Gonzales strode to the microphone and tapped it a few times. The auditorium grew quiet and he paused for maximum effect.

"Ladies and gentlemen, let me introduce you to Tom Marr – a great Texas legislator, my lifelong friend and the next governor of Texas," he said. The crowd applauded politely.

Marr got up, acknowledged the applause with a quick smile and started speaking slowly in a resonant baritone. Annie saw traces of sweat on his forehead and realized that he was nervous. He's a bit shy, she thought, like me. But his confidence seemed to grow as he talked, and she listened closely.

"Fellow Texans, I come before you as a proud native with ancestors who fought and died in the Texas Revolution. This land of ours is precious to me, as I know it is to you. There's nothing more beautiful to me than the Chisos Mountains of Big Bend or the Rio Grande River threading through our desert lands. I love the majesty of our state Capitol in Austin, the bustle of the Riverwalk on a San Antonio summer night and the wonderful smell of citrus fruit blooming in the Rio Grande Valley. I've always lived in West Texas, except for a few wonderful years in Austin, and I can't imagine living anywhere but Texas.

"But our beautiful state and wonderful way of life have never been in greater danger," he said. Unaccountably, he fastened his gaze on Annie again and she couldn't help staring back. She thought he was the handsomest man she'd even seen, but why was he looking at her?

"In the last two months, the violent feuds of the Mexican drug cartels have spilled blood across our border at least three times," he went on. "Rival gangs are attacking each other and it's poisoning life in cities like Brownsville, Laredo and Del Rio. People are scared to cross the border in the daytime, or to venture outside in their own cities at night. Bodies end up in our deserts with bullet holes, and with heads and limbs hacked off."

"How long will it be before all of our towns and cities are battlegrounds? Will the drug violence creep from Laredo to San Antonio? Brownsville to Houston? Del Rio to Kinston?"

"The U.S. Border Patrol can't do the job that Texans have a right to expect," he said. "We must control our borders – first, foremost and always."

Marr paused as business people applauded and some students cheered and whistled.

"Texas is what is known as a 'tax donor state.' Every dollar you and I pay in income taxes, we get much less in services.

"That's because God blessed the state we love with abundant resources. We still have 5 billion barrels of oil within our borders – one-fourth of the nation's supply. We still have the most farms and the highest acreage farmed of all states. We still have our lovely rivers, lakes and the wonders of the Texas Gulf Coast.

"We have the nation's second highest gross state product, more than $1.15 trillion. That's an economy that's bigger than that of most of the world's countries.

"Just think what we could do if we could use most – or even all – of those resources to support our twenty-five million Texans."

A hum of approval rippled across the auditorium and some in the audience stood up. Annie estimated that about two-thirds of the listeners seemed mesmerized. Marr seemed energized by their attention. His eyes shone with the kind of passion she had heard about, but rarely seen, in politicians giving speeches.

"If Texas had control of its resources, we could make sure that every child got a great education, from pre-kindergarten through college, and parents wouldn't have to pay a dime," he said.

"Every Texan who contributes to the state economy would get tax rebates -- instead of having to pay exorbitantly through the grossly unfair U.S. tax system. We could support our old and sick Texans in a way that gives them dignity instead of shame."

"How do we accomplish this?" Marr asked. "If I am elected governor, we would immediately press our legal case for secession from the United States – and I believe that we can succeed.

"That's because the Texas constitution says, 'The faith of the people of Texas stands pledged to the preservation of a republican form of government, and, subject to this limitation only, they have at all times the inalienable right to alter, reform or abolish their government in such manner as they may think expedient.'"

He stopped to let those words sink in.

"If you're like me, you're sick and tired of the partisan snarling that has driven the United States government to its knees in recent years. Politicians posture and ramble and delay. Nothing gets done – and our country is lost – maybe forever.

"By contrast, Texas is a place where men spilled their blood, and people fought to the death for their land. We have the land, the people and the spirit to make Texas the greatest of countries.

"So please join our crusade to make Texas a republic once again. Let's give Texas back to Texans!"

Many in the audience sprang up, applauded Marr and some took up a chant, "Texas for Texans." But others looked disapproving and a few left quickly. She heard a woman sitting behind her saying, "I'm getting out of here. There's no way I want to be part of this." Her heels clicked across the wooden floor as she moved to the end of the row.

Marr led the singing in his distinctive voice as the college band struck up "Texas Our Texas," the state anthem. Many in the audience could remember at least the first part of the song from elementary school days. They joined in:

"Texas, our Texas. All hail the mighty state. Texas, our Texas, so wonderful, so great. Boldest and grandest, withstanding every test, O empire wide and glorious, you stand supremely blest."

"Sounds like something the Nazis might have come up with, doesn't it?" Maddy whispered.

"It's a bit over the top," Annie agreed. "But what an amazing speech!"

"He nailed it," Maddy said.

Annie gathered her purse and laptop and she and Maddy hurried to the stage to interview Marr and Gonzales. Gonzales greeted them with icy politeness and said Marr was leaving to catch a plane. As they'd arranged between themselves, Maddy talked to Gonzales about the turnout and Annie ran over to catch Marr as he was leaving the stage.

"Hello, I'm Annie Price from the *Houston Times*," she said, shaking his large hand. "I'll be interviewing you on Friday in Marfa."

"Yes, I have it on my calendar," Marr smiled. "I'm looking forward to talking to you. I've enjoyed reading your stories on the *Times*' website, Miss Price."

She smiled. He kept looking at her face and didn't release her hand. Finally, she eased it out of his warm grasp.

"Call me Annie."

CHAPTER 11

Annie rushed with Maddy into the small corner room the college public relations people had reserved as a press office. Since Middle Texas College never got much press, the room didn't offer many refinements – just two old metal desks, three worn office chairs and a dark green faux-leather sofa so old, it looked 1950s retro. But they were glad that today, they didn't have to share it with other journalists. A few reporters and photographers from the local paper and TV station had shown up for Marr's speech, but had left quickly at the end.

They made a quick list of politicians and others to call for reaction, then both got on their cell phones to conduct quick interviews. Marr's public embrace of secession drew the mix of comments they had anticipated. Some called his remarks wrongheaded or even treasonous, but a few applauded what they said was his courage and vision. Annie got the feeling Marr had won a measure of respect and liking during his four years in the state legislature. Some politicians were quick to voice disagreement with him, but called Marr a friend and a hard-working legislator. She didn't know why, but that pleased her.

She called the governor's office for comment, getting Barb Anthony, a seasoned public relations aide she knew slightly. Annie was amused at Anthony's reaction when she told the aide about Marr's speech.

"He said what?" Anthony shouted into Annie's ear. "Uh, I need to get back to you on that. I'll consult with the governor first."

But time was ticking away, so Annie hurried through her calls to start writing. She and Maddy had agreed during the drive to Kinston that Annie would put the story together and Maddy would insert her reporting into it. Writing a deadline story with another reporter was sometimes tricky. Egos could clash, reporters could disagree on important points and the process could drag out a lot longer than necessary. Annie and Maddy rarely had problems with the direction of a story because they had worked together often. When they disagreed, Annie usually yielded to Maddy because her friend had more experience.

Annie drafted the story on her laptop at one of the beat-up desks and stepped aside to let Maddy add quotes from the people she had called. Then they both sat in front of the computer screen as Annie read the story aloud. They discussed it and tinkered with wording before sending it electronically to the newsroom, where Cilla quickly retrieved and edited it. She asked them a few questions before moving it to the copy desk for another read-through. Later, either the managing editor or top editor would read it before deadline.

"Guys, this is great stuff," she said. "It's on the page-one list. Is it exclusive?"

"Just one local paper and a TV station showed up," said Annie. "We didn't see anyone from Dallas or Austin."

"Excellent," said Cilla, who particularly enjoyed scooping the bigger papers. "And ladies, you should see the photos from the Kinston stringer we hired to shoot the speech. I thought all West Texans were pug-ugly with mullets and buck teeth, but Marr is Greek-god gorgeous."

"Yeah, Marr's a looker all right," Maddy said. "I saw him making googly eyes at Annie."

"Maddy, that's not true," Annie said. "We barely had time to speak before he left."

"Cilla, don't believe it," Maddy said. "He was squeezing her hand like he wished it was her boob."

Cilla snorted with laughter. "Take yourselves out for a nice dinner, girls, but skip the wine and hurry home. There's a newsroom meeting tomorrow at 10 a.m. Be there or be square."

"What's going on?" Annie asked.

"Big announcement about the future of the newspaper. Not sure what we'll hear, but I wouldn't miss it."

"We won't," Maddy said. "Should we all wear black?"

Though they had gotten back to Houston late, Annie and Maddy both made it to work early the next day, anticipating a big turnout for the standup at 10. The standup was the newsroom's slang for meetings where the managing editor or editor stood at a designated spot to brief the staff on important news. Annie was nervous about the meeting. She had skipped breakfast, feeling nauseous about what the day might bring.

Amanda Weeks, the newspaper's top editor, signaled for quiet after about 100 staffers had gathered, most standing before her with anxious faces.

Annie regarded Weeks as attractive, albeit in a severe way. The petite editor always dressed in expensively cut pants or skirts with great blouses and jackets. Her closely cropped, black hair and tall leather boots gave her an appropriately commanding air. Annie regarded Weeks as intelligent and fair-minded, with good journalistic instincts. Like most reporters, she kept her distance to avoid the editor's quick temper and fluctuating moods. But she knew that Weeks cared deeply about the newsroom and the paper.

Annie thought she looked more nervous and less sure of herself than usual. Her eyes restlessly roamed the room, as if searching for something elusive, like certainty.

"Folks, I have an important announcement," Weeks began. "The *Times* has been sold to McKnight Publishing."

Quickly she ran through the details in the shocked silence of the newsroom. In a few weeks, the paper would become the largest publication in the medium-sized McKnight newspaper chain. The California-based chain, which had bought several papers in recent years, would pay the Carter family $400 million for the Houston daily. Annie thought that seemed like a low price for a large paper, but she knew prices for newspapers were sinking like stones in the ocean's depths.

Barry McKnight, the 42-year-old son of McKnight's CEO, would become the *Times'* new publisher. He would move to Houston to assume the top *Times'* job within a month.

Annie thought buying the *Times* seemed like a bold move for the McKnight chain, whose debt was already approaching $1 billion. If the stagnant newspaper industry rebounded in the next year or so, analysts would praise it as a smart move. But it could easily go the other way.

With dozens of pairs of worried eyes staring at her, Weeks belatedly offered words of reassurance.

"No immediate changes have been announced. The company values the *Times*, obviously. But over the next few months, the company will be evaluating future needs in this newsroom and others.

"I have time to take a few questions," she said.

"Why did the Carter family decide to sell?" reporter Jim Merrill asked.

"Well, you know, Jim, that the last few years haven't exactly been a stellar time for this newspaper – or any other. I expect that the family thought it was a good offer at a difficult time."

"Will there any layoffs?" Annette Driver, a young copy editor, asked, drumming her fingers restlessly on her desk.

"I don't know, Annette. As I said, McKnight will study our operation carefully to see what, if any, cost savings can be achieved. I'm sure that buyouts, layoffs, furloughs and other measures will be considered."

"What about our pension plan?" Gary Melton, a photographer nearing retirement age said.

"As you know, traditional pensions are becoming a thing of the past," said Weeks. "I wouldn't be surprised if the plan changes, but you won't lose what you've put into it, of course."

After a few more questions, she ended the standup. Annie thought Weeks realized that her lack of information wasn't exactly boosting the confidence level in the room.

"We'll be talking about this in more depth in the weeks ahead," Weeks said. "But let's keep our focus on what really matters – our work."

Annie returned to her desk, her stomach churning. She searched for an antacid in her cluttered middle drawer. Was this the beginning of the end for her career in newspapers? What would she do, and what would her dad say? She managed to force down the tension and started making calls to follow up on the Marr story.

At the close of the day, she joined about a dozen other reporters who wanted to digest the news at La Carafe, a cramped but beloved old bar a few blocks from the paper. Inside its exposed brick walls set off by a long, battered wooden bar, Annie and her colleagues ordered beer and wine.

She and the others speculated on why the Carter family had agreed to cash out. John Carter, the current publisher, was more interested in ranching in the Hill Country than newspapering in Houston as he approached 65. His father was almost 90. The younger members of the family didn't want to continue the struggle to keep the newspaper profitable, they agreed.

Annie listened carefully as talk centered on Barry McKnight, the relatively young McKnight family member who would become the *Times* publisher. The reporters at La Carafe drafted Jim Merrill, the political reporter and a skilled researcher, to dig into archives and public records to find out everything he could about the new leader. Annie and her colleagues knew McKnight had worked at other company papers in various positions, but never as publisher.

"Great, we get a publisher-in-training who has never lived in Texas," Jim said. "Wonder what new and innovative management techniques he'll be trying out on us?"

"At least he can get the attention of the top brass at McKnight," Annie said. "Maybe that will protect us. Since we're a big acquisition, maybe they won't cut many people from the newsroom."

"We're hardly overstaffed," Maddy said. "I don't see how we could lose any people."

But Seth Anderson, the City Hall reporter and a veteran of three other papers, shook his head.

"Look at what has happened at some of McKnight's bigger papers in the west. Management has done everything it can to pinch pennies. It'll do whatever has to be done."

Annie trudged back to the newsroom feeling sick at heart.

Reporters tended to be more pessimistic than most employees, but she had heard nothing at La Carafe that made her feel hopeful about the new ownership.

She wanted to check her messages and talk to Cilla before she headed home. As she walked along the sidewalk towards the *Times* building, she saw a crumpled newspaper in the gutter. She looked at the banner headline: "Marr stirs Kinston crowd with talk of secession."

She had almost forgotten their big front-page story that day. The sight of the castoff paper in the gutter seemed an especially bad omen.

CHAPTER 12

Dan Riggins stood outside the door of the auditorium in Kinston, watching and listening as the last of the audience filtered out. He wanted to gauge the impact of Marr's speech, so he strained to hear to whatever snatches of conversation he could pick up. He was excited, though no one would have guessed. His years at the CIA had taught him to keep his emotions under wraps and it was rare that anyone could tell what he was thinking. Marr usually knew, because the two of them shared a closeness that Riggins never felt with other men, even his brothers. Riggins thought Marr represented his better nature, perhaps the more generous and open person he could have been if the CIA hadn't soured some of his beliefs. The feeling that Marr was his alter ego had persisted since college and continued to be something that kept them close.

Two men strode out of the auditorium, talking about Marr's speech. Both looked middle-aged, with sports coats and ties a shade louder than they'd wear in a more sophisticated city. Riggins thought they were probably local businessmen.

"He made a lot of sense when he talked about the border threats," the taller, balding man said. "But I can't imagine leaving the rest of the country. What would happen if somebody attacked us?"

"Didn't he say something about contracting with the U.S. government for military protection?" a man with a graying moustache said. "It's just too complicated to work, in my opinion."

"Yeah, it's kind of a crazy idea, but probably people said the same thing when the colonies wanted to split from England," his companion replied.

"You have to wonder if Marr is nuts. He looks good, but you never know about these loners from West Texas."

Riggins felt his anger burning. He grabbed the taller man by his ugly tie and said, "You have no idea what you're saying. Tom Marr's a true Texas hero. If you had any love for your state, you wouldn't talk like such an idiot."

"Hey buddy, calm down," the man said, staring at Riggins and pulling away. "Are you crazy?"

Riggins glared at the man, who left quickly with his companion.

He stood still for a moment, trying to regain his composure as a tall, slim woman with feathered brown hair approached with a smile. He straightened up and returned it, appraising her stylish figure in a well-tailored magenta outfit.

"Dan Riggins, right?" she said. "I'm Margaret Redmond, dean of students at the college."

She presents herself well, he thought. Her skin was slightly freckled and her nose and mouth were too large for her face to be considered beautiful. But when she smiled, she projected warmth and intelligence.

"Hello, Margaret. You're supposed to show me some of the newer parts of the campus, aren't you?"

"Yes, Ed'll be tied up for a while, talking to his business friends who came out for the speech. How do you think it went?"

"More importantly, how do you think it went?"

"He's a very engaging man whose ideas seemed to excite the crowd," she said.

"You sound like you have reservations."

"Well, I'd like to hear more – and I'm sure I will. It's a long time until the election."

He matched her brisk steps as they strolled around the school grounds, with Margaret pointing out buildings and other landmarks. He appreciated her enthusiastic patter about the campus and its history, since he hadn't spent much time there in recent years. When he met with Marr and Gonzales, it was usually at Marr's ranch. If he went to the college to confer with Gonzales, he went straight to the executive suite in the administration building and didn't hang around afterwards. Margaret intrigued him, so he used a slightly friendlier version of his usual interrogation technique.

"How long have you worked here, Margaret?"

"About 15 years."

"What brought you to Kinston?"

"My husband was assigned to Fort Kinston, so I looked for a job teaching English while we were here."

"Is he still there?"

"No, he was killed in Afghanistan six years ago."

"I'm sorry."

"Thank you. After he died, people here were so nice to me, I ended up staying longer than I thought I would. Ed promoted me to department head and then, two years ago, to dean of students."

"Where do you call home?"

"I'm originally from California, but most of my relatives there have died. I consider myself a Texan now."

She smiled at Riggins as they walked through the planetarium, one of the newer campus attractions. He wondered if she could be useful during Tom's campaign. They needed women to convince other women of the necessity of secession.

"Ed Gonzales has been good to me and good for this campus, as you can see. But I'd like to hear about you, Dan. Ed mentioned that you have twin sons in college."

"Yes, my sons are at Washington and Lee University in Virginia. My wife Karen and I are moving back to San Antonio after living in Washington for a long time. I'm glad to be coming home and working with Tom Marr's campaign."

"He certainly has unorthodox views. Do you really think he has a strong chance statewide?"

"Of course," Riggins said. "We'll make it happen. He's the man Texas needs desperately."

He knew he sounded brusque, but her words made him bristle. What did she know about politics? He forced himself to remain calm this time.

"I'm sorry," Margaret said, noticing his change in mood. "I don't mean to sound dismissive. It's just that I've never heard a candidate call for secession. With Fort Kinston, this is a pretty patriotic part of the world."

"I've worked for the U.S. government all my life," Riggins said. "I love this country. But that doesn't mean that I can't love Texas even more. Texas could be the kind of country the United States used to be and was meant to be."

"Well, I know the United States isn't perfect, but my husband died serving this country, so I could never condone secession," she said.

He didn't care for her words, but he forced himself to smile.

"You're entitled to that opinion. But keep listening to Tom Marr. You may change your mind before the campaign is over."

He felt angry, so he changed the subject.

"Tell me about your job. Do you deal with the college's military contracts?"

"No. Ed put the vice-president, Will Ward, in charge of the contracts business. I run the Kinston campus. We don't overlap. I think Ed likes it that way."

Good, Riggins thought. She shouldn't come anywhere near the contracts, especially now. She's too nosy – and probably too smart.

They walked through more academic buildings and chatted about Fort Kinston, talking about people they knew in common there. It seemed Margaret had as many contacts at the huge military base as Riggins.

"Dan, can I show you anything else? I think we've seen most of the buildings now. I can take you back to Ed's office."

"That would be great," he said.

She brought him back to the administration building and walked away, slim legs moving with athletic grace. She's not bad looking, he thought. Maybe I should seduce her and teach her a lesson or two.

Perhaps because he had managed to keep his relationship with Alicia going for so long, Riggins felt he could conquer almost any woman. But he usually suppressed those impulses because in his heart, he didn't really want anyone except Alicia. He forced himself not to look back at Margaret, to keep moving toward Gonzales' office.

Riggins found Gonzales behind his desk, looking satisfied with himself.

"Tom did a wonderful job with his first big speech," Gonzales said. "I thought it went over pretty well."

"Reaction was mixed, as we knew it would be, but the majority really liked him," Riggins said. "The border issue was especially effective. We'll have to keep punching away at that."

"Yeah, it's our trump card," Gonzales said.

Riggins switched to another subject festering inside his head.

"Why were those two reporters from the *Houston Times* there? How did they know about Tom's speech?"

"We invited the local reporters, but as you instructed, we didn't send out a statewide press release. The idea was to let Tom find his voice with a mostly handpicked local audience. And he did well, so there's no harm done.

"Maddy Daniels has covered politics and politicians at the *Times* for a long time, so probably she heard about it from another politician," Gonzales added.

"I didn't like it," Riggins said. "Who knows what they'll write?"

"The speech was pretty straightforward. They could hardly fail to mention that Tom got plenty of applause and enthusiasm. I expect the story'll help our cause."

"Don't be so sure. Isn't Daniels the reporter who wrote the story about the gold mine? That was really damaging. Isn't she hounding the college for information about the contracts?"

"Yes, but that's under control. Our lawyer has been stalling, giving her access to records a little at a time. She'll never be able to figure anything out."

"I think you're being overly optimistic about Daniels, but we'll talk about that later. I'm heading to Tom's ranch to sit in on the interview he's giving to that other *Times* reporter, Annie Price. We need to be vigilant."

"You requested a more specific contracts briefing with Will Ward, right?" Gonzales said. "He's waiting for us in his office."

"I'm running late," Riggins said. "Could he give me a lift to Austin? We could talk on the way to catch my plane."

"Sure. I can't go with you, though. My board meeting's in 30 minutes."

"No problem," Riggins said, shaking hands with Gonzales. "I'll stop by Will's office."

Gonzales had hired William Ward as vice-president when he became president ten years previously. Riggins knew Gonzales enjoyed his role as the top leader, being the public face – and mouthpiece – of the college, but didn't like to work too hard. So Gonzales left most of the poky administrative and financial work to Ward, whose fascination with numbers went hand in hand with a reclusive – and obnoxious -- personality. Gonzales trusted Ward with the college's secrets and rewarded his unorthodox accounting skills with generous bonuses.

Ward, thin and slightly stooped with a graying ponytail and thick granny glasses, stood up as Riggins entered his office. Even for small-town Texas, his fashion sense was execrable. He wore a tan polyester jacket and wide tie that might have been considered fashionable in the 1970s. Gonzales had made a quick call asking him to take Riggins to the airport, so Ward was ready to leave.

They headed out of Kinston in Ward's ten-year-old Crown Victoria, their conversation centering on the college's military education contracts and the profits that could be extracted from them.

Ward knew more about the contracts than anyone, even Gonzales, and Riggins enjoyed their frequent conversations. He saw Ward in Washington fairly often on business involving the contracts. During his years at the CIA, Riggins used his influence to help the college gain advantage in bidding to the military. Ward repaid him with inside information on the college – and on Gonzales.

Riggins understood people like Ward, who were driven mainly by greed, better than he understood Gonzales, whose motives tended to be more complex. He worried about Gonzales' unpredictability and used Ward to keep an eye on his lifelong friend. Ward understood and appreciated that instinct and didn't mind being interrogated.

"Has Ed visited his father-in-law in Matamoros lately?" Riggins asked.

"They went just before Christmas and he's supposed to go back next month."

"How's Ed's home life?"

"He seems restless and not as happy as he used to be."

"Does he talk about Cecilia and Manuel?"

"Not so much. He complains about Manuel's crying keeping him awake at night."

"Is Manny Lopez happy with Gonzales?"

"If he wasn't happy, we'd know it in a hurry," Ward said dryly. "Ed worries about being under the thumb of his father-in-law. He calls it the deal with the devil."

"Well, he should worry," Riggins said. "He got us into this. But the money's good, so he'll have to live with it."

"Yeah, but he's basically a pussy," Ward said. "He wants a lot, but he doesn't want to pay the price."

"Is he worrying about Maddy Daniels, that reporter from the *Times*?"

"Not as much as he should be," Ward said. "She's smart enough to keep asking questions and pressing us for more documents. She's getting another batch of college records later this week."

"Can't you keep that from happening?" Riggins asked.

"I've stalled as long as I dare. The lawyer says we have to give them up under the Texas open records law."

Riggins could feel his chest tighten with tension as he considered Ward's words. He reminded himself to breathe deeply and keep his temper.

"Do you think she knows anything?"

"Not much so far, but she'll be calling me in a few days. Don't worry, Dan. I'll call you if I hear anything from her that sounds worrisome."

"Please do. I'm afraid Ed's overconfident about his dealings with reporters."

"Of course. I know you'll know what to do if that situation gets out of hand."

"I'll count on you, Will," Riggins said. "And you can count on me. You know I'll make it worth your while."

CHAPTER 13

After a tumultuous week marked by Marr's speech in Kinston and the newsroom's angst over the paper's sale, Annie hit the road on a Friday to West Texas. She was looking forward to interviewing Tom Marr. By noon, she had passed San Antonio and headed out Highway 90 toward Marfa.

Annie had never traveled in West Texas and she marveled at the sense of peace she felt as traffic fell away and the landscape turned increasingly stark and rugged. She'd heard people joke about West Texas, calling it miles and miles of miles and miles. But after a half-hour of seeing no cars, trucks or people, she felt purified, almost spiritual. There was something alluring about solitary spaces. The sky shone a brighter blue than in most of the smoky cities she'd left behind, and the open land framed against the horizon stretched endlessly. By late afternoon, she passed through the small town of Marfa and drove westward into Marr's ranch.

Cilla had told Annie she could take just four days to travel to West Texas, interview Marr and return to Houston where plenty of other assignments awaited. Annie felt lucky to get a jump on other media that were suddenly interested after the publicity over Marr's secessionist speech in Kinston. Since the paper's finances were limited, she had accepted Marr's offer to stay in the ranch's guesthouse near the big house where he lived with his daughter.

She knew that the Marr ranch included tens of thousands of acres of rolling grassland, but she wasn't prepared for the power of its wide-open spaces. She turned off the highway and drove back into the Marr property for several miles before the landscape opened into his two-story, Spanish-style stucco house. With the Davis Mountains to the north and the Chinati Mountains to the south, large oak trees and minimal landscaping framed the unpretentious-looking home. She looked closer and spotted Marr sitting on the long front porch with a pretty blond child.

She stopped her car and got out. They quickly came over to greet her.

"Hi, Tom," she said, extending her hand. "It's good to see you again. Who's this young lady?"

"This is my daughter Betsy," he said. "She just turned 10 and likes visitors a lot."

"Hey, Annie," Betsy said. "We don't have dinner until 7. I'll show you your room in the guesthouse."

"Great, Betsy."

"Would you like to go swimming in our pool on the patio?" The girl asked. "Dad and I swim almost every afternoon when the weather's hot."

"I'd love to, but I didn't bring a bathing suit," she said.

"There's an assortment of bathing suits inside the hall closet of the guesthouse," Marr said. "If you'd like to swim, I'll get Maria, our cook, to serve dinner poolside later."

"Sounds good," said Annie, thinking it would help her work on the profile to see Marr with his daughter.

The small stucco guesthouse featured two charming bedrooms, two baths, a well-equipped miniature kitchen and an airy living room with white wicker furniture. Betsy said her great-grandparents had built it a long time ago and her father had fixed it up for company five years ago. She said Annie should take the nicer room with the red coverlet and the bigger bed, since she was tall.

Betsy opened the walk-in hall closet and started pulling out women's clothes from a chest of drawers.

"These are some of my mom's things," she said. "She died of cancer when I was four."

"I was so sorry to hear that," Annie said. "Do you remember your mom?"

"I remember some things, but not as much as I'd like," said Betsy. "Dad tells me stories about her and I look through the picture albums sometimes."

"That's good."

"She was tall and pretty, like you. But she had blonde hair, like me. People say I look like her."

Betsy held up three bikinis for her to try on. Annie winced.

"Is there a one-piece bathing suit somewhere in those drawers?"

"I think so." She rifled through the chest of drawers again and held up a black stretchy bathing suit that looked more modest. Annie went into the bathroom and put it on while the girl waited.

"Oh, you look beautiful," Betsy said, handing Annie a beach towel and a black lacy sarong that went with the suit. She took Annie's hand and led her to a stone patio and large pool in back of the ranch house.

Marr, dressed in royal blue swim trunks, looked tanned and exceptionally fit, she thought. He and Betsy dove into the water while Annie settled into a lounge chair. She felt a bit uncomfortable and wondered whether she should be intruding on their time together.

"Annie, come in and play volleyball with us," Betsy said. "You and me against Dad."

"You sure? I'm pretty rusty," said Annie.

For the next hour, Annie laughed and played with Betsy and Marr in the pool. She couldn't remember the last time she'd relaxed and had so much fun. She played every pool game the three of them could come up with. She finally got out, leaving Betsy to practice swim strokes with her father while she went to change.

Back in the guesthouse, she looked at her wet, sun-flushed body in the mirror and suddenly felt uneasy. Probably she should have passed up the pool fun. She was a reporter with a serious job to do and he was her story's subject. There was a narrow line between putting a source at ease and becoming too familiar with him. Had she crossed it? She hoped not.

She showered, blow-dried her hair and selected a modest outfit for dinner – black Capri pants and a red cotton blouse that was summery without being overtly sexy. She added a long strand of black beads and simple black sandals.

Over a dinner of steaks especially butchered for the family from the ranch's prize herd, she enjoyed listening to Betsy chattering about her school, her friends and her horse. Later, Ana, the nanny, came out to take the girl to bed. After hugging Betsy, Annie and Marr were alone for the first time. He had donned a white T-shirt and looked relaxed in his dry swim trunks.

"You were definitely a hit with my daughter," he smiled. "I hope she wasn't too much for you. Since it's just the two of us most of the time, she loves having company."

"She's a wonderful girl. You must be very close. She obviously adores you."

"She's been a blessing to me since my wife died," Marr said. "She's a lot like Elizabeth, her mother, but also very much her own little person."

"What happens when you go to Austin for the Legislature?"

"I hate to leave her, but she's got Maria and Ana here to take care of her. I come back most weekends."

"She must miss you – not having a mother at her age must be very tough."

"I really should remarry for her sake, but I haven't found anyone, and it's hard to make the time to look for a life partner. Now that I'm running for governor, I'll have even less time."

He leaned back in the lounge chair as they sipped after-dinner brandy. A cool breeze rippled across the patio as the sky began to darken.

"My friend and campaign manager, Dan Riggins, is coming over at 10 a.m. tomorrow. He'd like to be there during your interview."

"Okay, that's fine," said Annie. She thought she'd better ask him a question or two while he was relaxed, before Riggins showed up in the morning.

"When did you start thinking about the idea of Texas seceding?"

"I don't know," he said. "When I was a child, I was always fascinated with the stories of King Arthur and the Knights of the Round Table. Camelot seemed to be the perfect place, where knights could do good deeds and take care of the people."

He took a sip of brandy, gazed at the midnight-blue sky for a moment and continued.

"When I got to college and took history classes, I always thought Texas could be a kind of Camelot. With the right kind of governing, this place could be close to perfect."

"You know, I've always loved those stories too," Annie said. "I remember reading a child's version when I was little. Then, when I got to college, we studied Tennyson's 'Idylls of the King.'"

"Did you have a favorite tale?"

"I loved the story of Gareth, the young man whose mother makes him serve as a kitchen scullion before he is knighted," Annie recalled. "He accepts a quest to help the lady Lynette. She scorns him at first, but later falls in love with him."

"That's a great one. I really enjoyed the character of King Arthur himself, trying to create a just and fair society through his code of chivalry."

"So you see yourself as a sort of King Arthur?" Annie asked.

He gave her a searching look, she thought, and seemed embarrassed. She rushed to put him at ease.

"I'm intrigued – and I'm being serious," she said.

"I probably should have skipped this last drink," he smiled. "But at least King Arthur is a better role model than the last few governors we've had. Most of our politicians are so plastic and self-serving. The king tried to help the poor and encourage his knights to serve Camelot's people."

"Yeah, but remember, eventually he failed," Annie said. "His wife Guinevere cheats on him with Lancelot, his knights are killed off and he's mortally wounded in battle."

"You have a good memory, Annie. But it doesn't have to end that way."

"You're right, Tom," she smiled. "In Texas, you can create your own history."

"You must think I'm silly," Marr said.

"I don't think you're silly at all," she said. "But I think you have the kind of ideals that are difficult to hold on to in the rough-and-tumble of politics. Are you sure you want to be governor?"

"Yeah, I have something unique to offer and I want to give it my best shot. Secession will be a long and complicated process, but it could make Texas the greatest country in the world. I've thought about it all my life."

He looked at his watch, said it was nearly midnight and offered to walk her back to the guesthouse. They strolled along a grassy path from the pool to its front porch. Tom put a hand on her arm before they reached the door and pointed to the dark sky.

"On a clear night, you can see so many stars here," he said. "This is what I love to come back to whenever I can. In Austin, the lights of the city drown out the stars."

"Houston's even worse," Annie said. "Is that Orion's Belt?"

"Yes." They stood silently, appreciating the moment. At the door, he squeezed her hand and smiled.

"I'll see you in the morning. Thanks for making it a wonderful evening for Betsy and me."

In the quiet of the guesthouse, Annie took out her laptop and started making notes about her day with Marr. But she was having trouble concentrating, so she slammed it shut after a few moments.

Instead, she watched a small black spider climb toward the whitewashed ceiling, settle into a corner and start spinning a web. That's like me, Annie thought, alone and spinning away my little life. She sat still, reviewing the afternoon and evening with Betsy and Marr. For a few hours, she'd felt like a cherished member of their family. Most of the time she didn't mind being single, but tonight she ruminated on missing a part of life that many people took for granted. Would she ever find the kind of man who wanted her and a lifelong commitment? She hoped she would, but she knew plenty of women in their thirties and forties who hadn't – and were losing hope they ever would.

She thought about Marr, his handsome face, trim body and their provocative conversation. She loved the image of him as King Arthur. He seemed smart, principled and charismatic. He would make an attractive, though controversial, candidate. She didn't quite know what to make of his stand on secession.

She wondered what he thought of her. Did he find her attractive?

Oh Annie, she scolded herself. Get over it. This isn't about you. Finally she got comfortable, burrowed under the soft white sheet and fell asleep.

CHAPTER 14

The next morning, she woke early, dressed quickly and hurried to the big house as light crept into the sky. The cook directed her to the large den at the back and said coffee and homemade sweet rolls would be served there.

She walked in silently and saw Marr and a man she recognized as Dan Riggins standing in front of floor-to-ceiling windows stretching across the back of the house. The large den was paneled in rustic wood planking and decorated with worn but comfortable-looking lodge-style furniture. Riggins' arm was thrown over Marr's shoulder as the two men stood silently, surveying the splendor of the West Texas sunrise with its pinks, oranges and blues creeping over the mountains.

"Hey, guys."

They turned and looked surprised to see her. Marr came over and clasped her hands, his eyes resting on her pulled-back hair and moving down her body. He looked approvingly at the simple white blouse and straight khaki pants she was wearing, and she was glad she hadn't added a jacket, heels and jewelry. From what she'd seen of him and the ranch house, she'd gathered he didn't go for the fussy and the formal. He put his warm hand on her elbow, guiding her to Riggins and the stunning view.

"This is my best friend and campaign manager, Dan Riggins," Marr said. "As you can see, we're enjoying the gorgeous sunrise. This is my favorite vantage point from the house."

Riggins was slim, balding and a shade taller than Annie. Up close, she noticed the intelligence in his dark brown eyes and thick, expressive eyebrows. She could detect only a trace of the wolfish look Maddy had mentioned.

He smiled, but it left his eyes quickly as he shook hands and looked at her appraisingly. She remembered the hateful look she saw him flash at Maddy before Marr's speech in Kinston. She would be guarded in his presence.

"How do you like West Texas, Annie?" Riggins said.

"I love it. I've never been anywhere where I felt so completely at home. The sweep of the land and the grandeur of the mountains really soothe your soul."

Riggins looked surprised and gratified. She felt she'd gone up a few notches in his estimation.

"I wouldn't expect a Houstonian to feel that way," he said. "Some people think West Texas is barren and ugly, but we feel that it's the spiritual core of our state."

"I'd agree with that. There's nothing else like it. Are you guys about ready to start talking?"

"Sure. Let me pour you some coffee first," said Marr. "Want me to get Maria to cook you some eggs?"

"No, I'm good to go as long as there's coffee."

"Amen," said Marr. They settled into the sunny den, the two men sitting on either side of her.

She went through a list of biographical and background questions. Marr told her about his boyhood on the ranch, college experiences at UT and his return to the ranch as a young entrepreneur with a sick parent. He was as open, charming and self-deprecating as the night before.

Riggins laughed as Marr talked about their first meeting at the university. The two of them had both shown up at a meeting of the Young Republicans and didn't like any of the speakers or the party rhetoric.

"I said something about how Texas meant the most to me, and why couldn't we organize a revolutionary party around our state?" Marr said. "Everyone looked at me suspiciously and I walked out. But Dan and Ed Gonzales got it. They followed me out the door."

"Yeah, we started meeting at your apartment instead," Riggins said.

"We called ourselves the triumvirate," Tom said. "We all liked Latin and modeled ourselves after the first Roman triumvirate – Julius Caesar, Pompey the Great and Marcus Crassus. Those guys were united against the establishment, the Roman Senate."

"So you consider yourselves rebels?" Annie asked.

"Well, we definitely don't fall into the traditional party lines," Tom said. "We'll always put Texas first."

That was the opening for her to probe deeply about their beliefs on secession, which she felt might raise Riggins's hackles. He surprised her by answering some of the questions himself.

"Secession is a drastic step for any state to consider," she said. "Why Texas, and why now?"

"Surely you've noticed what's been happening in the United States over the last five or ten years," Riggins said. "Congress has lost its way, political parties run third-rate candidates and shoddy campaigns, and the American people have lost the spark that made this a great country when we were growing up."

Riggins looked at Marr, who picked up the thread.

"Here in Texas, we still have the will to grow and prosper. We've got to move fast to encourage that dynamic spirit, before our people become the impotent whiners that seem to dominate the rest of the country. Who knows what we could achieve if we harness the wealth and brains and spirit of Texas?"

"Texas, by itself, could be as productive and powerful as the rest of the country combined," Riggins said.

"How would you protect Texas from the dangers in the rest of the world without the U.S. Department of Defense and its powers?" Annie asked.

"We'd contract with the U.S. for services like national defense that would be impractical for Texas to provide," said Marr. "But we'd have our own police and armed forces."

"How would that work?"

"We're still studying that issue," Riggins said quickly.

The two men shared a look that Annie interpreted as a question about her. How much should we tell this reporter? She wondered why they seemed to shut down on the subject of police and armed forces.

Annie continued asking questions until Riggins looked at his watch.

"Let's break for lunch," he said. "Tom and I need to confer and check our messages. We really need to wind this up soon."

"Fine," said Annie. "But I need at least an hour more of your time."

"Annie, help yourself to sandwiches in the kitchen while Dan and I talk in my study," Marr said.

He followed Riggins out of the room, leaving Annie alone. She had recorded their conversation and had also taken notes. She went through her notes quickly, underlining key points and figuring what else she needed to ask.

Riggins seemed more approachable than she would have guessed, as eloquent as Marr and almost as eager to express his views. She wondered about the dynamics of the two men's relationship. Granted, college friendships could be defining and long lasting, but it seemed more than that, as if they were two halves of a whole. They seemed extraordinarily close and not afraid to express it.

She also suspected they had secrets they wouldn't share with her. Perhaps they hadn't quite figured everything out in this secession plan of theirs – or perhaps they had and didn't want to reveal controversial details yet. They both were smart and interesting, but she wasn't going to take anything they said on faith – especially anything from Riggins. She thought of the investigative reporter's maxim: If your mother says she loves you, check it out.

She checked her messages instead and noticed she had a text from Rob Ryland, the *Times'* newsroom clerk, asking her to call the newsroom immediately. She got him on the phone.

"Hey, Rob. Does Cilla need me?"

"She's out right now, but she wanted me to tell you to get on the road back to Houston. She said there's an emergency and she needs you back at the office tonight."

"What's going on?" Annie asked.

"She didn't say. She said she'd call you later when she got a chance. But she wants you back as quickly as you can make it."

"Okay. Tell her I'll be on the road shortly."

She hung up and sat for a moment, trying to figure out what the conversation meant. She'd been hungry for one of the big turkey sandwiches on the kitchen table, but now her stomach felt full of anxiety. She tried to shake it off as she looked for Marr. She found him relaxing on the front porch.

"I've had a call from my office and my editor needs me back right away," she said. "I'm going to have to cut our interview short and call you back."

He walked her to the guesthouse where they had stopped to look at the stars the night before. He waited for her in a rocking chair on the porch while she packed quickly, then carried her small bag to her car.

"Betsy and I hoped we'd get another evening with you," he said. "Can you call me and let me know you got back safely?"

"Sure. Please give Betsy a hug and tell her goodbye for me. And tell Dan I'm sorry I had to leave early."

He opened her car door before kissing the top of her head and squeezing her shoulders. His big hands felt warm and steady.

"Take care, Annie."

CHAPTER 15

Maddy Daniels glanced at the big newsroom clock. Nearly 6, time to get on the road if she wanted to make it to Dallas before midnight. Since it was Friday, traffic coming out of Houston for the next few hours would snare her in its vise. The 240-mile trip wouldn't be easy or fun.

She was headed for a long weekend with her parents, not her favorite destination. Her parents were divorced, so she would shuttle between their neglected houses in hoity-toity Highland Park and listen to their harangues about each other. They had split up ten years ago, but hadn't put their grievances to rest. Consequently, she and her sister, who lived in Tulsa, didn't relish spending time in Dallas. Still, both her parents were aging poorly, had serious health problems and since they had rejected each other, needed the help of their daughters to keep living independently.

She slid her latest documents into her bulging Middle Texas College files and squirreled them away in her bottom desk drawer. She needed to touch base with her editor before she left, which made her nervous. She considered him attractive, so she flirted with him to get her way, if for nothing else. But unlike most men in her universe, he appeared immune to her charms. She couldn't understand why, but she never knew where she stood with him. It made her crazy.

She walked over to his office, half-hoping he wouldn't be there. No such luck. Greg Barnett, tall, lanky and bearded, was the paper's investigative editor. At 50, he commanded considerable respect after just two years in the *Times'* newsroom. He distinguished himself as a deep thinker, a Harvard graduate in a sea of UT and Baylor alumni, and a spotter of special talent in a newsroom filled with people who were more than competent. Maddy and the two other reporters assigned to him valued his good judgment and ability to sell their stories at news meetings. A shortage of editors meant that they had to share his time and attention with enterprising beat reporters skillful enough to pursue an investigative story with his guidance. Maddy didn't mind sharing him, but the other two investigative reporters resented it.

She didn't want the daily handholding that her colleagues demanded, so it wasn't uncommon for her and Greg to go a day or two without talking much. She believed that the best editor was one who cherished her talent, charm and salty wit, rarely pestered her with picky questions and signed her outsize expense reports without complaining. She'd had some like that, but Greg wasn't one of them.

He sat in his small office talking to Jim Merrill, the politics reporter and her good friend. They seemed to be chewing the fat rather than discussing weighty matters, so she stuck her head in the door.

"Hi, Maddy. What's going on?" Greg said, taking a large, boot-clad foot off his desk.

"Hey, fellas. Just wanted to remind you that I'm leaving for Dallas to see my folks and won't be back until Tuesday."

"Right. What's on tap for next week?" Greg asked.

"The continuing saga of Middle Texas College. Since I finally got the download of contracts records, I've been going through them, looking for patterns."

"What have you found?"

"No answers, but I feel like I'm close to a breakthrough. I talked to Will Ward, the vice-president and obfuscator-in-charge, yesterday and asked new questions. He said he'd get back to me next week."

"Sounds good. Let's meet Tuesday morning. You can brief me on the latest and we can discuss our strategy."

"Aw, a meeting? Okay, if you insist. What are you guys talking about, anyway? The Maddy problem?"

She winked at Greg, who didn't respond to her clowning.

"We're just talking about the McKnights and what the new ownership might mean to us," Jim said.

"Well, I refuse to worry about such trivial matters this weekend. Instead, I'll worry about the big problems like my parents."

"Oh, the fighting Danielses? What's the pride of the Highland Park geriatric set doing these days?" Jim smiled. As a longtime friend, he'd heard her rant about her crazy relatives for years.

"Just trying to get separate cemetery plots so they won't have to be together for eternity."

She rolled her eyes and mimed shooting herself in the head. Jim laughed and she finally got a smile out of Greg.

"Well, have a great trip," he said. "Don't drive too fast. Remember, the *Times* won't ante up for your speeding tickets."

"I know better than to try that again," she grinned.

"And keep your flask hidden," said Jim.

"Now that's just a vicious rumor. Ciao for now."

She headed to the parking deck and her well-worn BMW, a gift from her parents fifteen years ago when their money flowed freely. She got in, opened her purse, took out a small flask of vodka and swigged some for the road. Maddy never drove drunk, but like many other Texans, she rarely drove sober either. Tonight, she drank just enough to take the edge off the irritation of bumper-to-bumper traffic heading up Interstate 45 North.

She had plenty to occupy her mind for a long road trip. God, she thought, Greg was such a stick-in-the-mud sometimes. He was a decent guy, but humorless. She tended to try too hard when she was around him. She knew he respected her work, but did he really like her? She never could tell, though he usually came through for her in a pinch.

She mused about her growing relationship with Mark Ingram, her longtime Texas Ranger pal in Austin. The friendship had turned romantic during a trip to Austin a few weeks ago. Now he wanted her to come back for another weekend. She liked him a lot, but for keeps? She wasn't sure. He was very smart, funny and sexy in a wonky kind of way. But she worried that his politics were too conservative, much different than hers. Plus, she had to be honest with herself – she was addicted to excitement, sexual and otherwise. Could she be content sleeping with just one guy the rest of her life? Too soon to tell, but she knew she wasn't getting any younger. She'd love to have a baby before it was too late.

She knocked down another belt of vodka after checking her rear-view mirror for cops. She noticed a black Suburban behind her following a bit closely. The national car of Texas, someone had called the Suburban. God, she hated those big-ass mom-cars. She had seen so many suburban moms at the wheel, feeding their progeny juice-boxes on the way to Houston's endless soccer fields. They ignored the needs of the drivers around them. She'd never be like that.

Two hours passed while she drove fast, but not dangerously so. She had outlasted most of the poky commuter traffic out of the Houston suburbs, so she could relax for a while. She speeded up through the swath of anonymous and boring countryside that stretched toward Dallas. The sky had darkened, landmarks had disappeared and the trip should be a breeze until she reached the outer limits of the big city. She just needed to keep herself awake because the drive was boring.

She drained the last dregs of vodka, stowed the remains of the flask in the glove compartment and turned on the car radio. A station playing '80s oldies blared John Mellancamp singing, "I fight authority, authority always wins. I've been doing it since I was a young kid, I come out grinning. I fight authority, authority always wins."

She turned the radio up louder and her lips curved into a smile. She loved that song's spunky celebration of the fighting spirit. It should be her mantra. She had always battered her head against closed doors. Small-town sheriffs, mayors, county commissioners, even governors – none of them liked women reporters, especially at the start of her career. Sometimes they said rude, sexist things just to throw her off her game. It didn't work.

She had shown them that authority didn't always win. Sometimes the reporter won – and the public benefited. Her mind drifted to the current contest of wills between herself and the horrid Will Ward at Middle Texas College. Who would win that? She was betting on herself. She knew her core of obnoxiousness equaled or exceeded his.

She was jazzed when she got the bulk of the records yesterday. Those contract documents hid a bunch of secrets, she thought, if she could just tease them out. She'd heard rumors about what might be going on, but didn't quite believe them. She needed Annie to sit down with her and sift through the records. Annie had the patience and the ability to see patterns when she couldn't.

She wondered how her trip to interview Tom Marr was going. On impulse, she grabbed her cell phone and punched in the speed-dial for Annie's cell. No answer, so she left a message. "Hey, Annie Girl. Hope you're enjoying yourself with Mr. Tall, Blond and Gorgeous. Don't do anything I wouldn't do. Or should I say, 'Don't do anything I would do.' I'm on my way to Dallas. I need to pick your big brain on those college docs when I get back. Love you, hon."

She looked in the rearview mirror again. Was that the same black Suburban that was behind her earlier? Was it following her? What kind of asshole would ride her tail like that? It was too dark to see.

She speeded up a bit. So did the Suburban. Now she was getting nervous.

What could she do? Not another car in sight to help her. The big car was practically attached to the rear of the BMW.

Suddenly, the Suburban tapped her car bumper, a chilling way of confirming it meant trouble.

Maddy went faster, sweat beading on her forehead, trying to shake her menacing black shadow. She hit a big pothole where the right lane joined the shoulder. Oh my God, she thought, as her car slid out of control. She screamed, but she knew no one heard. The BMW bounced off the road, skittered in the brush beyond the shoulder and hit a large tree. She felt a flash of fear as her head hit the windshield. She passed out.

The Suburban left the road too, much more carefully. The driver put on distress lights and stopped where the BMW had hit the tree. In her last moments, Maddy dimly heard a voice and smelled a musky perfume as a woman opened the BMW's door and sat beside her.

"I'm so sorry," she said in accented English. "I've called 911, dear."

"Just lie back and let me massage your neck a moment. Everything will be all right."

CHAPTER 16

Annie faced a ten-hour drive from Marfa to Houston – perhaps nine if she didn't stop much – but she was determined to make it that day. Cilla didn't interrupt her during an assignment, especially on a Saturday, unless she really needed her. What could she want? She kept fiddling with her car radio, trying to find music or news that would either confirm or assuage her feeling that something bad had happened.

After driving for a few hours without hearing back from Cilla, she pulled into a rest stop and called the newsroom. Again, she got Rob, the news clerk. He was a University of Houston student who worked part-time at the *Times*. About 24, he was capable and smart and she had a good rapport with him. She pressed him harder this time.

"What's going on, Rob?"

"Honestly, I don't know. Cilla, Greg Barnett and a couple of others have been meeting with Amanda in her office for a little while. Nobody has come out to say anything yet."

"Are there any big news events today?"

"No, it's the usual kind of Saturday in Houston. You know how it is, very slow. There's nothing much on the news budget."

"Anything unusual on the wires?"

"Not that I can tell."

One of Rob's Saturday duties was to monitor the wire services for stories that cropped up unexpectedly. She knew he was conscientious about that. He always knew what was going on.

"Well, call me if you hear anything."

"Will do, Annie. Stay safe."

She was about to hang up the phone when she noticed she had a message from Friday night. She smiled as she listened to Maddy's sassy greeting, then tried to call her cell phone.

No answer. She left a message.

"Hey, Mad, something weird is going on at the office. Cilla called me to come back from West Texas. Do you know anything? Hope your folks are okay. Call me when you get this."

By early evening, Annie was still an hour away from Houston on Interstate 10 when she finally got a call. Cilla sounded tired.

"Hey, Annie. Sorry I haven't been able to call you back. Can you pull over on the shoulder so we can talk for a moment?"

"Sure. Hold on. There's an exit just ahead."

Her heart pounded as she exited the freeway not far from the small town of Sealy. She could hear the trucks speeding down the freeway as her mind worked frantically. Cilla was about to fire her, or tell her that the company had gone under.

"Okay, I'm off the road now."

"Annie, this is going to be hard. Maddy Daniels has been found dead in a car accident. They identified her body."

"Are you sure? Could it be someone else?" Annie couldn't think straight. She felt like an anvil had landed in her chest and was cutting off her breathing.

"Yeah, the highway patrol is certain. You probably know that she was going to Dallas to visit her parents for the weekend. It happened late last night, on a fairly quiet stretch of Interstate 45 in Freestone County near Dew."

"What happened?"

"She ran off the road and hit a tree. The cops think she was going too fast, hit a big pothole and lost control."

"Oh, God. Did she die instantly?"

"They think she did. She had multiple injuries and it looks like her neck was broken. Another thing. They found an almost-empty flask of vodka in the glove compartment. It looked like she'd been drinking."

"Maddy always kept a little flask for long trips, but I never saw her drink much."

"Well, the cops don't know yet how much of a factor that was. They're going to do an autopsy tomorrow or Monday."

"Were there any witnesses?"

"They haven't found any, but they're still looking," Cilla said. "Where are you?"

"I'm about an hour from the office. I'll come straight in."

"If you don't mind. We're writing the obit for tomorrow's paper. Since you know Maddy better than anyone, I'd like you to look at it before the last deadline."

"Sure, Cilla."

"Drive carefully. I can't stand the thought of losing another good reporter." Annie heard the sob in the back of Cilla's throat before she hung up.

Don't think about this yet, she told herself. You have to get to the office. You can break down and cry later. She drove quickly to Houston and parked her car in the newspaper garage shortly before 9.

Upstairs, in the fifth floor newsroom, some of the more veteran reporters had gathered after hearing the news on local radio and TV. They wanted to help if they could, or at least be with their colleagues. The solemnity that hung in the air was strange for a Saturday night. Jim Merrill put his arms around her.

"It's terrible news, isn't it? As soon as the obit is finished, a few of us are going over to La Carafe to toast Maddy. Will you come with us?"

"Sure," said Annie. "Let me see what Cilla needs."

She headed over to the small office, where Cilla stood up and gave her a rare hug. She was editing the draft of the obit written by Jamie Pierson, the night cops reporter, with inserts from Rob Ryland. The atmosphere was tense but focused.

Jamie and Rob hugged her too and the three of them crowded around Cilla's computer for a read. She read the draft aloud. Annie thought they had done a good job with the obit, using personnel records and quotes gathered from editors and public officials who knew Maddy. It would run on the Metro front, indicating the high degree of respect that the top editors held for her.

Cilla, the night editor on duty, said the obit looked complete and cleared them to leave, saying she'd call them at La Carafe if she needed them.

Annie took Rob aside briefly.

"Did you know about this when we talked while I was driving?"

"No, I didn't," he said. "I would have at least found some way to warn you. I know how close you and she were."

Greg Barnett, Maddy's editor, led Annie, Jim, Jamie, Rob and a couple of others on the short walk to the bar on Congress Street. They found a table and Greg bought everyone drinks in Maddy's honor. La Carafe had been her favorite place. She especially loved the jukebox with its great old classics. So they played Edith Piaf, Ella Fitzgerald and other singers that she'd enjoyed. It wasn't quite a wake, but it felt like something they all needed.

Annie drank two glasses of Chardonnay quickly and began to feel anesthetized against the shock of the day.

Then her cell phone rang. It was Tom Marr.

She walked outside quickly so they could talk privately.

"Annie, I'm sorry to be in touch so late, but you had said you'd call to let me know you got back safely. I wanted to make sure you were okay."

"Tom, I'm sorry. I forgot to call because I found out that my best friend died."

All of a sudden she began sobbing so hard she couldn't talk. The tears she refused to shed earlier came pouring out. She held the phone aside for a moment.

"Annie, I'm so sorry," he said. "Tell me about it."

Between sobs, she blurted out Maddy's name and a few details about the accident.

"I'm so sad for you and me and for this state," Marr said. "I didn't know Maddy very well, but she seemed like a funny, real person. I know that she was a great reporter whose work did so much to improve Texas over the years."

Annie stopped crying. Marr's words about Maddy comforted her, at least for the moment. She tried to compose herself, but found she couldn't talk any longer.

"Thanks, Tom. I better go now. I'm with a group of people at a bar. I better get back."

"Annie, can I call you back in a few days? I want to make sure you're all right."

"Okay, Tom. Bye."

She returned to the bar where her group was ordering more drinks. She felt odd, drinking at La Carafe without Maddy – or even drinking at all. But she didn't want to go home and be alone.

CHAPTER 17

Annie opened her eyes reluctantly. Her head felt like it was being beaten by twin sledgehammers and her stomach quivered with nausea that threatened to spill out. But the worst pain was in her heart when she remembered that Maddy was dead. She recalled that when her grandmother died five years ago, she understood for the first time what heartache meant. Her heart, or at least something in her chest, had thrummed with pain when she had heard the news. That's the way she felt now, in addition to the fierce hangover that enveloped her body.

She looked around, seeing the familiar antique furnishings in her pale green room and the door ajar to her ivory-colored bathroom with the old-fashioned pedestal sink and the large claw-footed tub. But she realized with a jolt of unease that she was naked under the sheet. What had happened last night? Had someone brought her home and put her into bed?

She groaned, both from her pain-racked eyes and memories that unspooled like a bad movie. She recalled drinking glass after glass of Chardonnay, sensing that if she stopped, she'd feel unbearably sad. It was such a relief to be with friends at La Carafe who had loved Maddy and could reminisce about her wicked wit and spunky exploits. Annie remembered almost falling as she stumbled out of the ladies room, and Rob Ryland offering to take her home, since she clearly couldn't be trusted to drive.

He had eased her into his car, driven the two miles from the bar to her house, located the keys in her pocketbook, unlocked the door and steered her straight to the bedroom. He kissed her forcefully and quickly took off her clothes. It wasn't what she wanted, but she didn't resist because she didn't want to be left alone. She knew his presence in that empty house would stave off the heartache a little longer. She had expected gentleness and comfort, but Rob's lovemaking was rough and insistent. Had she passed out before it was over? She couldn't remember it all, just the overpowering need to sink into oblivion for a long while.

The door to the bedroom was shut, but she sensed that Rob was still in the house. She smelled the aroma of coffee and heard muffled noise she thought came from her TV in the kitchen.

She heard him knock tentatively at her bedroom door.

"Yes?" She said nervously.

"It's Rob. Can I come in?"

"Okay."

He opened the door, bearing a cup of coffee and a conspiratorial smile. He was shirtless and his thick brown hair was tousled, but his hazel eyes shone with the robust health of a young man who could carouse all night without looking dissipated. His tall, toned body exhibited the near-fanatical dedication she knew he had to working out. She thought he had the clean-cut choirboy look of a young Paul McCartney.

"Hey, Rob. Tell me about last night." She spoke quickly to forestall any intention he had of climbing into bed with her.

"It looked like you were about to pass out at La Carafe. I got you into my car and inside your house, but I was afraid to leave you here alone. I saw someone almost choke to death on their vomit one time after drinking too much."

He looked at her with concern.

"Do you remember everything that happened?"

"Not everything. I must have passed out, or blacked out."

He looked almost relieved. But he joked, "I sure do know how to make an impression on a woman, don't I?"

"Rob, I'm sorry. Tell me everything. But give me that coffee first."

She sat up in bed, holding the sheet over her breasts. He sat beside her, put his arm around her shoulders and held the steaming cup to her lips. She sipped a little at a time, afraid that it wouldn't stay down, but it did.

"You, me, Greg and a couple of others shut down the bar at 2 a.m. You'd been laughing and telling great stories about Maddy, but that last hour, you started to slump in your chair and I was afraid you'd pass out. I told Greg I'd take you home and make sure you were okay.

"When we got to your house, you told me not to go," he said. "Annie, how could I resist?"

"Rob, I'm sorry. I'm embarrassed."

"Don't be. You were beautiful and sexy."

"I'm old enough to know better."

"Annie, you're what, thirty-five or so? I'm twenty-four. There's not a huge difference in our ages. And I'll tell you something that I wouldn't have told anyone before yesterday. Maddy and I were lovers for nearly a year."

"You were? She never told me that."

"She had her secrets. I know you were her best friend, but since we worked together, she and I both agreed we'd never tell anyone. Just as I'd never tell anyone about you."

"Well, that explains a few things. She was always telling me with absolute certainty that I should have a friend with benefits."

"She worried about you a lot. And she knew I had a crush on you."

"You did?"

"Well, I can't resist those long legs. I was always hoping you'd come to the office in short skirts. Anyway, she told me a reporter had broken your heart a few years ago and she worried that you wouldn't let anyone get close to you again."

Her eyes stung and she became tearful, thinking about Maddy. He hugged her quickly.

"I'm grieving too, Annie," he said. "Maybe we can comfort each other today. Why don't you get a shower while I make us some breakfast? You'll feel better after you eat something."

She took her time showering, soaping herself several times, removing the faint scent of his cologne from her body and some of the sluggishness from her brain. She was puzzled by Rob's attentiveness and concern. He could have left during the night or before she had waked. His solicitous attitude today didn't quite square with the aggressive behavior she remembered from last night. She wondered about the relationship he had described with Maddy. She knew Maddy had liked Rob, as she did most younger, fit men who were nice to her. Annie never understood her propensity for young lovers, since she rarely found herself attracted to younger guys. Rob was nice-looking and bright, but she felt a strong sense of embarrassment. She was angry with herself for drinking so much that she had been unable to say no to him.

By the time she reappeared in clean jeans and a plain black T-shirt, Rob had set the kitchen table and produced scrambled eggs, toast, grits and coffee. She ate with more gusto than she thought she would feel, but realized it was already the middle of the afternoon.

"Rob, I'm impressed that you threw together a breakfast with so little food in the house."

"Hey, I'm a poor college student. I know how to make do."

"I also get the feeling that you know how to take care of women," she said. "You must have a lot of practice."

"My mother was an alcoholic. After my father died, she just lost her way. I felt like I was always picking up the pieces for her. She passed away three years ago."

"Oh, I'm sorry. How did you hook up with Maddy?"

"You know how flirtatious she was. It just happened one night after a drinking session. Then I started getting together with her on Sunday nights. She felt like it was the loneliest night of the week and we enjoyed spending it together. It helped me too, since I was still sad after my mom died."

She picked up dishes and took them to the kitchen where Rob had started cleaning up. When she put them down, he grabbed her shoulders and pulled her in for a long kiss that felt pretty good. She kissed him back. Then she heard the distant ring of her cell phone.

She sprinted to the bedroom and got it from the pocket of her crumpled jeans on the floor. She had missed the call, but Jake Satterfield had left a text.

"So sorry about Maddy. Will call later."

She stood there a moment, wanting to fall back into bed and erase the rest of the day. Her best friend had died and instead of behaving with dignity, she had gotten stinking drunk and slept with a colleague twelve years younger.

It wasn't that she and Jake had an exclusive relationship. She didn't know what they had right now, but she didn't need to sabotage it with an alcohol-fueled encounter with someone barely out of his teens. Jake's message brought her back to the land of grownups. She walked back into the kitchen where Rob was wiping the counter.

"Rob, can you give me a ride to the *Times'* parking deck to get my car? I've got a lot to do today."

He looked surprised and tried to pull her into his arms again.

"I thought you might want me to hang out here with you for a while," he said. "We could go back to bed and just enjoy being together. No pressure or anything."

She stepped away. "I don't think that's a good idea."

"Why not? I'd like to spend the day with you. I know the circumstances are weird, but I think we could be good together."

"Rob, I appreciate you bringing me home last night, but I made a mistake in having you stay."

"Why, Annie?"

"For one thing, you're a newsroom colleague and those relationships never work out for me. Someone always gets hurt."

"I don't think Maddy had any regrets."

"People are different. I'm not Maddy."

"Okay, I get that. But I'm worried about you."

"Worried?"

"You blacked out last night, and that's a terrible sign. I saw my mom slide deeper into alcoholism after she started blacking out. You should slow down or stop drinking."

She bristled at his words. How dare a 24-year-old pass judgment on her behavior? Was it because she wasn't ready to jump back into the sack with him again? She felt a wave of cold anger.

"I don't need your advice on drinking. It's something I can figure out on my own."

"I don't mean to tell you what to do. I'm just concerned. What if you'd blacked out with a stranger? He could've hurt or killed you."

"I'm just glad I was there last night," he added. "Promise me you'll call me if you're drinking and I'll take you home."

"I appreciate all that you did for me, Rob," she said with sarcasm. "But you got what you wanted, didn't you? Consider us even."

The muscles in his jaw tightened and he glared at her.

"That's a really bitchy thing for you to say, Annie. I know you're feeling sad, but you shouldn't take it out on me."

"Just go, please."

He walked out the front door, slammed it and gunned his car down her quiet street.

She cried a little, wishing she could confide in Maddy and laugh at her salty advice. Then she dried her face with a kitchen towel and went into her bedroom. She stripped off the pale green sheets, stuffed them in the washer and turned on the hot-water cycle. She would obliterate the last reminders of Rob's presence. She called a neighbor to take her to get her car.

Given his experiences with his mother, she could see where Rob might have a genuine concern about her drinking. But the whole episode had left her shaken and furious.

CHAPTER 18

Annie stayed home Monday, calling the office to see if the cops reporters had found out anything new about the accident. The autopsy was being done, but results wouldn't be out for a few days.

She also called Maddy's sister Diana in Tulsa, Oklahoma to offer condolences and to see if she needed help with the memorial service. Diana sounded sad, but seemed pleased to hear from her. She said Maddy's body would be cremated Tuesday morning and the service would be at 4 p.m. that day.

"The memorial service will be short and simple because as you know, she wasn't religious. My parents aren't in great health, so it's best just to get it done," Diana said.

"That sounds like the right thing to do," Annie said.

"I know how much you meant to Mad. I'll be glad to see you."

And she briefly talked to Jake, who promised to be at the funeral if he could get away from the legislature for a few hours.

Tuesday morning, she dressed carefully in her best outfit. It was a short, low-cut black sheath with a matching bolero jacket and strappy black heels. Was it too sexy for a funeral? She didn't care. Maddy had shopped with her the day she found the outfit on sale and had loved it. She remembered her voice in the dressing room of Neiman's just a month ago when she tried it on. "Take a chance, Annie. You have the perfect figure for this dress."

Some of the top editors were flying to Dallas for the funeral, but she'd accepted the offer of a ride from Jim, her newsroom pal. Not many reporters were going because they'd have to take a day off and pay their way there. But she guessed the editors had a slush fund that would pay their expenses.

She'd arranged to meet Jim in the newsroom at 10. She got there early and signed on to her computer to check her email. She found lots of condolences from friends, but nothing from Rob. He was working at his desk about ten feet away and didn't look in her direction. But she'd seen his eyes flick her way when she walked in.

Jim drove carefully to Dallas and they both sat quietly for a while. He had befriended her when she first came to the newsroom and they'd been good friends for six years. At forty-two, he was married with two young children. She always found him easy to confide in and discreet about personal problems. So she broke the silence with a question.

"Jim, do you think I drink too much?"

"What brought this on? It's not a question of what I think. Do you think you drink too much?"

"Probably, but I don't want to stop."

"Who thinks you should stop?"

She gave him an edited version of her weekend and her last conversation with Rob.

"Well, you looked pretty wasted Saturday night. I saw that Rob was taking you home, so I didn't worry about you. I know about his background with his mother."

"Do you think he's right about the drinking?"

"Annie, if you blacked out, you know that's dangerous both for your health and your personal safety."

"Yes, but I can handle that."

"You're a grownup, so I'm not going to tell you what to do. And right now is a hard time for you. But at the very least, I'd think about cutting back."

He hesitated a beat or two and spoke again.

"I'd be careful about Rob. He's quite a bit younger than you and you know newsroom relationships can be volatile."

"I know," she said. "I don't think you have to worry about that. I made it clear that a relationship wasn't going to work for me."

"I'm glad. Your work has been so good lately, you shouldn't jeopardize it with newsroom distractions and gossip."

"Thanks for the advice, dude."

She felt relieved that she'd confided in him. When they got to the Dallas funeral home, she was pleased to see a decent turnout, about 80 people. There was even a smattering of politicians.

Annie felt someone grab her from behind and hug her tightly.

It was Jake. Though they had talked briefly, the last time she had seen him was their dinner several weeks ago at Chuy's. It seemed like a lifetime ago, but the feel of his strong arms soothed her. He looked sharp in a dark gray suit and a blue tie.

"Hey, Annie. The only thing good about this is getting the chance to see you."

"Hey, Jake. I'm glad you made it. I know how much you enjoyed working with Maddy when she covered the sessions."

"Yeah, she was quite a gal," Jake smiled. "She was a great reporter and a smart and funny person. What's the latest on the accident?"

"They're still investigating, but I don't know of anything new," said Annie.

"I heard you were in West Texas talking to Tom Marr."

"Yeah, I had to rush back to Houston, but I enjoyed meeting him."

"What did you think of him?"

"Nice guy. Not so sure about his ideas."

"When's the profile coming out?"

"Don't know yet. I'll have to get back to the office and regroup."

He still had his hand on her arm, so she let him lead her to a pew in the funeral home's ornate chapel. They sat together quietly as the music started. Jake grabbed her hand, squeezed it and held it.

The service began with Handel's "Water Music" piped through the sound system. It was a quirky but cheerful choice, she thought. Maddy's sister Diana read poems from writers Maddy had liked, including selections from Emily Dickenson, Robert Frost, Walt Whitman and Shakespeare. As promised, Diana used nothing from the Bible and Annie didn't see any ministers hanging around.

The only other speaker was John Daniels, Maddy's 78-year-old father. Diana brought him from a front pew to the podium in his wheelchair. Daniels, who had muscular dystrophy, was a retired oilman who had made a fortune in the wild 1970s and lost most of it during the downturn in the 1980s. Annie knew him as a colorful man who spoke plainly, drank heavily and swore prodigiously. Daniels looked frail, but his voice sounded surprisingly strong as he talked about his younger daughter.

"My darling Madeleine was stubborn from the day she was born. When she was little, she used to hold her breath if she didn't get her way. When she got a little older, she bit other kids when she didn't think they were playing fair."

Annie laughed along with most of the gathering. It certainly sounded like the Maddy she knew.

"She was a wild kid, but she didn't mean any harm," he continued. "She always had too much energy to sit still, so she would constantly get into trouble. We were forever being called to her school when she misbehaved, but the teachers liked her, so they always gave her another chance. I worried that as she grew up, she would get into more trouble than we could handle and waste her life with drinking or drugs.

"But I needn't have worried, because when Maddy went to college, she found journalism. When she got to SMU, instead of joining a sorority, she channeled her energy into working for the student newspaper. We could see that she had found her calling. We never had any trouble from her again.

"Not to say that Mad became an angel. She still loved her wine and Scotch, and I think she always had more than her share of bad boyfriends. I thought she would get married, become a great mom and give us lots of grandchildren. But when I mentioned that, she would just smile her sweetest smile and say, 'Daddy, I'm gonna take my time and find the right one.'

"She loved the newspaper business, and she made a name for herself at the *Houston Times*. She could tell a great story, but more than that, she wanted to correct the injustices of the world. Now, there are a lot of injustices, even in Texas, and I don't reckon she got to them all. But she did as much as she could in her limited time on earth.

"I just wish she hadn't left us so soon. If I had my way, I would have gone before she did."

He lowered his head to hide his welling eyes and Diana wheeled him back to his corner of the front row. Annie was weeping quietly into a tissue and Jake put his arm around her waist. She heard the sounds of sniffling across the church.

"John Daniels really was a powerful speaker," Jake said, guiding Annie to his car for the short drive to the family's reception at a nearby golf and tennis club. "I can't imagine his pain."

"Yeah, he really seemed to get Maddy. She was always a lot closer to him than her mother."

She walked into the club with Jake and Jim, who had followed in his car. She spotted Mark Ingram, Maddy's Texas Ranger friend, across the room. He looked pale, serious and out of place. She would make sure to talk to him.

Jim drifted away to talk to politicians while Jake steered her to the bar, looking into the low-cut bodice of her dress.

"You look beautiful, honey, but this is a memorial service, not a high-class bordello," he smiled. "Not that I'm complaining."

"Maddy loved this dress and helped me pick it out," she said.

"Yeah, it looks more like Maddy than you, baby," he said.

"This is the new me, Jake," she said. "If you don't like it, tough."

"Besides, look at all the women around us," she added. The wealthy Dallas crowd that socialized with the Daniels family was dressed to the hilt. Plenty of sexy outfits on gorgeous women in their thirties and forties showed lots of cleavage and leg. Maybe memorial service receptions were the new pickup bars.

"I love the new you, just like I loved the old you," Jake whispered. "If you come back with me to the Palomar Hotel, I'll show you."

"Did it occur to you that I'm grieving?" she said.

"Of course. There's nothing more life-affirming than sex."

She looked into his eyes and thought she saw sadness and longing that contrasted with his flippant words. But it wasn't the time or place to explore what that meant for her -- or for them.

"I'm riding back to Houston with Jim in an hour," she said. "Besides, we're agreed that you're just a friend and source right now, remember?"

"Okay, honey," he said. "Can I get you a Chardonnay?"

"No, I'll just have a Diet Coke, please."

CHAPTER 19

The reception was thinning out. Annie looked out the French doors at the back of the club. To her surprise, Mark Ingram now sat slouched on a bench by himself in the glaring sun.

She looked at her watch. Jim would be pressing her soon to leave for the long trip back to Houston. She better catch the Texas Ranger while she could.

"Excuse me, Jake. I need to go outside and talk to someone."

"Okay. I'll look for you later."

The club featured a large back patio area with teak benches, lush plantings and beyond that, trees and the sloped parking lot. Because it was hot, most people stayed inside for the air conditioning. But Mark Ingram seemed oblivious to the heat. He rose to greet her as she walked over. She hugged him hard.

"Oh, Mark. I'm so glad to see you. Did you drive up from Austin?"

"Yeah. I'm glad to see you. I need to talk to you privately."

"Let's find a place in the shade. You shouldn't be sitting out here in the hot sun. With your fair complexion, you're really going to get sunburned."

"It doesn't really matter to me, but whatever you want," he said.

She signaled a waiter, who brought over a tray of drinks. She looked with longing at the Bloody Marys and Screwdrivers, but chose two iced teas. She led Mark gently to the back of the patio, where the benches were shaded by big trees and no one could hear them talk.

They sat down. She looked at him closely, struck by his somber face and low voice that sounded mechanical and emotionless. He looked wrung out, as if he'd had a few sleepless nights.

"Mark, I know Maddy thought you were very special. I'm hurting for you and for all of us."

"Thanks. We were going to spend next weekend together and

figure out if she should transfer to Austin and live with me. She was everything I wanted in a woman. It just took me a while to convince her to give me a chance."

"I know. Sometimes Maddy could be difficult to pin down, but she was really happy that you and she had found each other."

"I appreciate you telling me that. I want you to know that I'm going to get to the bottom of her death."

"Tell me what you've learned. You probably know some people in the Highway Patrol that wouldn't talk to us."

"Well, the autopsy turned out to be inconclusive. The cause of death officially will be head injuries sustained when she hit the tree, including a broken neck. But some things don't add up."

"Like what?"

"Why did she run off the road? The patrol finally got a call from a witness who said a large black vehicle, possibly a Suburban, was following her awfully closely."

"What do you think happened?"

"Well, Maddy was pretty good at maneuvering her little car. I don't see her just running off the road unless something happened. Did the Suburban nudge her off the road, or something like that? I don't know."

"Did the witness get a license plate?"

"No, apparently it was too dark. But the witness said the second vehicle pulled off the road right behind Maddy. So she assumed the driver would call 911 and Maddy would get help quickly."

"Did that happen?" Annie asked.

"Apparently not right away. By the time the ambulance came, it may have been as much as ten minutes after the accident. Maddy was dead."

"Do you think her drinking had anything to do with it?"

"Well, I know she kept a little flask in her car, but I don't think she drank that much. I used to lecture her about it. Still, I knew she was basically a good driver and I never saw her impaired."

"What are you going to do?"

"I'm going to interview the witness myself and go through the reports looking for other threads. Maybe something was missed. I want you to keep in touch with me about it."

"Who'd want to harm Maddy? She was such a wonderful person." Annie felt tearful again.

"Lots of people might want to hurt her because of the tough stories she's done. You know she was always at odds with people."

"Yeah, she didn't mind making enemies," said Annie.

"The last time I saw her, Maddy told me some things about her investigation of Middle Texas College that made me worry," Mark said. "I'm going to be looking closely at that."

"When we went to the college for Tom Marr's speech, they made it clear that she wasn't particularly welcome," Annie said. "Do you think someone at the college had it in for her?"

"Who knows? She thought something funny was going on with the college's contracting business. Her death and the college president's connection with a secessionist candidate give me the justification I need to open a state investigation."

"That's great, Mark. Will the Rangers back you up on that?"

"As I told you, my job is to monitor secessionist activity that might conceivably be a threat to Texas. All of this is off the record, by the way."

"Of course," Annie said. "You don't think Tom Marr could have been involved, do you?"

"I have no idea. But I'll find out."

"I'm really glad. Will you keep me up to speed?"

"Sure. We need to help each other out on this."

"Will you take care of yourself? I'm worried about you. Do you have friends in Austin you can talk to about how you're feeling?"

He brushed back a stray tear and nodded. He stood up and she hugged him again. He was such a good guy. It was so unfair that he and Maddy had found each other too late.

Out of the corner of her eye, she saw Jim waving her to the door.

"Mark, I have to run. Talk to you soon."

Jim was sipping the last of his Diet Coke, looking anxious, and for someone so good-humored, slightly impatient.

"We need to hit the road in 15 minutes if we want to get back to Houston before midnight."

"Okay, Jim. Let me say a few goodbyes."

She hugged Maddy's pitiful parents in their twin wheelchairs and told Mr. Daniels how much she appreciated his eulogy. She found her sister and embraced her for a moment.

"I'll be talking to you soon, Diana. You did a lovely job with the service."

She saw that Jim was deep in conversation with Jake. They'd known each other for years and enjoyed talking legislative politics when they were together. Jake beckoned her and turned to Jim.

"Jim, I need to talk to Annie privately for a moment."

He motioned to what appeared to be a small conference room near the bar. She went inside with him, wondering what she'd hear next. The day had been full of revelations.

He shut the door and took her into his arms. He kissed her hard, putting one hand into the cleavage of her low-cut dress and cupping her bare breast. She kissed him back, letting herself enjoy the unexpected pleasure. She pulled away reluctantly.

"I've got to go. Jim's waiting."

"I want to spent more time with you, Annie. But I'm tied up with the legislature six days a week, and Jeannie and I are still fighting over the separation agreement. Be patient with me."

"I want to see more of you, Jake. The next few weeks at work will be awful. But call me and we'll figure something out."

"Okay, babe."

She opened the door and saw Jim looking their way.

"Hey, I'm ready to go," she said, smoothing her hair and dress.

They got in the car and Jim shook his head. He looked at her with a mixture of amusement and exasperation.

"Annie, your life is getting way too complicated. Getting involved with Jake carries a lot of baggage. Slow down and try to figure out what you really want before you do anything you'll regret."

She buckled her seat belt and turned to him.

"I hear you, dude, and I'm grateful for your advice. But you're an old married guy and you've forgotten what it's like to be single!"

CHAPTER 20

Annie looked forward to getting back to the newsroom and to the relative calm of her work. She'd heard on the morning TV news about another strange incident along the border. Two men in a pickup truck in Brownsville had fired shots at a school bus as it stopped to pick up a dozen students waiting at a suburban street corner with their moms. The shooting had left a few holes in the top of the bus, but no injuries. It reminded Annie of the attack few weeks earlier on the elderly churchgoers in Laredo. She thought she'd probably be assigned to look into this one.

She was wrong. She'd barely signed on to her computer when Cilla asked her to stop by her office. To Annie's surprise, she wasn't alone. Greg Barnett, the investigative editor who had worked with Maddy, sat in Cilla's office too.

"Annie, Greg and I wanted to talk to you together," Cilla said. "Now that Maddy's gone, we've decided you should take her place temporarily on the investigative team. If things work out, we hope we can move you there permanently."

"Gosh, I didn't expect this," Annie said. "She was such a great reporter. I feel strange stepping into her shoes."

"You're eminently qualified to do this with your particular reporting and computer skills," Greg said. "Are you up to it? I know you were great friends with Maddy and her death came as a horrible shock. But we need to continue the fine work she was doing."

"I've always hoped for this chance," Annie said. "Are you giving me a trial period?"

"I'd like for you to take over the Middle Texas College investigation," he said. "Since you went up there last week and already know a lot about it, you're the best person to push it forward. We'll see how that works out. I don't have permission to fill her position permanently yet."

Annie thought a moment and decided she better lay out everything Mark Ingram had said about Maddy's death. She spent some time briefing them.

"I don't know if he's so addled by grief, he's just being paranoid or what. But he's worried that someone deliberately harmed Maddy. If the college had something to do with it, I'd be at risk too."

"I doubt that," Greg said. "She'd been drinking and mostly likely it was just a terrible accident. Most sane people don't try to kill off a reporter, especially bureaucrats. In this day and age, it'd be hard to get away with something like that."

"I guess you're right," said Annie. "I'd love to take over the Middle Texas College investigation. But I need to get my profile of Tom Marr finished."

"That's why we wanted to talk today," Cilla said. "Amanda wants it for the Sunday paper. If you work it really hard for the next few days, can you get it done? Marr's people gave you an exclusive interview, but you know other reporters are on it by now."

"You bet," said Annie. "I'll have it done Friday afternoon. It may not be as comprehensive as I had planned, but I want to be first."

"That's the spirit," Cilla said.

Annie got to work quickly, reviewing notes on her interview with Marr and making a list of people she needed to talk to that day.

She called Marr on his cell phone and he answered immediately.

"Hi, Annie. I'm really glad to hear from you. I've been worried."

"Thanks. Life goes on. I've been asked to get our profile of you finished quickly. I'm taking over Maddy's spot on the investigative team."

"Is that a promotion for you?"

"It's a temporary thing right now. But I'll be talking to your friends at Middle Texas College a lot."

"I know Maddy did some stories on the college that weren't too flattering to Ed Gonzales and his folks. But I don't have anything to do with the college. I hope you won't hold its actions against me."

"I understand, Tom."

She launched more questions about secession to round out her interview. She was impressed by how much thought he had put into it. He sounded sensible and pragmatic.

"Thanks a lot for your time," she said. "I'll call you back if I need anything else. I'm sure you've got other interviews lined up by now."

"I'll be talking to the *New York Times*, *Wall Street Journal* and some network TV reporters soon," he said. "But we made a promise that you'd get the exclusive, so I didn't want to talk with anyone else before I heard back from you."

"I appreciate that," she said. "Look for the story in the *Times* on Sunday and let me know what you think."

"I'd like to see you again and so would Betsy. Since you presumably won't be writing about me after this story, would that be possible?"

"Let me think about it. Right now, I need to just work."

Her voice broke.

"I still feel so lost without Maddy."

"I understand that you need some time. Take care of yourself and I'll call you back soon."

CHAPTER 21

Annie worked two 12-hour days before finishing the Marr profile. As usual for a major Sunday piece, it had to pass muster with several different editors – Cilla, Greg and Amanda Weeks, the paper's top editor.

She thought she had done a decent job with the story, despite the tight deadline. She read through it, looking for any evidence of bias. She always worried about writing too favorably about someone she had grown to like during the interview process. She thought Marr's quest still seemed strange, but propelled by sincere belief. She had talked to other politicians to get their opinions about Marr. Some supported his views, or at least respected his stand. Others regarded him as hopelessly misguided and possibly dangerous. It seemed balanced to her.

At 6 p.m., she headed to La Carafe with a half-dozen other reporters for a drink. She'd tried not to drink since the awful night after Maddy's death, but she craved the company of her friends and perhaps just one light beer.

"I'll be back in an hour or so to see if there are any more questions," she told Cilla. "I just need to get out of this place for a while. My head's spinning."

"Well, don't drink too much, or your head will be spinning a lot more," Cilla smiled. "Go on, you deserve it."

At La Carafe, her friends toasted her move to the investigations team, though she protested that it might not be permanent.

"I may fall flat on my face," she said. "Maddy was so tough and so good. I'm not sure I'll scare anyone the way she did."

"Annie, you're pretty intimidating in your own way," Jim said. "I've heard your phone interviews. You disarm them with your polite southern charm and before they know it, they've screwed themselves by blabbing everything they shouldn't."

"You should talk, Jim Merrill," she laughed. "Your down-home Texas drawl makes people think you're just another good old boy. Then you hit them with your killer questions."

"Annie, you're lucky you're so tall," said Jamie Pierson, a reporter who barely topped five feet. "People take you seriously. They think I'm a kid they can just brush off."

"They'll just have to learn the hard way that dynamite comes in small packages," Annie smiled.

Just then, Rob Ryland walked into La Carafe and sat down across the table. She almost choked on her beer. She had avoided him all week.

She quickly drained her glass.

"I need to get back to see if Amanda's got any questions on my story," she said. "Thanks, guys, for coming and for buying me a beer."

She was half a block away when she realized Rob was following her. He stopped her at the next corner and put a hand on her arm.

"Annie, let's talk a minute. You haven't spoken to me all week. Why are you acting like this?"

"You're the one who stalked out the door after accusing me of being a hopeless drunk," she said, recoiling from his touch. "You said you worried about men taking advantage of me, but it didn't seem to stop you."

Rob pursed his lips and glared at her. "When I brought you home, you asked me to stay. In fact, you practically insisted on it."

"Yeah, I'm not denying responsibility. But you didn't seem to worry about jumping me when I was about to pass out. That was pretty creepy."

"I didn't hear any objections."

"You didn't even use a condom. That makes me really angry."

"I'm sorry, Annie," he said, looking embarrassed. "But I'm clean and I assume you're on the pill."

"Why do you assume that? You didn't bother to ask. And you know what? I don't believe you and Maddy had an affair."

"I can't believe you would say that. I wouldn't lie about her."

"How do I know that?" Annie said. Her face turned red and her voice rose in frustration, drawing a stare from a man who walked by them. "I hardly know you."

She looked into his eyes, seeking honesty but doubting she'd get it.

"You thought if you mentioned her, I'd jump back into bed with you, you creep."

"You're being totally unreasonable."

"You bastard. Just stay away from me."

She marched back to the newsroom, feeling glad she'd confronted Rob. She saw Greg in his office and stopped by.

"Did Amanda have any questions about the story?" She asked.

"What do you think? Doesn't she always? Just go by her office."

"Is it bad?"

"You'll survive."

So much for smooth sailing, she thought. Questions from Amanda were never easy. She knocked on the editor's door and Amanda motioned her inside.

"Annie, good job on the story. But it's too long and it feels a bit too favorable to Marr's candidacy. We want to be scrupulously neutral. Sit down and I'll show you places I've marked for cuts."

Annie suppressed a sigh and sat beside Amanda in front of her computer. Within a half hour, Amanda had whacked twenty inches from the story and some of the more flattering parts, including Marr's warm interactions with his daughter Betsy, had gone.

She couldn't argue with the cuts – or rather she knew better than to argue with the top editor. From previous experiences, she knew it would get her nowhere. In spite of Amanda's lack of warmth, Annie knew her judgment was impeccable.

She stopped by Greg's office and reviewed the cuts with him. They knew that Amanda disliked long stories, since she believed readers didn't spend the kind of time with the Sunday paper that they would have even a few years ago. Readership habits had changed for the worse.

But Greg brightened up when he remembered the rest of his conversation with her.

"I told her everything you had heard about Maddy's death," he said. "We talked for a while about making sure you're safe, just in case there's something going on that we don't know about."

"What'd she say?"

"She's arranging for Rob Ryland, the news clerk, to shadow you while you work on the Middle Texas College story. He'll help you with research and drive you every time you leave the office. Isn't that great?"

Annie was chagrined, but chose her words carefully.

"That's totally unnecessary. I can take care of myself just fine."

"We'll all feel better if Rob is with you. Besides, on a big story like this, we need all the help we can get. Rob's a great researcher and a promising reporter."

"Why Rob? I don't mind having the extra help and company on the road, but how about a more seasoned reporter, like Jim Merrill or Jamie Pierson?"

"They've got beats and can't be spared. You know how understaffed we are. Amanda said we can use Rob and she wanted him to work with a veteran reporter before we decide whether to hire him permanently."

"Well, I don't like it."

"What have you got against Rob? Everyone in the newsroom seems to like him and he's definitely got the skills."

Annie gave up. She wasn't going to confess to Greg that she'd gotten drunk and slept with the youngest person in the newsroom. She knew she was screwed. But at least she'd be the one in charge. He'd have to toe the line – or else.

"All right. But if I have any trouble with him, I'm coming back to you."

"I can't imagine that will happen."

CHAPTER 22

Secessionist candidate wants to 'save Texas'
By Annie Price
Times Reporter

Tom Marr says he loves the United States for its natural beauty, strong traditions and the diversity of its people.

"But I love Texas even more," says the 48-year-old West Texas rancher. "It should be a country of its own – and it will be if I'm elected."

That's why Marr recently announced his candidacy for governor of the state – and why he thinks he can "save" Texas by making it a republic. He wants it to operate as an independent nation – as it was for ten years after its heroic countrymen defeated the Mexican Army at the Battle of San Jacinto in 1836.

His surprise entry into the wide-open governor's race – Texans won't elect its next governor for two years – has turned Texas politics upside-down. But Marr, who was elected four years ago to the Texas House from Presidio County, comes across more as an unassuming, plain-speaking rancher than a firebrand political rebel.

Since he made his landmark speech in Kinston a few weeks ago endorsing secession, Marr's candidacy has caught fire. He has already attracted promises of big money from oil and other major business interests, united a dozen ragtag groups that call themselves secessionists and forced even traditional politicians to talk about how secession would work – or not.

During a recent visit by the *Times* to Marr's ranch in West Texas, the six-foot-five politician with the distinctive white-blond hair and luminous blue eyes seemed certain he'll have no trouble attracting supporters from both political parties and all regions of the state.

"Most Texans, even ones who are relatively new to the state, value Texas as unique. It has the superior resources, the can-do spirit and the pride of heritage that will bring people together as a republic."

Marr, who is running as an independent, offered a tantalizing clue about how he might govern. If elected, he said, he'd like to see Texas become "a new Camelot." He's not harking back to the Kennedy era, but to the ancient legend of King Arthur and his Knights of the Round Table.

"Texas needs a leader who would share the power with his round table of intelligent and principled men and women," he said. "The state could do worse than model its society after Camelot, where people were motivated to work hard for peace, justice and a good life for everyone."

Marr's roots as a Texan are as firm and emphatic as his strong handshake. His ancestors came to Texas in the 1820s, and a distant relative fought and died at the Alamo. His grandparents bought up hundreds of acres of land near Marfa and founded the Marr Ranch in 1920. The Marr family has gone on to acquire thousands of acres more and now the family's ranch is almost as large as the famed King Ranch in South Texas.

Thomas Robertson Marr was born on June 2, 1967 to Knox Marr and his schoolteacher wife, Mary Davis Marr, their first and only child. By that time, the Marr family was well established in Presidio County as producers of Black Angus and Longhorn cattle. Their markets stretched across the United States and into South America. Knox Marr became known as a civic leader and a philanthropist.

By his teachers' accounts, Tom Marr was an extremely bright child who excelled in school and sports, including track and football. He became an Eagle Scout by age 14 and led a troop of younger boys while in high school. He said he recalls his boyhood as a happy time, helping his father raise cattle and tame horses for nearby auctions. He graduated number one in his class from the small Marfa High School.

For him, the path was clear. It was supposed to lead to the University of Texas and an academic career in philosophy and political science. He graduated Phi Beta Kappa with a double major in those fields. While a student, he would meet three people who would have a major impact on his life: Elizabeth Barnard, Dan Riggins and Ed Gonzales.

Elizabeth Barnard, a philosophy major from Alpine, became his girlfriend their freshman year and they married a few days after their graduation in June 1988.

Dan Riggins and Ed Gonzales, both political science majors at UT, were his best friends and confidants and have continued in that role through the years. Riggins, from San Antonio, and Gonzales, from Mexico, became inseparable with Marr. The triumvirate, as they called themselves, reflecting their love of ancient history, talked about Texas politics through their college years before deciding to make secession their lifelong goal.

Marr said he intended to stay in academia, pursuing advanced degrees before writing and teaching and some day getting into politics. But his sick father led him back to West Texas.

By the time he graduated, his father had been diagnosed with a slow-growing stomach cancer. Knox Marr asked his son to come back and run the Marfa ranch. He died four years later and by that time, Tom Marr had modernized the cattle operations and had begun to open slaughterhouses in Oklahoma.

Six years ago, tragedy struck the family again. Tom Marr's wife Elizabeth died of breast cancer, leaving him with a young daughter to bring up alone. Betsy is now 10.

Marr postponed getting into politics for a while after his wife's death. Then, four years ago, he won election to the first of two terms as a Texas House member from Marfa.

He became active in public school finance, helping to restructure the state budget to ensure that all low-income children were eligible to go to preschool at no cost by age four.

Marr said most of his friends know of his long-held conviction that Texas should secede from the United States and make the most of its ample natural resources.

"Tom Marr has made no secret of his plans to run for governor, and once elected, to lead Texas down a path to secession," said

Timothy Weaver, a longtime political science professor at UT and an advisor to Marr.

"He's a genius, smart enough to make it happen, and savvy enough to make it work when it's in place," said Weaver.

But Ronald Ray Fox, who leads the Democratic Party in Texas, characterizes Marr as foolish and naïve for thinking that the United States will ever release Texas from the union.

"He's baying at the moon like an overeager hound dog, thinking of untold riches that would come our way," Fox said. "He's a charlatan who will stop at nothing to get ordinary citizens to swallow patent nonsense."

However, many other politicians who respect Marr's intellect and ability to unite disparate personalities under common goals said they'd like to hear more about his quest before passing judgment on it.

Marr said he's not afraid to make enemies, but is encouraged at what he calls "a growing grassroots movement to reclaim this state.

"I realize I'm a controversial guy. But I'd be sorry if I didn't try to do my best for Texas."

CHAPTER 23

Dan Riggins drove from San Antonio to Marfa feeling increasingly excited about the weekend ahead. It had been a month since he had luxuriated in the arms of his lover and he could hardly contain himself. He made his way to Alicia Perez's simple adobe home built on some of the acreage Tom Marr had given him near Marfa. His own vacation home not far away was much grander than Alicia's, and the stately residence he and Karen had moved into in San Antonio's finest neighborhood qualified as a mansion. But Alicia's little house tucked away in the ranchland was the place he loved best. He parked his pickup truck in its graveled driveway and paused to take in the sight of the welcoming light in the front windows. He let the anticipation of the night ahead envelop his whole body for a moment before getting out of the car.

Alicia came to the door smiling, her lustrous black hair with its odd white streak in the front hanging around her shoulders, wearing tight black jeans and a tank top. He stepped inside, shut the door and wrapped his arms around her tightly. He unzipped her jeans and began tugging them off.

"You should wear a skirt, so that I can get to you faster," he said.

"Mi hombre," she said, pulling his shirt off and jeans down in a few deft actions. They collapsed into a hot, writhing heap on the living room rug. Only later did they get to the bedroom for a second round of lovemaking.

The next few hours went by in a blur. Even after eighteen years, the passion that cemented their relationship still felt intoxicating. It always happened this way if Riggins had gone more than a few weeks without seeing her. She had spoiled him for other women, even his wife. Not that Karen seemed to mind that they rarely had sex. Their married life had never been filled with wild lovemaking, even at the beginning.

Alicia always came alive after a killing mission, particularly one that had gone so well there was little likelihood of tracing it. She took pride in her professionalism. She never talked about her feelings to Dan, but he sensed that her deadly missions satisfied something primal and twisted. As usual, he felt excited and a bit repelled by this. He wondered idly how he could still care about Karen, cherish his two sons and yet be so dependent on Alicia for the pleasure that turned his world from everyday gray to vivid colors when they were together. But that was the reality.

They lay in bed together, smoking potent marijuana from her native Peru, which she often purchased through her contacts in San Antonio.

She told him about the latest reports of illegal border crossings along the Rio Grande just hours from their property. Alicia hated Mexico and the stream of illegal aliens who took advantage of the porous borders of Texas. Riggins thought her anger seemed ironic for someone who had sought refuge in the United States and regularly committed heinous acts that went far beyond illegal crossings.

But Riggins didn't say that because he also deplored illegal immigrants. Ever since Santa Anna and the Alamo, lower-class Mexicans had wanted to despoil Texas with their drugs and inferior culture. He had nothing against educated people like Ed Gonzales, who moved from Mexico legally and wanted to contribute something. But worthy immigrants like Gonzales were few and far between. He knew that Tom Marr believed in strict control of the Texas borders, but he would draw the line at some of the stronger methods Riggins favored.

Never mind. When Tom got elected and secession became a reality, Riggins would persuade him that draconian action was necessary. He and Alicia often talked about the need to build an electrified fence across Texas to repel unwanted immigrants. If Tom balked at electrocuting the interlopers, perhaps his regime could scatter land mines across the border area as a warning.

Riggins felt confident that once the secessionists were in power, he could manage things behind the scene and basically do what he wanted. Tom possessed the charismatic personality people sought in a leader, but once in power, he would need a strong man like Riggins to enforce his agenda. Tom was a smart guy, but a former CIA operative like Riggins always would be the smartest guy in the room – or the state.

The next morning, Dan lingered in bed with Alicia, enjoying their playful conversation. He wondered again, as he did occasionally, whether he would be happier if he divorced Karen and married Alicia, or at least lived with his mistress full-time. He always felt so at home in her house, even though it was messy and he loved order. But conversations with Alicia in the past about living together never elicited much response. She enjoyed living alone and compartmentalizing the different areas of her life.

She had taken a recent trip to San Antonio for her crafts business, and as she talked about it, he wondered whether she had slept with anyone. He believed – or at least hoped – that Alicia wasn't attracted to other men, but he knew that she thought women were a harmless diversion. He was aware that she pursued short-term affairs with women she met in the crafts business, but she generally kept those activities confined to San Antonio. He thought he would sense it if Alicia brought anyone to the home he had helped her to build. He knew he shouldn't be jealous of the women she slept with, but he hated to think about her being close to anyone but him. He mostly didn't talk about those feelings with her, because he knew she would shrug them off.

He got up and went online to read the Sunday *Houston Times*, looking for Annie Price's profile of Tom he knew was slated to run. It was the top story on the website and he read it quickly, seething with anger. She portrayed Marr as a kind of Texas Don Quixote tilting at windmills, he thought. He particularly disliked the part in which Marr talked about his appreciation of King Arthur and Camelot. It made Tom sound weak and effete.

Damn that woman. Jake Satterfield had recommended giving her the exclusive on the story, and look what she had done with it! Jake would hear from him.

Alicia, wrapped in a black silk robe, silently put a cup of coffee for him on the kitchen table.

"Alicia, I will see you tonight. I must go meet with Tom all day."

"Tonight, mi hombre, will be even better."

He drove to Tom's ranch house and the two men sat down to catch up. Tom seemed cheerful, even ebullient. The only times Riggins remembered him being unhappy were during Elizabeth's long siege with cancer and the months after her death. Tom didn't worry much about things that drove Riggins crazy. Today was no exception.

"Did you read the profile of you that the *Times* published today? I can't believe they did such a lousy job," Dan said.

"I read it online this morning and thought it was pretty good."

"You did? What about that stupid stuff about King Arthur and Camelot? I can't believe they put that in."

"Well, I said it and Annie quoted me accurately. What's wrong with that?"

"I don't think many Texans would relate to the whole Camelot thing. It sounds too highfalutin, like someone who went to college in the Ivy League."

"Hold on. You're not seriously saying I'm like the Bushes, are you?" Tom laughed.

"Well, it sounded more Kennebunkport than the South Texas coast."

"Did you see the comments online?" Tom asked. "Most readers seemed to like the story."

Riggins called up the *Times'* website on his BlackBerry and sure enough, the story was getting mostly favorable comments from readers. He guessed the haters weren't up yet.

"Dan, when we agreed I'd run for governor, I said I was going to be myself," Tom said. "I'm just a West Texas guy who tries to be true to the values I was raised with."

"I know that. But we need to polish a few rough edges here and there. You've never run a statewide campaign."

"Hey, if the voters don't like me or the secession message, there's not a lot we can do. We can lead that horse to water, but can't make her drink."

"Okay, I hear what you're saying. I wanted to talk about our early campaign ads for television, radio, newspapers and billboards."

"What is this costing, Dan? You know I've got a nice cattle business, but I'm not made of money, particularly with times being as tough as they've been for the last few years."

"Don't worry about it. Ed's in charge of the fundraising and he's doing fine. You just leave that side of it to us. You work on your speeches."

"Did you hear that the *Times* reporter who was looking into things at Ed's college was killed in a car accident?" Tom said.

"Yeah, I did hear that," Riggins said carefully. "It wasn't in the papers out here, was it?"

"No, Annie Price told me. Remember when she left in a hurry last weekend? The *Times* wanted her back after the accident. Her best friend was the reporter who died, Maddy Daniels."

"I remember seeing them together the day you made your speech in Kinston."

"Well, I talked to poor little Annie after she found out and she was crying her eyes out. She seemed a little better this week."

"Oh, did you talk to her again?"

"Yeah, she's been assigned to take over Maddy's work on the *Times'* investigative team. So I imagine Ed will see a lot more of her."

"Are you serious? Somebody should tell Ed."

"He'll know it soon enough," Tom laughed. "I told Annie I'd like her to come back to the ranch soon. She's the first woman I've wanted to see in a long time."

"Really? That might be a good thing. You could keep an eye on what she's doing in Kinston and control our message with the *Times*."

Tom laughed even louder. His trademark good humor should have been infectious, but today it just irritated Riggins.

"Control Annie?" Tom said. "You're joking. She has a mind of her own. That's one of the things I like best about her, along with those beautiful legs."

"I'm surprised," Riggins said. "You sound like you're in love, or at least in the throes of lust."

"It's too soon for that. But she's the first woman in a long time that I could visualize as a wife and mother for Betsy. Maybe even a first lady for Texas."

"A reporter?" Riggins said. "She'd be prying into everything."

"Danny Boy, back off. That's my decision. But no matter – it's too soon to think about that stuff. I don't want to jinx anything."

After he finished meeting with Tom, Riggins called Will Ward at Middle Texas College. He told Ward the news about Annie.

"Damn, I thought we'd be rid of those interfering reporters for a while," Ward said. "I guess Price also got the contracts records we downloaded to Maddy Daniels."

"Did the reporter's death cause much talk?" Riggins said.

"None that I heard. Ed didn't say much. I don't really know what he thinks or suspects. But it wouldn't look right at this point if a second reporter investigating the college met with a tragic accident."

"I appreciate your judgment, Will. We'll see."

CHAPTER 24

Annie started the new week in better spirits. The profile of Tom Marr, despite the last-minute cuts from Amanda, had turned out to be a hit. The Associated Press picked it up and a number of statewide papers carried it. It generated brisk traffic on the *Times* website and hundreds of comments online, which she knew the bosses particularly liked.

She wondered what Tom Marr thought about it, but she didn't have to wonder for long. She signed on to her computer and found a nice long email from him. He told her he really had enjoyed the story, though he'd put up with a lot of teasing from his friends about Camelot and King Arthur.

"Please come back to Camelot in its purest form – West Texas," he said. "If you can get a few days off, I'd love to show you my kingdom! Seriously, Annie, I want to see you again and Betsy can't stop talking about you. I know you're starting a new assignment, so I'll wait a few days until the dust settles. I'll be calling you."

She smiled as she read the email and thought about that carefree afternoon with Tom and Betsy in his pool. She wanted to see him again, to explore whether there was a chance for a relationship. But could she really do that in her new job? She'd be investigating the college run by one of his closest friends and supporters. Tom had emphasized, however, that he had nothing to do with the college. She would think about that a little longer before she made up her mind.

Jim got it right. Her love life was getting too complicated. She had enjoyed kissing Jake at the funeral – nobody kissed her the way he did. But Jake had baggage and seemed to pop in and out of her life unexpectedly. Could she trust him to be there for her when she needed him? She wasn't going to pass up a chance to see if she could really care for Tom if Jake took forever to get divorced and commit to her.

Then the fiasco of her night with Rob Ryland still needed fixing.

What an idiot she had been to fall into bed with him! She could only plead temporary insanity because of her grief over Maddy. The next thing on her agenda was to meet with him. She'd seen Greg Barnett talking in his office with Rob, probably about their forced partnership. She took a deep breath and walked over to his desk.

"Hey, Rob," she said. "Do you have time to meet with me in the rubber-hose room?"

The rubber-hose room was a longstanding joke with the reporting staff. It beckoned as a small conference room near the elevator, the kind of out-of-the-way, nondescript place that reporters imagined existed in corrupt police departments for the clandestine torture of suspects.

They walked in silently, settled in chairs across the table from each other and Rob waited for her to speak. She thought hard about her words, needing to get the tone right.

"Rob, I'm really sorry for calling you a bastard. I take full responsibility for what happened between us."

"No, I thought about what you said. Maybe I took advantage of the situation and I shouldn't have. But when you told me to stay, I really thought you wanted me."

Annie blushed. This wasn't going according to her plan. She needed to get him back on track quickly.

"It wasn't your fault," she said. "You're right about the drinking. I'm cutting way back and probably will stop altogether. I promise that will never happen again."

"I know I made you mad, but I was worrying about your drinking," Rob said. "I went through a lot with my mother. I think Maddy probably was an alcoholic too, though she never would have admitted it."

"Maybe so," Annie said neutrally. She didn't want to talk about her.

"I did have a relationship with Maddy, though I don't know how much it meant to her. You have to believe that I was telling the truth."

"Okay, Rob," she said. "Let's move forward. We're stuck with each other for a while. We have to make it work."

"I know," he said. "Greg said I need to make a success of our partnership to get a reporting job on staff. So I'll do my best."

"Okay, I'm glad to hear that. Let's look at Maddy's files together."

For the next two days, they combed through everything Maddy had collected about the college. They reorganized her files and reread the three stories she had written. One was a Sunday takeout on the college's mysterious military contracting empire, a scene-setter designed to draw attention and cultivate sources. Another focused on its executive travel expenses, showing that the president and chancellor were spending lavishly in a time of lean budgets. The third one was her blockbuster about the gold mine in Las Vegas.

They were all good stories, but the best by far was the gold mine expose. However, she knew Maddy had put her hopes into finding interesting new stuff in the contracting documents. She and Rob began studying the thousands of pages of computerized contract records the college had made available to them online.

Annie loved her new investigative reporting assignment. General assignment reporters got a variety of stories to do, all with specific deadlines. That usually meant producing them too quickly and without much depth. But on the investigative team, Greg wanted her to take her time to engage her brain and her computer-assisted reporting skills to dig out exclusive stuff. The stakes became higher with an investigative project, but the reporter could work on stories that really mattered.

Annie had set up a get-acquainted interview with Gonzales and Ward, so later that week she and Rob scheduled a Kinston trip to meet with the two college leaders. Rob would drive and Annie would use the time to prepare.

"Have a good trip," Greg said. "If they give you any trouble, remind them that we've got a pretty good lawyer."

Annie had thought a lot about the interview, carefully choosing the outfit she was wearing. Her navy blue pants, tweed blazer, silky white shirt, knotted red scarf and conservative closed shoes were a departure from the more casual office attire she normally favored.

"You look nice," Rob said as they settled into his car for the four-hour trip. "But personally, I like you best in a short skirt and heels."

"Rob, I need you to stop making comments like that. We're not going to sleep together again."

"Hey, you should never say never. I thought we were back on good terms."

"Yes, we're work partners now. That's all."

"Well, since we're traveling together, what's wrong with enjoying our down time together at night? I'd never tell anybody. I know you liked the sex."

What was wrong with him? Couldn't he take no for an answer? She wasn't about to get into another argument, so she patiently plowed ahead.

"Yes, sex anesthetizes the pain when you're hurting," she said. "Maddy's death really threw me. But falling into bed with someone attractive isn't enough for me any more.

"I want a relationship that has a chance of lasting. Despite what you think, the age difference between us is a killer. You need a woman who'd share your love of softball games and salsa dancing."

"I've always enjoyed older women a lot more than women my age," Rob said.

"Yeah? You'd get tired of me pretty fast. My idea of a good time is to watch World War II documentaries on the History Channel with my cat in my lap."

"I love your cat. Mr. Marbles is cool."

"This subject's officially closed. I'm your mentor and I'll show you everything I know about reporting. Doesn't that mean more to you than a few cheap thrills in a bad motel room?"

"I'd rather have both," Rob grinned.

She laughed and shook her head.

"Drive on, Rob."

They rode in companionable silence to Kinston and Annie had another chance to examine the college campus. The 1960s Spanish-style architecture Maddy had complained about looked dated, and with few students around in mid-afternoon, a curious lifelessness enveloped the place. They found the small administration building and a clerk directed them to a conference room.

Three college leaders stood up to introduce themselves to Annie and Rob. She recognized Gonzales and Ward from Tom Marr's speech. The third person introduced herself as Margaret Redmond, dean of students. She was tall and nicely dressed. Annie thought she seemed more welcoming than either of the men.

Annie and Rob sat on one side of the long conference table with the college leaders on the other side and a TV technician at the end. Steve Timmons, the college's public relations director, explained that the campus TV station was recording the interview for Gonzales. Annie thought that was odd, but she went ahead and turned on her tape recorder without commenting.

"We were sorry to hear about your colleague's death in a car accident," Gonzales said. "But we still don't understand why reporters from a big-city newspaper would be interested in our little college in Kinston."

"Thank you for your kind words about Maddy," Annie said. "The *Times* covers subjects of interest all over the state. Your military contracting program seems unique among the state's community colleges, so of course, we're interested."

Annie believed that the best way to conduct interviews was to start with easy questions and work up to more sensitive issues as trust developed. She showed genuine interest in her subjects and usually that was enough to win them over.

She launched into her long list of questions, leading with the blander ones. Gonzales and Ward answered some, poked fun at others and joked about turning the tables on her by taping the interview. Annie ignored their comments and kept going down her list, using her most evenhanded tone. Redmond said little and Rob took notes silently, as Annie had asked him to do.

About 45 minutes into the interview, Gonzales and Ward began to bristle. They clearly weren't used to hard-hitting questions, she thought.

"Your salaries appear to be nearly double those of leaders of other Texas community colleges," Annie said. "How do you justify that?"

"We have a worldwide presence," Gonzales blustered. "We're entrepreneurs who bring in the money. We deserve every dime."

"Some people contend that the college teaches secret courses for select groups of military recruits," she said. "Is that true?"

"We never dignify ridiculous rumors by commenting on them," Gonzales said.

"Can you explain to us how your military education contracts benefit a community college supported by taxpayers? Do the contracts make a profit for the campus?"

"We don't have to explain anything to you about the contracts. We've honored your request for computerized contract files. They're self-explanatory," said Ward.

"Dr. Gonzales, I understand that you and Mr. Ward support the secessionist movement. Are you contributing any financial support to Tom Marr's candidacy for governor?"

"Our political opinions are our own. We have no obligation to disclose anything about our beliefs and practices as private citizens," Gonzales said.

"Does the state of Texas financially support the college's contracting business in any way?"

"Of course not," the chancellor said. "The state should have more enterprising colleges like Middle Texas. It would be better off."

Gonzales had turned visibly angry during the last fifteen minutes of questioning. His face kept getting redder. He stood up from the table and the other two leaders quickly did the same.

"You're persisting with questions that are way out of line. This interview is over."

Gonzales stormed out of the room with his colleagues. Annie followed them down the hall, asking more questions that they ignored. The three leaders went into a private office and slammed the door. Timmons, who had chased all of them, told Annie she'd have to submit other questions in writing. He escorted Annie and Rob back to their car, standing there to make sure they left the campus.

Rob closed her door, then got in behind the driver's seat. He looked at her with astonishment and, she thought, new respect.

"Wow, that was incredible. I can't believe they just walked out."

"They don't like being asked tough questions. It's obvious that the local media doesn't press them on anything." Annie said.

"Has that happened to you often?"

"I can honestly say I've never had an interview quite like that."

"I've never seen you so fired up, Annie. You were great."

"I just want to get at the truth. Those guys are hiding a lot and it makes me really mad."

CHAPTER 25

A few days after Annie's interview on campus, Gonzales noticed that Margaret Redmond had scheduled an hour-long meeting in his office. He was curious, because he saw her frequently on campus for shorter chats. But he was receptive, because he had always considered himself her mentor and friend.

She appeared a few minutes early, looking more serious than usual, he thought. Gonzales greeted her warmly and told his secretary to bring a pot of her favorite Earl Grey tea for them to share.

"What's on your mind, Margaretta?" he asked, using his pet name for his longtime colleague.

"Ed, I'm worried about our reputation. I don't think we should have walked out on those reporters. We just played into their hands by refusing to answer their questions."

"Go on," said Gonzales.

"I think we should give them all the information they want about the contracts business and explain it in ways they can understand."

Alarm bells sounded in his head. What was going on with her?

"We don't have to explain it to them – it's entrepreneurial, not a part of state government. We've sent them the required open records. Let them figure it out for themselves, if they can," he laughed shortly.

"I think that's dangerous, Ed. When reporters ask questions, I think we should make sure to give them answers that show the college in its best light."

She leaned forward earnestly and smiled, to his chagrin. He needed to shut this down.

"Will and I disagree with you, Margaret. The reporters will get discouraged and find another target."

"We don't have anything to hide, do we?" she asked.

"Of course not. But we don't want their meddling."

"Can I be completely open and confidential in what I want to say?"

Gonzales sat up straight, all attention. "Of course, dear. You know you can tell me everything."

"I know that Will means well, but it's hard to get him to focus on the campus needs," she said. "The contracting program is important, but we're giving short shrift to the needs of the students here in Kinston.

"You know we need more academic courses for the students who can't afford to go away to a four-year college," she added.

"Margaret, I promise you that we'll work on that. But we need the money that the contracts bring in."

"Of course, Ed. But the faculty and staff complain that Will isn't interested in what they're doing. They think the contracting business has grown too big. It's the tail wagging the dog."

"I hope that as their leader, you tell them otherwise," Gonzales said.

"I do, of course," Redmond said quickly. "But there are always rumors going around about the contracts. It's hard to stop them."

"What do you hear, Margaret?" Gonzales leaned in again, concern in his eyes. He had always trusted her to repel such nonsense.

"Well, the rumors are always changing – that some of the courses are top-secret, that the contracts use unqualified people – and..."

She hesitated.

"Go on, Margaret. It's important that I know what people are saying."

"Well, people wonder where the money goes. If we're doing such a big contracting business, why doesn't the campus ever get any of the money?"

"It's a very complex business," Gonzales said. "Are you worried about the contracts?"

"I trust your judgment. I always have. But Will is very secretive. Sometimes I wonder if he keeps you fully informed."

"I'm glad you brought these concerns to me. You can be sure I will be asking Will questions. But let's keep this conversation just between us for now."

"Sure, Ed," she said, getting up to leave. "I hope you don't think I'm out of line here. I really care about the college."

"Of course, Margaret." He showed her out of the office.

A few minutes later, Will Ward walked in – without asking, as usual.

"What was the meeting with Redmond about?" He asked with his usual measure of suspicion. There was no love lost between Ward and Redmond – and never had been. They regarded themselves as ceaseless competitors for the president's attention.

Gonzales outlined much of what Redmond had told him, omitting specific criticisms of Ward. He didn't want to fan the antagonism between his two subordinates.

Gonzales and Ward handled the contracting business mostly by themselves, which gave them ample opportunities to fiddle with the money. He had purposefully kept Redmond away from the contracting business because he knew she would disapprove of its unsavory aspects. He valued all that she contributed to the success of the Kinston campus and hoped to keep her focused on that.

Sometimes he hated Ward, who was standing there in his horrible 70s clothes, his greasy ponytail hanging down his back, glaring through his granny glasses like the know-it-all he was.

"She's becoming a danger," Ward said bluntly. "I think you should get rid of her before she starts talking to people who could get us into trouble."

"That's not true," Gonzales said. "Margaret's too loyal to me and the college to do anything that could lead to trouble. And she does a great job with the campus. We need her."

"No, we don't," Ward said. "There are a half-dozen people on the faculty who could do her job."

"I'll be the judge of that," Gonzales said.

"I think we should ask Riggins's opinion," Ward said. "He could easily have this problem fixed."

"Will, if you go behind my back again, I won't be responsible for the consequences," Gonzales shouted. "If I hear another word from you about this, you're fired."

"Okay, don't get your panties in a wad," Ward said, sliding quickly out the door. "And don't say I didn't warn you."

CHAPTER 26

Annie felt so nervous she couldn't finish the first cup of coffee cooling on her desk. Barry McKnight, the *Times'* new publisher, was about to make his first visit to the newsroom and the tension felt sludge-thick in the air.

She stacked the random piles on her desk into neat rows, trying to make it look organized, pausing to answer the jazzy ring tone of her cell phone. She smiled when she heard the West Texas baritone of Tom Marr.

"Hi, Annie. I'm in Houston today and I'd like to take you to dinner tonight, if you're available."

"That sounds lovely, Tom. What're you doing in town?"

"Fundraising and schmoozing the rich and powerful, the most hated task on this politician's agenda. I'd rather walk across a dozen rattlesnakes barefoot in a 110-degree desert, but I can't get out of it."

They chatted briefly before deciding to meet at the Rainbow Lodge for dinner. Annie hung up and felt unexpectedly happy. There was something about Marr that felt so safe. It was hard to pinpoint, but probably related to his West Texas solidity – the big frame, the booming voice and the certitude that enveloped him. Annie met very few people who seemed genuinely confident about their beliefs, their life and their place in the universe. Though she didn't understand his obsession with secession, she admired him.

Rob walked up and leaned on her desk. "Hey, Price, what're you grinning about? Did Middle Texas College just ship you a few thousand more documents we won't be able to understand?"

"Yeah, they're all written in Kurdish." She smiled. "You up on that?"

"Kurdish is my second language," he said. "Bring it on."

"I'm thinking how great it'll be when this command performance is over and we can get back to work," she said in a low voice.

"No kidding. There's a bad vibe in here today."

The sale of the *Times* had moved quickly and rumor had it that Barry McKnight had already settled into a palatial home in River Oaks, Houston's swankiest neighborhood. But this marked his first official week of work.

During the first few weeks of the new ownership, the McKnight chain hadn't announced any changes in the newsroom. But Annie had noticed a few differences she thought were revealing. The supply cabinets in the mailroom that held notebooks, pens, staples and other necessities weren't restocked as often. And when they were, the quality of the goods looked discernibly lower. As a left-hander, Annie used quick-drying, felt-tip pens to take notes. Now someone with an eye on the budget had replaced them with cheap ballpoints, which smeared her writing across the reporter's notebooks she used for interviews.

She noticed that the newsroom's more obsessive reporters were checking McKnight's stock prices online a few times a day. The markets hadn't liked the purchase of the *Times*, sending the big company's stock price down to record lows. Today she registered that the New York Stock Exchange price had dropped from $3.67 to $2.19 since the purchase.

The top brass had muted preparations for Barry McKnight's first week at the paper, but Annie noticed some pitiful attempts to impress him. The cranky elevators leading to the newsroom sported smart gray carpeting, replacing the dirty brown carpet that had sufficed for a decade. And the office spread for the 11 a.m. reception looked a little more sophisticated than usual. Instead of someone running out to get whatever cheap supermarket sheet cake was available, an administrative assistant had ordered platters of fresh fruit and gourmet cookies from a deli.

But the atmosphere in the newsroom felt anything but celebratory. Annie saw that editors of both sexes wore their best gray, black or navy suits. Even the more disreputable-looking reporters were cleaned up and nervous. Annie had dressed in a black skirt, pink blouse, pearls and a rose-colored blazer, an outfit she normally saved for the most formal of interviews or meetings. She didn't like to feel confined, though, so she had draped the blazer across the back of her chair until the reception started.

Usually by mid-morning, reporters had left the building for meetings or visits with sources. Today everybody waited.

Finally the message went out that the editors wanted to start the standup. At the front of the newsroom, Barry McKnight was shaking hands with Don Waters, the managing editor, and Weeks, the top editor. Everyone in the newsroom gathered quickly.

Barry McKnight was a slightly overweight man in his mid-forties whose California origins showed in his longer, blondish-gray hair, gold chain around his neck and studied air of casualness. As the youngest great-grandson of the founder of the McKnight chain, he had worked at several of the organization's papers. He had trained for his newest position in key roles like managing editor and advertising manager. He had earned the reputation inside the chain of being productive and smart, but also offbeat and unpredictable.

He gave a short speech and the message comforted the gathering at first. He loved Houston, the *Times*, the talent in the newsroom and the strength of the daily paper.

Then he got to the worrisome stuff. National and local advertising continued to plummet, newsprint costs had soared and the *Times'* costs were higher than those of other McKnight papers, he said.

"I expect we'll have to cut about 150 jobs, about 15 percent of the 1,000 or so employees working here now," he said. "Of course, that'll include people from all departments, not just the newsroom."

"When do you anticipate making those cuts?" Jim Merrill asked.

"Probably within the next two months," McKnight said.

"How will those decisions be made?" Reporter Jamie Pierson asked.

"Seniority will be a factor, but also each type of job will be evaluated. Is it really necessary to have some of the jobs we've always had in the newsroom? Can we share more resources with our sister papers in Oklahoma, for instance?"

Annie looked around, noticing stricken faces among her colleagues. She gave McKnight points for trying to be candid, but his bluntness was scaring everyone.

"We'll ask each *Times* employee with a salary above $70,000 to take a 10 percent pay cut this year. If your salary is less than $70,000, your pay'll only be cut by 5 percent."

"Will there be any furloughs?" Seth Anderson, the city hall reporter, asked.

"Yes, a mandatory one-week furlough in this first half of the year and another in the second half, unless revenues improve."

"Will there be any changes in the *Times'* pension plan?" Jim asked.

"Regretfully, the McKnight Company is going to freeze the pension plan. What you have, you'll keep. As you may be aware, traditional pensions are disappearing in the workplace."

Annie noticed several middle-aged copy editors looked grim when McKnight said that. She heard quiet whispers among the older reporters.

"Will the *Times* keep contributing to our 401-k plans?" Jim said.

"Not this year. Maybe we can restore the contributions in a few years," McKnight said.

Annie could feel the 100 or so newsroom employees straining to digest the painful news. Even the most vocal reporters who rarely hesitated to confront senior managers over changes appeared to be shocked into silence.

Amanda stepped in smoothly, changing the subject from the dire economic measures McKnight had laid out. She looked a bit nervous, Annie thought, even in her sleek black, confidence-building suit. She probably sensed how battered the staff was feeling, but wanted the meeting to end in a more positive direction.

"Barry, can you explain your philosophy of news and what you hope to see from this newsroom?"

McKnight puffed out his chest and fairly bristled with his own importance, Annie thought. Score one for Amanda in her brazen attempts to curry favor with the new regime.

"I'd like for this newsroom to become as vibrant and open to new ideas as the city and the state it covers. It strikes me that this newspaper is hidebound and overly traditional in the way it decides what to report."

"Can you give us examples?" Jamie Pierson asked.

"Sure. The *Times* should lead the state in covering the secessionist movement that's coming to the forefront with the governor's race. I sense that the paper is slightly dismissive of such ideas because they aren't considered mainstream. I think that's a mistake."

"In what way?" Seth Anderson said.

"Secession isn't automatically a crazy idea. It could inject new life into our economy and make it much stronger than that of the rest of the states. You have to remember that I'm from California, a state that's been ruined by bad politics. Its eagerness to hold statewide referenda on any outlandishly liberal idea that comes down the pike has destroyed a wonderful place.

"I'd like to see this staff be open enough to new ideas to thoroughly explore secession and other emerging philosophies that might help the state – and our newspaper business at the same time. We shouldn't just keep doing the same boring, do-gooder stories on the environment and social issues. We need new strategic thinking."

After another twenty minutes of McKnight expounding on Texas and his philosophy of the news business, Amanda called a halt.

"Barry, we appreciate your dynamic thinking and look forward to your leadership. I know you have a luncheon engagement, so we'll let you go. Staff, how about a round of applause for our new publisher?"

Annie joined the rest of the staff in polite but tepid applause.

"Remember that I appreciate everything you do. We'll come out of this terrible period in journalism with a better product, because we'll learn how to play to our strengths," McKnight said. He left quickly.

"What was that all about?" Jim asked Annie quietly. "He sounds rather taken with the secessionist movement. Wonder what that means for our political coverage?"

"It was all rather strange," Annie agreed. She didn't tell Jim she was meeting Marr, the most prominent secessionist in the state, for dinner. Suddenly she felt uneasy. Should she cancel? No, she thought. I need to learn more about him.

Annie and Jim drifted back to their desks, but many others lined up for the cookies, fresh fruit and Diet Coke refreshments that had gone untouched by Barry McKnight.

"I guess after hearing about all the cutbacks, folks are at least going to take advantage of the free food while we have it," Jim said.

"Yeah, who knows when we'll get fresh fruit again?" Annie tried to joke. "But maybe the awful sheet cakes will go away."

Late in the day, she slipped out to meet Marr for dinner. She drove four miles from the paper to the Rainbow Lodge, a restaurant housed in a century-old log cabin with three fireplaces and an acre of beautiful grounds. With its fishing and hunting memorabilia, the place had the feel of old-money Houston. It was the kind of place that journalists like Annie rarely could afford, though she'd been taken there on a few dates.

Since it was still early, the restaurant was half-empty. She spotted Tom quickly at one of the best tables near a window. He stood up to meet her, kissed her cheek, pulled out her chair and seated her across from him. She loved the fact that he was so tall, he bent slightly to kiss her. He smelled wonderful too, a fresh, citrusy scent of something she couldn't quite identify. She smiled at him for a moment without speaking, thinking it was a treat to be taken to a beautiful place with a handsome man.

"I'm so glad to see you, Annie. Have you had a good day at work?"

"It was kind of a strange day, to be honest."

She told him about the staff meeting with Barry McKnight and the cascade of bad news about the planned cutbacks.

"Oddly enough, he also mentioned the secession movement. Your ears should have been burning," she joked.

"What did he say?"

"He seemed interested in more coverage about it. Even though he's fairly new to the state, he apparently knows a good bit about the secessionist movement and your campaign."

Tom looked a bit uncomfortable.

"Barry McKnight showed up at a luncheon we gave today for Houston business people at the Petroleum Club. He seemed welcoming, and as you noticed, very interested in the secessionist movement."

"That's interesting. It sounds like your candidacy is attracting a lot of interest among the movers and shakers here."

"It seems to be striking a chord, especially among the oilmen and oil business folks. They can see how much better their future could be if they could escape federal regulation."

"Did Barry McKnight promise anything?" Annie asked.

"Not specifically, but he indicated the *Times* would provide wall-to-wall coverage of our campaign and he personally would give money."

"Hmmm. That's not exactly comforting to hear, when he's talking about cutting people, salaries and benefits at the paper." Annie frowned. "When publishers get involved in politics, it's usually not a good thing."

"I'm sorry, Annie. Since you wrote the first profile about me, I thought you'd be kind of excited to hear that."

"You've gotten quite a lot of press since then, including stories in the *New York Times* and *Washington Post*."

"I enjoyed your story the most. Can't you get assigned to the campaign trail, so I can see you every day?"

"That wouldn't be a good idea. I'm a little worried about having dinner with you as it is. The only way I can justify it is that I'm not covering your campaign."

"Okay. By the way, I heard that Ed Gonzales walked out on your interview last week. That was really stupid and rude. But I've got to stay out of the college's business."

"I understand. It's probably best that we don't talk about Middle Texas College at all. And you shouldn't tell me anything about your campaign you wouldn't want a reporter to know, because I'd probably feel obligated to share it with our political writers."

"You're right," Tom smiled. They talked instead of books, movies and Annie's childhood growing up in southwest Virginia. Annie, who had held herself to two glasses of wine, stood up to go after dessert and coffee.

"I've had a great time," she said, squeezing his hand. He kissed her cheek again, his soft lips lingering on her face for a moment. She thought he might want to prolong the evening, but she wasn't ready for intimacy yet. He seemed to sense that.

"Can you come to the ranch soon for a weekend?" Tom asked. "I want to see you again when we have more time to get to know each other."

"Maybe, Tom. I've got a long weekend coming up in a few weeks. Let's see how things go between now and then."

"Okay," Tom smiled. "I'll be talking to you and looking forward to your visit. My kingdom awaits your bidding, lovely Guinevere."

CHAPTER 27

Annie got to work early the next day, eager to meet with Rob and Greg to figure out their next step. But before she could scroll through her email, she got a call. She noticed it was a private number.

"Is this the reporter who came to Middle Texas College last week to interview the president?" A male voice she didn't recognize asked.

"Yes, this is Annie Price. Who's this?"

"I can't tell you who I am yet, but I work at the college and don't like what's going on there. My friend and I would like to meet with you. It's too dangerous to talk on the phone for long."

"When do you want to meet?"

"How about this afternoon after work at 5:30? We'd have to drive somewhere away from Kinston to feel safe enough."

"I'll need to bring my reporting partner with me."

"Okay, but will you both protect us as sources? Our jobs and our lives could be at stake." His voice sounded tense and worried.

"Yes, we always protect our sources. Where do you want to meet?"

He gave her some specific instructions that she jotted down. She hung up the phone, feeling excited and jumpy. She raced across the newsroom, collected Rob and they went into Greg's office and closed the door. She reviewed the phone call with them.

"This could be the break we need after that awful interview with Gonzales and Ward last week," she said. "We've got to go for it."

"What makes you think this guy is on the level?" Greg said. "Could it be some kind of trap?"

"I'm going on intuition, but I think it's the real thing. He sounded well-educated and desperate to make contact. We've got to give this a shot."

"I agree," Rob said. "We'll be careful."

"Okay, but I want you to call me after the meeting, so I'll know you're all right," Greg said.

Later in the day, Rob drove in a fast three hours to a strip shopping center near Austin. They circled the parking lot slowly and Annie looked for a silver Honda Accord. She saw one with two people inside, parked near the Dollar Store. She and Rob got out and walked to the car. She tapped on the window of the driver's side. A middle-aged man rolled down the window.

"Hi Annie. I'm Ben Weatherby, chairman of the English Department at the college, and this lady is my boss, Margaret Redmond. I think you met her last week."

Margaret, the tall, stylish woman who had impressed Annie during the ill-fated interview, smiled nervously from the passenger side. Ben looked like a typical English professor, bearded with glasses and a little paunchy. She liked his soft hazel eyes.

"Hi, Ben and Margaret. Do you want to talk here?"

"Not really. Can you and your partner get in the back seat? We'd feel better if we drove a little further off the beaten track, to a café a few miles away. Is that okay?"

Annie made a split-second decision to trust them. They seemed perfectly rational, if a bit paranoid. Rob locked his car and left it parked at the shopping center. Ben drove down a quiet country road with her and Rob in the back seat. He parked the Accord in the lot of a dilapidated, closed cafe. He said he felt safer talking inside the car.

"I'm sorry Ed and Will were so hateful to you two at the interview last week," Margaret said. "I told them it was unprofessional. Then I had a heart-to-heart talk with Ed after your visit and felt angry that I couldn't get answers from him."

Annie smiled, hoping Margaret felt safe enough to go on.

"That's why Ben and I wanted to meet with you secretly and tell you what we know, and what we wonder about. But you must give us your word that you'll protect us."

"Absolutely," Annie said. "I realize that your jobs are at stake."

"It's more than that," Ben said. "The last Middle Texas employee who asked a lot of questions ended up drowning in Galveston Bay."

"Oh, my God!" Annie said. "Please tell us more."

"His name was Doug Pender. He was an English teacher who

chaired the Faculty Senate and was openly critical about the college's contracting business. Doug was gay and used to go to Houston pretty often to meet guys in the gay bars. One weekend about two years ago, he drowned in Galveston Bay, apparently while boating with someone."

"The case remains unsolved after two years. The consensus of the cops and faculty gossip was that he ran into some rough trade in a bar and got killed after a sexual encounter. But a few of us on campus wondered if somehow his death was connected to his criticism of Gonzales and Ward," Ben said.

"Wow," Annie said. "Do you mind if we take notes and record this session on my cell phone?"

"Please don't record anything," Margaret said. "But I don't mind if you take notes. Is that okay with you, Ben?"

"I guess so."

"I'll take the notes, Annie," Rob said. "You should ask the questions."

"Tell us whatever you can about Gonzales and Ward," Annie said.

"They're ripping off the college right and left," Ben said. "Gonzales is getting older and lazy, so now he mostly gets Ward to do his dirty work."

"I run a pretty tight ship," Margaret said reflectively. "But I only manage the Kinston campus. I don't know what goes on with the military contracts. I do know there's big money in those contracts and it never benefits the campus.

"I've tried to beef up the college's offerings, but it seems like we have less money to run the local campus every year. At the same time, Ward brags about all the new contracts he's gotten. It's just not right."

"Since the college is getting the contracts money through federal sources, the state doesn't have any oversight," Annie said. "That's the problem. Nobody is accountable to anyone."

"Both Ed and Will are extremely sympathetic to the secessionist movement," Margaret said. "They're very close to Dan Riggins, the strange friend of Ed's who's running Tom Marr's campaign."

"We do have one solid tip for you, from a friend in the accounting department," Ben said. "He thinks the college is cheating the state's teacher retirement system."

"What do you mean?" Annie said.

"Pay attention to this, because it's hard to understand. You need to check the state's retirement rolls. If the college is asking the state to pay into the retirement accounts of people who are working outside the state under federal contracts, that's illegal," Ben said. "The college should be getting money in its contracts to reimburse the state. State law requires it.

"I know the college has sent you the contract documents. You need to cross-check the names of employees listed in them with the state retirement rolls."

"Why aren't they including the retirement contributions in their bids?" Annie asked.

"Because they might not get the contracts," Ben said. "They want to make sure the college gets them because that's the way they skim off money for themselves."

"They probably figure the overworked state bureaucracy would never check up on them," Annie said.

"Exactly," Margaret agreed. "It's a story ripe for the picking."

Annie and Rob looked at each other with excitement. Finally, a tip they could actually prove – or disprove.

"We can definitely do that," Annie said. "We'll get on it immediately and see how it pans out."

She talked to them for another hour before Ben started looking at his watch.

"Margaret and I need to get back," he said. "You guys probably need to hit the road, too. But I'll be back in touch."

"Thank you, thank you," said Annie. "We appreciate your efforts and we'll work hard to get to the bottom of things."

Ben dropped them off at the shopping center and left. Annie and Rob got into his car, high-fived and talked through what they had found out on the drive back to Houston. They began planning what to do.

Annie got Greg on his cell phone to assure him they were safe.

"You're not going to believe what we heard – it's incredible, but scary."

She gave him an abbreviated account of their meeting, including the Galveston Bay drowning Margaret and Ben thought was suspicious.

Annie hung up and reflected on the day's events. She noticed the highway traffic still going strong at 10 p.m. Was someone following them? She watched the traffic flow behind them for a moment and decided that all the cars were just going fast.

But anxiety stabbed at her stomach as she thought about the interview. What if Tom Marr was involved in this whole messy business? It could be a disaster.

CHAPTER 28

Margaret Redmond nursed her second glass of wine and thought about calling it a night at an officers' club party at Fort Kinston. She sat on a sofa in one of the quieter areas of a suite of red and gold party rooms, resting her tired feet.

She had come to the party hoping it would be a bit more exciting than usual. But the gathering disappointingly consisted of the core group – officers and their spouses and friends from the base. Occasionally the parties attracted interesting visitors from Austin, San Antonio or Washington. Tonight, however, she saw mostly the same divorced or married men who sometimes hit on her after a few too many drinks. She always talked to the eligible men, such as they were, but she was pretty picky about going home with any of them. It had happened occasionally, but Margaret was choosy.

Tonight she felt preoccupied with work problems. Perhaps she was being paranoid, but ever since her conversation with Ed Gonzales about the military contracts doing harm to the college mission, she felt his warm feelings for her had shifted. He seemed to be avoiding her, though she couldn't single out a specific incident.

She had asked Will Ward to have coffee after she had talked with Gonzales, partly as a peacemaking move and partly to try to extract more information. She peppered him with questions. How was the contracting business this year? What were the profits? And where was the money going? He quickly clammed up and changed the subject, so all she probably accomplished was to put him on guard.

She had felt jumpy when she and Ben had met secretly last week with Annie Price and her reporting partner. But Ben, who also was paranoid by nature, swore that no one had seen or followed them. She felt no qualms about talking to the reporters because she had finally gotten angry enough to do something about what she passionately believed was injustice. Middle Texas could be a great school if

Gonzales and Ward would focus on its core academics and local students, instead of chasing federal dollars all over the globe.

Suddenly she saw a new face standing over her – a stunningly beautiful Hispanic woman with a lustrous cloud of dark hair enlivened with an unusual white streak. The woman smiled and spoke.

"Hello, you look very comfortable sitting there. I'm Alicia Pereira. May I join you?"

Margaret stood up and shook hands with the slender woman in the red cocktail dress. Alicia stood nearly as tall as she in stylish black patent-leather stilettos.

"Of course, please join me. I'm Margaret Redmond, dean of students at Middle Texas College. I was thinking about leaving, but perhaps I'll get another glass of wine."

Margaret talked to Alicia for the next hour and it turned out they had much in common. Alicia was fifty, just a few years older than she was at forty-seven. Like Margaret, she had suffered the grief of early widowhood. She said she still mourned the loss of her husband two decades earlier in Peru. She said he had fought bravely against the Shining Path and the communist group had tortured and killed him.

Alicia had told her hair-raising tales of her escape from Peru to South Texas eighteen years back. She said she had never married again because she hadn't found a man as brave, strong and intelligent as Jose Pereira.

Margaret had bared her own deep feelings with the story of her beloved husband Peter, who had died six years earlier in Afghanistan after a surprise bombing. Alicia had put a sympathetic hand on her arm when she talked about how hard it was to find love again – how men in their forties or older were either attached, alcoholic, gay or too neurotic.

Alicia poured more cold Vouvray into their glasses and said she had drunk too much to drive to the hotel room she had booked an hour away in Austin. Margaret found herself urging her new friend to stay with her, saying her condo was just ten minutes away. It would be no trouble and they could continue talking at home without interruption.

Alicia agreed enthusiastically and they quietly slipped out of the party. Margaret giggled when she saw that Alicia had filched another bottle of good Vouvray from the bar to drink at home. Out in the cold air, Alicia hugged her and they laughed joyously at their escape from the loud, overheated party. Alicia kissed her on each cheek and softly pushed Margaret's feathered hair away from her freckled face. Alicia's thick hair rippled in the breeze and she smelled faintly musky.

Alicia pointed out her car, a black Suburban parked several rows behind Margaret's blue Toyota Corolla in the parking garage.

"I will follow you to your condo, mi amiga bonita," she told Margaret.

Margaret felt excited, but nervous, as Alicia followed her home. She would drink more wine with Alicia, enjoy her company and see where the evening took them. Margaret wasn't gay, but she had lesbian friends and was comfortable around them.

She felt that Alicia was flirting with her, but Margaret wondered if perhaps she was misinterpreting a desire for friendship for sexual interest. She had known other Hispanic women who seemed much more physically expressive than her Anglo friends. But Alicia was especially warm.

Margaret drove her car into the one-car garage at her condominium complex in Kinston. She had purchased the two-bedroom townhouse ten years ago with Peter. After he was killed, she saw no reason to move, even though her rising salary at Middle Texas could have gotten her something better than the flimsily constructed frame units near Fort Kinston. Other than the occasional splurge on nice business attire and a few overseas vacations with other single women, she lived simply.

She came into the kitchen through the door connecting the garage, threw her car keys and handbag on the counter and swayed dizzily. As tipsy as she was, she felt glad she hadn't driven far. She opened the front door and Alicia stood there smiling with a floral cloth bag Margaret guessed held clothes and overnight supplies.

"Mi amiga, your condo is so lovely," she said. "Show me all of it."

She exclaimed about Margaret's good taste as she walked through the first floor of the condo, furnished in a mixture of antiques and traditional pieces in blues, browns and reds. She opened the kitchen door to the garage and surveyed the parked Toyota neatly flanked by precisely arranged utility shelves.

"Very nice," she said appraisingly. "You don't have to go outside when it's raining. And you keep everything neat."

Margaret felt gratified, continuing the tour upstairs. Before she could tell Alicia to put her bag in the spare bedroom, her new friend walked into the master bedroom with its king-sized bed and blue satin coverlet. She put her cloth bag on the bed and said how pretty and feminine everything looked.

Then Alicia kissed her softly on the lips, her hands caressing Margaret's tired back. Margaret knew she wasn't gay, but there was something about Alicia she'd never felt with another woman. She seemed so alluring and so comforting at the same time. Margaret felt blissfully relaxed, her softness blending into Alicia's slender body.

"Margaretta, put on your nightgown and we can have our wine up here," Alicia smiled. "I will get glasses."

Margaret slipped into a blue lacy nightgown, climbed into the bed and propped up pillows on each side. Alicia came upstairs barefoot, with two large goblets of wine, which she set on a bedside table. She unzipped her red dress, stepped out of it and stood smiling in a red thong and matching bra. She had well-toned arms and muscular long legs.

She got into the bed and handed Margaret her wine. They both sipped quietly for a moment.

Margaret felt sudden prickles of anxiety. What was she doing with this woman? What did she know about Alicia?

"Alicia, I've never done this before. I'm not sure I'm really comfortable being with you like this."

"Don't worry, Margaretta," Alicia said softly. "We will delight in each other's company with no feelings of pressure. Just leave everything to Alicia."

They clinked glasses and Margaret sipped from her large goblet. She felt good as Alicia drew closer and traced the outline of her face.

CHAPTER 29

Greg Barnett scrolled through the Associated Press weekend stories on his computer Monday morning in the quiet newsroom. It was his duty to make sure the *Times* wasn't missing anything interesting in the Texas hinterlands. He spotted a surprising item from Kinston. After a quick read, he walked over to Annie's desk and asked her to call up the story. He stood there silently while she read it on her computer.

The story detailed the deaths of three people from carbon monoxide poisoning. The bodies were discovered Sunday in a condominium complex in Kinston, where a 47-year-old woman apparently had left her car running after coming home from a party at nearby Fort Kinston.

The woman, identified as Margaret Redmond, was found dead in her upstairs bedroom. The carbon monoxide gas emanating from her garage also had killed an elderly couple in the adjacent condo. Apparently, Redmond, dean of students as Middle Texas College, had ingested a large quantity of alcohol before returning from the party and accidentally leaving the engine running in her Toyota Corolla. Police were still investigating.

The discovery of the bodies Sunday afternoon led police and fire officials to issue dire warnings about the dangers of carbon monoxide in closed spaces. They said the tragic accident should be a worrisome example to others who lived in condos or apartments that weren't especially well constructed. They cited similar deaths across the country. College officials said they would hold a memorial service for Redmond on Wednesday.

Annie quickly messaged Rob, who joined them at her desk and read the story over her shoulder.

"I can't believe Margaret is dead," she said. "We just saw her last week. What a terrible thing to happen."

"I thought when I saw the story it must be your source – the woman you guys met with who talked about the college contracts," Greg said.

"Yeah, I really liked that woman," Annie said. "She seemed to be the only person in the college administration with brains and class."

"She was really smart – and brave to meet with us," Rob said.

"On the face of it, this sounds like a terrible accident," Greg said. "But you should call your sources and see what they're hearing."

Annie called Ben Weatherby on his cell phone. He was working in his office at the college's English department. He said word had spread fast about Margaret's death.

"Hold on a minute." After a pause, he said, "I shut my door. Now we can talk more freely."

"Do you think it could be foul play?" Annie asked. "Both of you were so worried about being discovered that day we met near Austin."

"I really don't think anybody followed us that day," Ben said. "I don't feel that I've been followed at all. But Margaret felt differently. She said she got prickling sensations at the back of her neck sometimes when she drove around town."

"Poor Margaret," said Annie.

"She had worried off and on about her safety since she confronted Gonzales about the contracts," Ben said. "She also had coffee recently with Will Ward to ask him questions. She said that didn't go well either.

"But it was an odd kind of accident. If you wanted to kill Margaret, why would you arrange something that would also kill and injure her neighbors. That seems so risky."

"Or smart, if you were a cold-blooded killer and you wanted to draw attention away from your intended victim," Annie said. "What are the police saying to the TV reporters?"

"The cops didn't notice anything out of the ordinary at her townhouse," Ben said. "Leaving your car running with keys in it is the kind of thing you'd do if you'd been drinking – and police confirmed she had drunk a lot that evening. Still, it doesn't sound like Margaret."

"Why not?"

"She enjoyed her wine at parties, and she had gone to a big one at

Fort Kinston," Ben said. "But basically, she took good care of herself."

"How are Gonzales and Ward taking it?"

"Gonzales seems genuinely upset, but it's harder to get a read on Ward. They didn't like each other at all. Margaret often battled Ward to get appropriate funding for academics – one reason the staff loved her and hates Ward."

"Gonzales just sent out a long email praising Margaret," Ben said. "I'll forward it to you. Do you think you'll come to the memorial service?"

"Probably," Annie said. "I'd like to see how Gonzales and Ward handle it, and pay my respects to Margaret. Will you be in touch if you hear anything else I should know?"

"Absolutely," Ben said. "Just pretend you don't know me at the memorial service."

"Of course!"

Annie planned to leave for Austin that day with Rob to look at the state's teacher retirement system records. She wanted to find out whether the college was cheating the state, as Ben and Margaret had suggested. She also wanted to meet with Mark Ingram to see what the Texas Ranger had found out about Maddy's death.

"What should we do?" She asked Greg. "Should we go to Austin and on to Kinston for the memorial service?"

"Definitely," said Greg. "There's no time to waste.

"I'm glad we have a solid tip to investigate," he added. "You should be able to get to the bottom of it pretty fast. That's good, because I don't know how long I can keep you guys on this story."

"What do you mean?" Annie asked.

"Our new publisher met with the editors yesterday and said some things I found troubling. He wants a lot of people covering politics. That might mean fewer people doing investigative stories. I gather his interest in politics means more stories covering the secessionist movement – and not in an investigative way."

Annie groaned. She saw that Rob also looked worried.

She knew that the investigative team's work depended on getting the time to pursue open-ended stories. The Middle Texas College investigation was a good example of a purely enterprise project. A political source of Maddy had tipped her that the college's top two had built a strange empire based on military education contracts. So a few months before her death, Maddy had convinced Greg she should investigate the college, not knowing what she'd find or how long it would take.

Annie believed – like most reporters – that if a newspaper didn't devote reporters to investigative reporting, it wouldn't uncover the great stories that needed telling. The reporting would become essentially a daily catalog of the mundane – incremental developments from governmental meetings, shallow crime stories and forgettable news features.

"You don't think Barry McKnight will dismantle the investigative team, do you?" she asked.

"He didn't say that," Greg said. "But if he demands that we put more reporters into covering other stuff, you know what might happen."

"Just my luck," said Annie. "I finally get to do some investigative work and it lasts about a minute."

"Guys, don't worry about it yet," Greg said. "I'm not doing anything different until they force me to. I just want to be candid about what's going on behind the scenes."

"I appreciate that, Greg. We'll work as hard – and as fast – as we can."

"I know. Just be careful about spending money, okay? Nothing raises red flags faster than expensive out-of-town trips."

"No problem," Annie said. "We're reporters. We can pinch pennies with the best of them."

She and Rob got to Austin by early afternoon and spent the rest of the day at the state's Teacher Retirement System offices. With both of them matching names in the state's records with names of college employees listed in the federal contracts, they found that the state was paying retirement contributions to at least 700 people who weren't working in Texas – and never had. Instead, the workers were assigned to military bases and ships throughout the world.

"This is brazenly illegal," Rob said as they left for dinner. "If the college has done this for five years, as it looks, it could owe the state $10 million."

"Maybe more," said Annie. "If the state of Texas makes the college pay this back, it could bankrupt Middle Texas."

"I can't believe the college thought it would get away with this," Rob said.

"Well, they apparently did get away with it for years," Annie said. "You know what Ben and Margaret told us. They didn't include this expense when they bid for the contracts because they wanted to beat their competition. So instead, the people of Texas are paying for their empire-building."

"What a story!" Rob said.

"Don't count your chickens yet. We need to tie up all the loose ends before we know this is a story. The college may have an explanation we haven't thought of – or state officials may say this somehow doesn't add up."

"Yeah, I know. Stories that sound too good to be true may not be true."

Annie felt good about Rob. Some reporters in training might complain about the tedium of spending hours matching names from two long lists. But Rob was patient and meticulous. He didn't try to be flashy or show off when he was dealing with people either. Annie disliked reporters who tried to throw their weight around with courthouse clerks or minor officials – or even major officials. Quiet resolve carried the day more often than self-important blustering.

She often thought that if more college students understood what reporting was really like – more painstaking research and grim office politics than colorful bursts of writing and front-page glamour – fewer would choose to major in journalism. She said that to Rob as they ate dinner at a cheap barbecue joint near their budget motel.

"Most journalism majors I know are going into PR," Rob said. "But for me, nothing could compare to what we did today – knowing we're finding out something that's wrong and having a hand in correcting it."

"I'm glad you feel that way. Remember that the next time you're writing briefs about garbage service changes or new chamber of commerce officers."

They both laughed as they made their way to separate motel rooms.

"You know, we could share one room and save money," Rob said as he waited for her to unlock her door.

"I thought of that," Annie said. "But I don't think the paper's that hard up yet."

"I could behave if I had to," Rob said, looking longingly at the queen-sized bed in her room. "It would be nice just to cuddle."

"I've heard that one before. Good night, Rob."

The next day, Rob finished up their work at the retirement system headquarters while Annie visited Ken Asher, the state's higher education commissioner.

Asher, one of her favorite public officials, was razor-smart, politically sharp and fearlessly quotable. He had been suspicious of Middle Texas College's contracting business for a long time, but his state agency didn't have authority over federal contracts. He gave her great quotes for the story she would write.

"We've told by Middle Texas College for years that the courses taught abroad and out of state would incur no state costs – that the taxpayers of Texas were not having to pay for any of these courses through state appropriations," he said.

"I doubt that the Legislature ever intended to create Texas retirement programs for people who do not even live or work in the state of Texas."

"That's great," Annie said. "Let me know what you hear from your board about this."

"I definitely will," he said. "I expect the college will say that it's just a mistake. It will be interesting to see what Gonzales does when this all comes out."

He paused for a moment.

"Can I say something off the record?"

"Sure, Ken."

"I'm really worried about the college's links with the secessionist movement. I think those people are dangerous, especially since Tom Marr seems to be gaining traction as a gubernatorial candidate."

"Do you know him?"

"No, I don't. But I think any movement toward secession is pure folly. The people in the Republic of Texas movement I've heard about tend to be right-wing oddballs, who dislike immigrants and want to push Texas back into the last century. But I should be asking you what you think, since you profiled Marr for the *Times*."

"He seemed like a good guy who wants the state to prosper, but I must confess I don't understand the secessionist movement very well."

She felt uncomfortable talking about Marr, so she ended the conversation.

But she respected Ken's judgment and she left his office feeling uneasy.

CHAPTER 30

The next morning, Annie joined Rob in the breakfast room of their budget motel, where they'd prepare for their meeting with Mark Ingram and later, the funeral of Margaret Redmond.

"Check out the bizarre story on Big Bend," he said, handing her the Austin newspaper.

She silently read the story on page two about an unsettling incident at Big Bend National Park, the large federal preserve along the Rio Grande, just a few hours south of Tom Marr's ranch. The day before, three men armed with rifles on the Mexican side of the river had taken potshots at park tourists floating down the river in rented rafts. One rafter was seriously injured, though most shots hit the rafts. The shooters had disappeared by the time the park rangers appeared on the scene. The park had suspended all rafting activity until further notice.

"That's just crazy," Annie told Rob. "You better call in, to see if they want you to do any reporting on this."

"I already did," he said. "Greg said to finish up the trip with you."

Because there was no one else in the newsroom to spare, Rob had been instructed to check with police if unusual border incidents continued to surface. But it had been relatively quiet since the odd school bus attack in Brownsville and the armed robberies of the Laredo churchgoers.

"What do you think is going on?" She asked Rob. "Big Bend is such a quiet, peaceful park."

"I have no idea. It sounds like a few Mexicans just got restless. I doubt that it amounts to much."

"Perhaps you're right," Annie said. But she felt uneasy about it and wondered if she should talk to Greg about sending them there. They really needed to go to Margaret's funeral, though. You can't do it all, she reminded herself.

They headed to the Texas Rangers headquarters, where Mark Ingram greeted them warmly in the reception area. He gave Annie a solid hug and invited her and Rob into his office. She hadn't seen Mark since Maddy's memorial service and had worried about him. He looked better, though she still detected a trace of sadness in his eyes.

"What've you found out since I saw you in Dallas?" Annie asked.

"I'm still in early stages, but some interesting things have come to light," he said.

"Like what?"

"As I explained earlier, I opened a two-part investigation under my authority as a Ranger," he said. "I'm trying to find out if Maddy's death was connected in any way to the reporting she was doing at the college – or elsewhere. And I'm looking at the college's relationship with Tom Marr and the secessionist movement."

"What have you learned about her death?"

"One witness called the highway department to report that she'd seen a black Suburban stop after Maddy ran off the road. She said she saw its female driver get into Maddy's car, presumably to help her. Police found fibers and hair that weren't Maddy's, but they could've been from anyone."

"That's discouraging," Annie said.

"If this person was trying to help, why didn't she call 911 and wait there?" Mark said. "If help had gotten there sooner, maybe Maddy would have had a chance."

His voice trembled and he stopped briefly to regain his composure before continuing.

"Did the mystery person try to hurt Maddy, or tamper with her car? Her neck was broken, presumably from the accident. But we may never know exactly what went on inside that car."

"I hate hearing that," Annie said.

"I'm also looking at Tom Marr's connections with Ed Gonzales and Dan Riggins," he said. "Riggins's background is pretty mysterious. He was with the CIA for years, which means we can't get answers about what he did there. You know the agency won't answer questions."

"Do you think Tom Marr has done anything wrong?" Annie asked.

"That's the second time you've asked me about Marr," Mark said, looking at her intently. "What's going on between you two?"

Annie blushed and looked down, wondering what to say. She saw Rob staring at her.

"We've had a dinner or two," she said. "He's a widower with a wonderful little girl. I liked being with them when I was at his ranch in West Texas."

"Annie, I'd run as fast as I could," Mark said. "Most of the secessionists I've investigated in the past are pure poison. I don't know that much about Marr, but I don't think he's surrounding himself with people who mean well for Texas."

"That seems a bit unfair," she said.

"Look, I don't know anything about your politics and I don't really care," Mark said. "But the secessionists are mostly extremists. Their literature tends to be full of hate for Hispanics, for instance. They're very big on border controls. That's fine until you start talking about electrified fences and other stuff that's clearly aimed at hurting people."

"Have you heard Tom Marr say anything against Hispanics?" Annie said. "Ed Gonzales is Hispanic and Marr picked him as his campaign finance director. I would say that's an indication that Marr's not prejudiced."

"No, I haven't heard Marr say anything prejudiced and we're monitoring his speeches," Mark said. "But he gets pretty worked up about drugs and violence along the border."

"Don't we all?"

"Yeah, but secessionists have their own language. They're always talking about training civilians to deal with their enemies, and that's a dangerous thing. The more we learn about them, the more we Rangers worry what they're doing."

"I hear what you're saying, Mark. But remember what we talked about at the funeral. You need to follow your heart sometimes."

She saw his eyes brimming and backtracked hastily.

"Mark, I wasn't trying to make you feel sad. I want to know everything you find out about Marr. But I won't turn my back on him yet."

"I'll keep you posted," he said. "But please be careful."

"I will." She was silent for a moment, checked her watch and changed the subject.

"Did you hear about the carbon monoxide death of Margaret Redmond, dean of students at Middle Texas?" she asked. "Rob is driving us to her memorial service this afternoon."

"I'm going to that, too," Mark said. "I didn't know her, but I'm curious about her death. Can I follow you in my car? It's very troubling that two women connected with that college have died recently in strange accidents.

"I don't want you to be the third, Annie," he added.

"I'm glad for you to go with us, but don't worry about me," she said. "I've got Rob with me whenever I go out of town."

She and Rob walked to the car silently and she got in. Once he settled in behind the wheel, he gave her a puzzled look.

"Annie, are you serious about dating Tom Marr? Wouldn't that be a conflict of interest? Plus, he just doesn't seem to be your type."

Because he was echoing her own worries, she felt irritated and couldn't keep the defensiveness out of her tone. Why did everyone feel compelled to drive her away from Marr?

"Rob, this is really personal. I'm not covering his campaign, and whom I date is my decision. If you really want to know, I haven't made up my mind yet."

"I'm just surprised," he said. "You've been acting like secessionists are the lowest form of matter."

"That's not true. I have an open mind. Maybe they're on to something. What do you think?"

He was quiet for a moment and seemed to choose his words carefully. "I think Texas could do a lot worse than those guys. But I'm trying to be an objective reporter."

They rode in silence until he turned off the highway to the college's main entrance. Annie dreaded going to another funeral just weeks after Maddy's memorial service. She felt her stomach tighten with tension. They parked at the same auditorium where she and Maddy had listened to Marr's big secessionist speech. Mark had followed them in an unmarked Toyota 4-Runner so that he could blend in with the crowd. The three of them walked into the auditorium and sat in the few remaining seats toward the front, where they could see clearly.

Annie counted about 150 people in the auditorium. She assumed that people in the front row were Margaret's relatives and close friends. She remembered that Margaret was from California and had been widowed a few years ago. So it was mostly Middle Texas colleagues and former students in the crowd, she guessed.

A big portrait of her rested on an easel on the stage. It was a formal one probably taken when she was promoted to dean of students, Annie thought. She looked at the woman's slightly freckled face framed by her feathered brown hair and felt a pang of sadness. In the picture, she was wearing a white ruffled blouse with pearls. She looked like the classy and vibrant woman Annie remembered from their meeting. Someone had placed an urn, which Annie assumed contained Margaret's ashes, beside the easel. Flower arrangements banked the stage and a lectern had been set up for speakers.

College luminaries, including Gonzales, Ward and their secret source, Ben Weatherby, sat in two rows of chairs on the stage. She assumed that the plump young woman in the too-tight maroon dress sitting next to Gonzales was his wife.

She scanned the audience and spotted Dan Riggins sitting toward the back of the auditorium. Beside him sat a striking Hispanic woman with long black hair featuring an odd white streak in front. She was wearing a silky black dress and large round sunglasses and was sitting a little too close to Riggins to be merely an acquaintance. Who the hell is that? She wondered. The woman looked about the right age, but too exotic to be Riggins's wife from San Antonio.

After a pianist played some hymns and a soloist sang "The Lord's Prayer," Gonzales got up and faced the room from the podium. Annie thought he looked sad and tired, and she listened carefully to his somber speech. After tracing Margaret's early life, educational trajectory and the death of her military spouse, he talked about what an asset to the college she became.

"Margaret put away her sadness after losing her husband and channeled all of her energies into helping the students of Middle Texas," he said. "She was never too busy to help a student find the right class, get scholarship money or even to find a babysitter if that's what it took to stay in school. Even with all of her administrative duties, she taught a class each semester to stay in touch with students.

"She was the best friend of the college and one of the best friends I have ever had," Gonzales said, his voice breaking and his eyes leaking.

"We are setting up a scholarship in her honor and I personally will contribute the first $10,000," he said, choking up before taking his seat.

The other speaker was Bobby Jett, the college's student body president. Tall and skinny with dark curly hair, he wore a navy blazer that hung a bit short on his long arms. He started out shaky, but by the end of his 15-minute speech, his voice had gained authority.

"Dr. Redmond was the most amazing teacher," Jett said. "Everyone wanted to be in her English course because you could tell she really wanted to teach it. She lit up the room when she talked about a Charles Dickens novel or an Emily Dickenson poem.

"She wanted to be around students and she listened to what they said with great respect, even if she disagreed. She wanted to see students succeed and go on to a four-year university, and she worked at making that happen for anyone who asked. She was just a terrific lady."

Annie noticed that many students looked moved when Jett finished. He obviously was popular with his peers. Gonzales's eulogy had drawn only the polite attention students accorded an administrator they didn't personally know, which told her the students didn't see much of him on campus.

But she'd been startled by the raw emotion in Gonzales' tribute. He seemed distraught over Margaret's death. She wondered about their relationship. She knew Margaret had considered Gonzales a mentor, but what had she meant to him?

In contrast, she had noticed that Will Ward looked bored and almost contemptuous on stage during Gonzales' speech. She wished she could decipher the complicated emotions in the room.

She got up to walk out with Rob and Mark. She glanced at the back of the room, where Riggins and the mystery woman had stood up to leave. Riggins acknowledged her presence with a cool nod. The woman seemed to be staring at her a little too intently from behind her sunglasses. Annie felt chilled. She couldn't quite put her finger on it, but there was an underlying presence of menace in that bland auditorium.

CHAPTER 31

Alicia Perez sat down on the bed of the plain motel room in Kinston and kicked off her stilettos.

Riggins watched her, his unease deepening. She had been too quiet since the memorial service ended. She had eaten almost nothing for dinner at a lackluster chain restaurant nearby, and said little on the drive to the motel. Usually after a successful mission, Alicia's excitement translated into a night of prolonged and inventive sex. But tonight her mood seemed sour and morose.

"You are awfully quiet, mi querida," Riggins said. "What's wrong?"

"I hated going to that service. Why do you insist on taking me?"

"I told you. I wanted you to see Annie Price, so that we could begin planning what to do with her."

She didn't answer immediately, just pulled her black dress over her head in one fluid motion. As always, he delighted in seeing her slim, well-toned body, but he also noticed the dark circles and lines under her eyes. She usually looked younger, but tonight she looked every day of her fifty years. She got into bed in her leopard-print bra and panties and pulled the coverlet up to her chin, shivering.

"Can you get us some wine from the mini-bar?" she asked.

"Of course, mi amor."

He found an acceptable bottle of Pinot Grigio in the decidedly low-range offerings of the mini-bar and poured two full portions into the thick, cheap goblets. He shucked off his clothes and slid in bed beside her. Her hands felt cold and he rubbed them briskly to warm her up.

It wasn't just her hands. Alicia's whole manner seemed chilly and detached. It bothered Riggins greatly. She was moody by nature, he knew, but mostly when they were together, she usually made their limited time fun and sexy.

They drank their wine meditatively while he searched frantically for ways to cheer her up.

"Tell me everything about your mission, mi querida. You are so clever to think of using the carbon monoxide from her car in the garage. How did you get into her place?"

"I met her – as you and I had planned – at the officers' club, using your membership card. It was easy to find her and to talk to her. She invited me back to her place. That was my big mistake."

"Why a mistake?"

"I made love to her. Then it was harder to kill her."

"Did you have to make love to her?"

"Yes. You know I like making love with women, and she was muy simpatica."

Riggins got out of bed abruptly and went into the bathroom. He badly needed a moment to think. He mustn't let his hair-trigger temper get away from him. He looked into the full-length mirror behind the door. In the cheap fluorescent lighting, he looked small, his penis shriveled, his desire gone. He had always known that he couldn't possess Alicia exclusively. So why did the news that she had seduced Margaret Redmond before killing the woman bother him so much? He remembered how he had desired Margaret that day at the college, but hadn't acted on it because of Alicia. Why couldn't she be faithful to him?

He tried to think logically. To his knowledge, she had never slept with another target. He was just bothered by the change in her behavior. He would get over it. He had to get past it because Alicia didn't permit jealousy. She had always been respectful of his marriage, probably because she knew Karen really wasn't much of a rival. Also, he thought, she didn't really care if he was married or not.

He walked back into the room and climbed into bed, edging closer to her delicious body. She moved slightly away from him and looked at the ceiling.

"I will not do that again," she said.

"You mean you won't sleep with a woman again?" He asked, a shade too eagerly.

"No, Dan. I won't get to know anyone I have to kill. And I won't kill any more women."

"Why not?"

"You know I'd rather kill men. Men killed my mother, my father, my brother and raped and took me away with them. Hijos de puta!"

Alicia rarely let the vestiges of bitterness show from her traumatic years with the Shining Path. When she did, Riggins realized how much emotional turmoil and –probably – mental illness remained under her hard-edged façade. He stayed quiet and listened.

"I am a professional, but you know I do not kill children. And I cannot kill women any more. All of the things they say about Margaretta at her service, I think they are true. She was a good woman, a smart woman. Why should she die and that pig Gonzales live?"

"Because she was our enemy," Dan came close to shouting. "I hardly ever ask you to kill a woman. What about the blonde reporter? You didn't seem to be upset about her."

"I do not know her," Alicia said, with a look that said he'd better lower his voice. "And I do not like her when I see her. She looked like a puta."

"I understand. I shouldn't have taken you to the memorial service. But I did want you to see Annie Price. Did you get a good look at her?"

"Yes. I will think about it. But give me a man to kill next."

Instead of the wild night of sexual abandon Riggins had anticipated, he could hardly sleep for his angst about Alicia's revelations. He wished she hadn't told him about Margaret Redmond. Lurid images of them making love in all kinds of exotic ways whirled in his head. Some men might have found such images prurient, but Dan saw the encounter as a dangerous crack in his relationship with Alicia. If she ever left him, his life would be worthless. He couldn't imagine an existence without her.

The next day, they sipped coffee in bed. Alicia seemed more like herself.

"I forgot to tell you, mi hombre. I took your soldier class to the border last week. They enjoyed their shooting. The best of the new men hit a fat Mexican."

"Did he kill him?"

"I don't think so," Alicia smiled. "But he won't try to cross the border again."

"Alicia, you can't let the soldiers shoot Mexicans right now. It could be bad for Tom's campaign. Please tell me you won't do that again."

"Okay," she said. "But they must learn these skills, no?"

"Yes, but let them shoot at animals. We must be careful until Tom is elected."

As always, he felt terrified, but thrilled, at Alicia's daring. What would she do next? He never knew, but it made being with her dangerous and unpredictable. Later, he walked with her to her Suburban and she kissed him softly.

"I will think about Annie Price," she said. "But you must let time pass, or people will become suspicious."

"Okay, mi amor. I'll see you soon."

He drove to the college for the meeting he had planned with Will Ward and Ed Gonzales. First he met with Ward to size up the atmosphere.

"How's Ed? I thought he might lose it yesterday at the service for Margaret."

"He was a pretty sad sack," Ward agreed. "But I think he realizes it was necessary. Margaret was out of control. Who knows what she was doing? She was even trying to get information from me."

"Yeah. Should we talk about her death with him?"

"Lord, no. He's too raw," Ward said with a grimace. "Before we go to his office, we should talk about Annie Price. I don't think we can risk another accident yet."

"You're right, of course. And I may have to find a solution other than Alicia."

"What's going on?" Ward looked interested behind his thick granny glasses. He always seemed intrigued by Alicia, though he had met her only a few times. Since Ward seemed even more ruthless than

Alicia, he doubtless admired her handiwork, Riggins thought.

"Let's not talk about it. Time to meet with Ed."

Gonzales welcomed him and Will into his inner office. He shut the door, looking considerably more composed than the day before at Margaret's memorial service. Following Ward's advice, Riggins tiptoed past that subject.

"I noticed Annie Price in the auditorium yesterday," Riggins said. "What do you think she's doing?"

"My spies tell me she's working on a story about the state's retirement contributions for our out-of-state military instructors. You know about that. We can talk our way out of that one, easily. She doesn't know anything about the important stuff."

"That would be a disaster, for us, for Tom and for the whole secessionist movement," Riggins said. "You must let us know if she gets close to the other stuff."

"It's not going to happen," Gonzales said. "And there better be no more accidents. Everything will be jeopardized."

"I hear you," Riggins said. "For now, we'll monitor what Annie Price does. But on a more positive note, Tom's doing absolutely great. His poll numbers are skyrocketing and he's getting huge attention."

"Yeah, our dream's going to come true," Gonzales said. "He's a hell of a candidate and he'll make a great governor."

"Of course, this'll cost a lot more, as we move into more active campaigning and advertising," Riggins said.

"Don't worry, things are going well in that department," Gonzales said. "How's the new military training class going here, Will?"

"We've got a class of about 50 right now, thanks to you, Dan. Your connections have helped us find good men who're going to be useful to the movement."

"Shouldn't we be moving faster on that?" Ward asked.

"We've got another 52 officers in training at Tom's ranch," Riggins said. "We're up to 700 now in the company. Of course we'll need more by the time Tom's elected. We'll step it up soon."

"What else do we need to talk about?" Ed said.

"I don't think I've mentioned it, but Tom has an itch for Annie

Price," Riggins said. "They seem to like each other, which is what we hoped when she did the profile."

"What if it goes further than that? Surely those two wouldn't last?" Gonzales said.

"No, I doubt it," Riggins said. "If it looks too serious, we'll figure out how to make her go away."

CHAPTER 32

A week later, the *Houston Times* newsroom got a message from Amanda Weeks that the publisher, Barry McKnight, would hold a standup in 15 minutes.

Annie walked over to Jim Merrill's desk to see what he'd heard. The bagel she'd eaten while driving to work sat in her stomach like a big rock.

"This can't be good news," he said. "My guess is that we're going to take a hit – buyouts or possibly layoffs."

"You're probably right," she said. "God, I hate these meetings."

People gathered quickly for the standup. It was at 10:30, so most of the day staff had arrived. Annie, Jim and Rob stood close together, as though they could protect each other from whatever was coming.

Barry McKnight came out of Amanda's office and stood at the intersection of the copy desk and photo desk, where stand-ups took place. Looking considerably less happy and animated than at his earlier appearance, he signaled for quiet.

"I have some bad news," he said. "We are laying off 19 in the newsroom today and about 100 companywide. We have notified some people already this morning, and we'll give the news to the rest before noon.

"I didn't think we'd have to take this step so soon, but quarterly results came out a few days ago and they're extremely disappointing. All categories of advertising are falling and the cost of newsprint just went up again. The only thing we can control right now is our personnel costs.

"I'll take a few questions, if you have any," he said.

"How did you decide who to lay off?" Jim asked.

"We looked at seniority in work groups. For instance, we're letting three news copy editors go. So the three in that particular work group with the least time at the paper will have to leave. The same would hold true with various reporting and editing work groups.

"In some cases, we looked at functions we could take care of in other ways. For instance, do we need some of our specialty writers, or can we use wire copy to fill more space in Features sections?"

"What kind of severance will people be getting?" Barbara Vick, the paper's film critic, asked nervously. She knows hers is a job that can be replaced using wire stories, Annie thought.

"The company will pay two weeks for each year an employee has worked," McKnight said. "We wish it could be more, but that's pretty standard in the industry."

"Is this the only round of layoffs you anticipate?" Jim asked.

"Probably not," said McKnight. "We'll see how the rest of the year goes. I must go visit with other departments now. But remember, we appreciate everything that you do."

He left quickly and people gathered in nervous little groups for a few minutes, then returned to their desks. Annie looked at her watch – 11 a.m. Would she get a message in the next hour that her job was gone?

It was one of the longest hours she could remember, but she tried to bore deeply into the complicated college story she and Rob were working on about state benefits for the out-of-state workers. Greg and Amanda had edited the story and she was rechecking each fact carefully.

At noon, Amanda sent out a newsroom message that all of the employees who were going to be laid off had been notified. The knot in Annie's stomach began to dissolve and she offered a silent prayer. She still had her job. She caught Jim's eye – he signaled that he was okay. She walked over to Rob's desk.

"Are you okay?"

"Yeah. I'm still employed as a news clerk. But the way the company is going, I may never get promoted to reporter."

"I'm not so sure of that. They'll figure out a way to lay off enough well-paid people to hire new reporters like you that they can get cheap."

"That's a hell of a way to get a job," Rob said glumly.

She saw a group of people around Barbara Vick's desk. She guessed that the film critic had gotten bad news. Barbara was energetic and a wonderful writer, but those qualities would hardly save a job the bosses had decided wasn't necessary. Annie would offer her condolences later.

Right now, she needed to see if Cilla had finished the draft of the college story. Greg had edited the story, but had asked her to read it as well. As Annie's former editor, she knew the most about Annie's reporting and writing.

She walked over to the glass office and knocked on the door. Cilla sat facing the interior wall, but motioned her in. When she turned around, Annie saw that the editor's face was streaked with tears.

"I've been laid off," Cilla said. "They apparently decided they could lose one assistant city editor out of four. I had the least seniority."

"Oh Cilla, I'm so sorry." Annie walked around the desk and leaned down to give her an awkward hug.

"I can't believe it. You've been here, what, ten years?"

"Ten years next month. I had hoped to spend my career here. But you know there's so little turnover in the city desk editing ranks. It's my bad luck to be the junior person."

"What can I do?" Annie asked.

"Nothing right now. I'm going to leave for the rest of the day. I'll come back tomorrow to pack up my stuff."

"What do you think you'll do?"

"That's a good question. You know my husband Jim works for an oilfield equipment company. His job's pretty shaky right now, too."

"I'm sorry. I didn't know that. How old are Fred and Frank?"

"They're four and six, and we definitely need two incomes with all the expenses of those two kids.

"I'll probably stay home for a few weeks to clean my house, then look for a job in editing at one of the smaller papers. Of course, you know they don't pay anywhere near what I make here."

"Yeah, I know, but you've got great experience. Hopefully something will turn up soon. I'd like to organize a lunch for you tomorrow. Would that be okay?"

"I don't think I'm ready for that. I'll see you tomorrow, but why don't the two of us have lunch later when things settle down?"

"Okay. Let's talk again tomorrow."

She walked out of Cilla's office, went back to her desk and sent Greg, Rob, Jim and a few others who would care an email about the editor's departure. She knew Amanda would not make public the names of people who were losing their jobs out of privacy concerns for those employees. But the word would get around.

She went into Greg's office and sat down, hoping for comfort.

"This is so depressing," she said. "Cilla was my first editor here. She taught me so much about reporting and writing and was always good to me."

"I know. She's really a great editor. It's a bad day – we're losing six reporters, including the film critic, book editor, agriculture reporter, two sports reporters and our wonderful night cops reporter, Jamie Pierson."

"Oh no, not Jamie," Annie lamented. She loved spunky, petite Jamie, whose crime reporting was accurate and colorful.

"It's going to be that much harder to put out the kind of paper that Houston deserves," Greg said. "The only antidote to a blow like this is to be true to our mission and do it well.

"That's why I'm proud of the story you and Rob are producing for tomorrow," he added. "You guys worked hard and uncovered something that will help our readers, maybe even save the state millions of dollars."

"Thanks, Greg. I can't help but wonder if I'll be in the next round."

"Any of us could, depending on what the publisher decides he values. But don't live in fear. Do your best work. That's all any of us can do."

CHAPTER 33

Ed Gonzales drove south into the Rio Grande Valley, the last leg of a 420-mile trip from Kinston to Matamoros, Mexico. Normally Gonzales loved road trips, but he preferred driving alone in his comfortable beige Cadillac. Traveling with Cecilia and two-year-old Manuel for a very long day had shattered his nerves.

Manuel alternately screamed and chattered. Cecilia hadn't done much to control him other than occasionally whipping out a large breast from her stained white blouse to nurse him. Though she had moved to the back seat beside Manuel's car seat while trying to perform the nursing maneuver, it still mortified Gonzales. Luckily it appeared that Manuel at last wanted to wean himself, a fact that cheered Gonzales and depressed Cecilia.

She was talking about getting pregnant with a second child. Gonzales carefully had refrained from saying anything against the idea, but it filled him with dread. He had enjoyed the babyhood of his first four children, but raising Manuel felt like a chore. He supposed it was because he had loved the mother of the other children, while he felt bored and increasingly impatient with Cecilia. It didn't help that Manuel acted like a brat.

He missed Marla and his other family intensely. He saw Kenny, his sweet twelve-year-old at the boy's weekly soccer games now, which he loved. He saw Sonya, his fifteen-year-old and Donnie, who just turned seventeen, much less frequently and sensed their coldness when he got together with them. He knew the divorce had affected them powerfully and that they harbored intense anger. But he hoped that would lessen in time. They refused to visit Cecilia or their little half-brother. Gonzales didn't press the issue.

He half-feared, half-hoped that Marla would remarry. He knew she had dated several officers at Fort Kinston, but seemed to be in no hurry to settle down. She wasn't glamorous, but in her mid-forties, exuded an understated attractiveness that drew men to her. In most ways, Gonzales thought, she and Cecilia couldn't be more different.

Finally, Manuel slept in the back seat. Gonzales pulled into a gas station to refuel, restock his stash of nerve-calming candy bars and restore Cecilia to her place in the front seat. Luckily, he and Cecilia accomplished this without waking Manuel. Perhaps they could enjoy quiet for the last two hours of the trip. Gonzales liked driving through the Rio Grande Valley with its flat landscape, skinny palm trees and the peculiar feeling that Texas was tilting downward into Mexico. He never quite understood why they called it the valley – it all seemed low to the ground. He wanted and needed it to be a pleasant trip. So he made an effort to pay attention to Cecilia.

"Are you enjoying the trip, mi chica?"

"Si, Eddie. You know I love coming home. You don't like to hear about it, I know, but I hate Kinston more and more."

Cecilia lately had stepped up her complaints about Kinston, which seemed like dangerous territory to him. She had acted happy enough when Manuel was a baby, but was becoming increasingly restless and dissatisfied as the baby grew and the novelty of new motherhood wore off. He resolved to listen carefully and do what he could to end her foolish talk.

"What would help you to like Kinston more?"

"You could come home for lunch every day, and take me out at night. When Manuel is sleeping, I walk around the big house and do not know what to do."

"I can do more, but you must get out to do more things on your own. What about yesterday? You went to the meeting of the faculty wives at the college, no?"

"Yes, but they are old and unfriendly. I can tell they do not like me."

"Chica, you're imagining that. Of course they like you."

"No. They do not like that I am young. They do not like that I am married to the president. They liked your ex-wife. And they do not have young children."

"Are you making more friends at Manuel's nursery school? I

know your friend Bianca moved to San Antonio. Are there other women from there who could become friends?"

"No, they are all Anglos. They do not like Mexican women. They seem proud and unfriendly."

"Would you like me to hire a full-time housekeeper? Since Barbara only comes two days a week, maybe I could find a Mexican woman who could come every day. Someone to speak your language and be company for you."

"Like Ramon?"

More dangerous territory. Ramon was their young, handsome Mexican gardener and Cecilia spent an inappropriate amount of time talking with him. He was there every other day and Cecilia always brightened up on the days he worked. She often followed him around the large property with Manuel in tow.

"Yes, except better. A woman you could talk to about cooking and children, the things that women like."

"Ramon likes to cook and he likes Manuel."

"Querida, you mustn't become too familiar with Ramon. You're my wife and Ramon is our servant. Please remember that."

"Of course, Eduardo. But I am thinking we should move to Matamoros. You could work for mi padre. I would have my family and Manuel would have his cousins to play with."

"That's not possible. I'm a Texan and so is Manuel. And my other children are there."

"I do not care about your other children. We will build our own family."

"Cecilia, my job's in Kinston and our future is there. You must make an effort."

Her selfishness angered him and lent an unaccustomed sharpness to his tone that momentarily shut her up. She lapsed into a sulky silence that ended only when he steered the Cadillac toward the Gateway Bridge connecting Brownsville with Matamoros. As they slowed for the border crossing on the Texas side, Manuel woke and started wailing.

Gonzales was inching along in line to the crossing booth when

Cecilia suddenly opened the passenger door and darted behind the car. She climbed into the back seat and began unbuttoning her blouse. Her moves caught the eye of several Hispanic men loitering at the booth. They nudged each other, alternately laughing and staring.

"Cecilia, people are watching," Gonzales pleaded. "Please don't try to nurse Manuel here."

"Eddie, he is hungry. Nobody will care."

She proudly hoisted a big breast toward Manuel, who eagerly sucked this time as the gaggle of men took it all in avidly. He felt like sliding down into the seat and disappearing. Instead, he moved the car forward and showed their passports to the smirking guards.

Soon he was driving through the urban streets of Matamoros, reflecting on the upcoming visit with his hated father-in-law. Gonzales regarded Manny Lopez as the creepiest human being he had ever encountered. Lopez came across as superficially charming and cultivated, with a taste for gourmet food, fine wines and American football. He didn't seem to smoke his own marijuana. He just produced it for the masses of gringos that clamored for his superior product up and down the East Coast.

Gonzales knew that the Lopez organization was smaller and considered less violent than the fearsome Zetas, who regularly dumped headless bodies in streets and public squares. But since Lopez ran a leaner organization, with a high-quality product, he lived in constant danger of being murdered by his larger rivals.

Consequently, his father-in-law rarely left the compound, but he welcomed a select few visitors like Gonzales and treated them well. Gonzales knew Lopez liked him inasmuch as the cold-blooded kingpin was capable of liking anyone. But Gonzales also knew enough to be deeply afraid of him. He remembered the horrible threats from Lopez's traveling henchmen when Cecilia got pregnant. Gonzales never doubted that his wife's father would get rid of him if it suited him.

He passed through the Matamoros suburbs and drove farther out into the hinterlands to the heavily guarded and gated Lopez compound. He coasted carefully to the guard gate, speaking briefly in

Spanish to several men armed with AK-47s. They bowed politely, recognizing his car from past visits and waved him inside. He drove for nearly a mile to a low-slung ranch house in the rear of the compound.

He and Cecilia got out of the car with Manuel. Several servants carried their bags inside, where more armed guards stood at attention. A guard took them through the house to the large office where Cecilia's father worked.

Manny Lopez stood up, hugged his daughter, kissed his grandson and shook hands with Gonzales. Lopez was a short, thickset man in his fifties with iron-gray hair and large, long arms. He had deep-set, dark eyes that constantly moved around the room.

Though it was late, Lopez had ordered a great feast of roasted goat and beef and many side dishes to celebrate their arrival. Lopez led them to the interior, open-air dining room where he poured margaritas made with the best tequila. His four sons and other family members had gathered to visit with his youngest child and her family.

"We welcome Cecilia, Manuel and her husband Eduardo to Casa Lopez," said Lopez, raising his glass.

Lopez had seated himself at the head of the table with Gonzales on one side and his sons on the other. The women and children sat farther down, chatting among themselves excitedly. Gonzales felt wary – he never knew which way the conversation would go with his father-in-law.

"Your contracts bring us very good business," Lopez said. "But you could do more for me. I have been thinking about it."

"Thank you, Manny. I'm honored to help the father of mi esposa bonita."

"My sons and I would like you to be the chief of our North American market, to find new ways to distribute our fine product. You would be handsomely rewarded."

"You do me such a kindness. But I am a college president, content to do my small part for your great organization."

"Do you refuse me?"

"Of course not, Manny. Let me think it over."

Lopez shook with soundless laughter, something Gonzales imagined he did while watching his enemies being tortured and killed.

"Think about it, Eduardo, but not too long. We will talk more about it during the coming week. You are one of us now."

CHAPTER 34

The next few days passed in a whirlwind for Annie and Rob. Their story that the college owed the state $10 million for failing to get contract money to pay the retirement contributions for its out-of-state employees created a sensation. College president Will Ward called it an honest mistake and said the college immediately would change its practice. The state attorney general announced an investigation, but so far no one was insisting that the college pay back the money to the state. It appeared that the college might dodge that particular bullet.

Annie felt exhausted. She had worked a lot of six-day weeks during the last two months and needed a break. Every few days, Tom Marr called her to chat, and she had agreed to come back to the ranch to visit. This looked like a good time, so she had made plans to fly the next day to Midland, where he would meet her and drive them to the ranch. She would stay in West Texas for five days, and he would take her to Big Bend National Park for canoeing, hiking and riding horses.

Her cell phone rang as she was preparing to leave the newsroom for her vacation. It was Jake Satterfield. She hadn't heard from him in a week and wasn't happy about it. Why did he keep putting everything in his life before her?

"Hi, babe. What're you doing Saturday?"

"I'm going out of town tomorrow for five days."

"Damn, this is the first weekend in a while I haven't had legislative committees or my kids. I wanted to drive over to see you. I've missed you a lot."

"I've missed you too. But as usual, I haven't heard from you much."

"Things are still tough, shuttling from Austin during the week to be with the kids in Kerrville on the weekends."

"I know it's hard for you. It sounds like the legislature has been crazier than ever. But are you always too busy to call?"

"No, but Jeannie is making the divorce harder than it should be. For a woman who wants out, she's being a royal pain."

"Is it ever going to happen?"

"Yes, honey. And spending more time with you is the first thing on my list as a free man. Where're you going?"

"Well, since you might hear about it, I'm going to spend a few days with Tom Marr at his ranch and at Big Bend."

"Annie, please tell me you're not going to do that."

"I *am* going to do that. Tell me why I shouldn't."

"He's not your type. To be honest, I'm disassociating myself with his campaign. I've found out some things I don't like."

"Don't tell me. I want to make up my own mind about Tom. Unlike you, he's been there for me."

"You can't sleep with him."

"Why not?"

"It will ruin everything. I can't share you with him."

"Well, so far Tom seems a lot more reliable than you, Jake. I'm not getting any younger. I can't wait forever for you to get free."

"It's only because of the divorce and the session that I haven't been able to see you. Things'll change."

"Yeah, I've heard that before."

"Remember what you told me about not getting involved with sources? You shouldn't get mixed up with him while you're investigating the college. They're way too connected."

"Don't tell me what to do. You're the one who introduced us, in case you don't remember."

"I made a mistake. I didn't know some of the things I've found out since then. You can't go, damn it."

"Jake, I'm going. And I'm hanging up. I've made my plans and I resent this. You're always a day late and a dollar short."

"You'll be sorry," he said before she slammed down her phone.

With a flushed face, she stalked to the ladies room to compose herself. He wasn't going to stop her at the last minute from seeing Marr. She wet a paper towel and held it against her hot forehead to stop her head from throbbing, but it didn't stop her uneasiness. Would

Jake really drop her just like that? He had rekindled her worries about a conflict of interest, though Tom kept assuring her he had nothing to do with the college.

Didn't her happiness count for something? Since Maddy's death, Annie had been haunted by the memory of her friend's exhortations to live in the moment. Carpe Diem had become Annie's mantra too. Since the *Times'* layoffs, she had felt insecure about her ability to keep her job. Could Tom Marr be the answer to her clouded future? Maybe it was time to get married and become a stepmother, and just maybe, a mom.

Rob walked over to her desk for some last-minute instructions.

"Here's the stuff I want you to work on while I'm out," she said, handing him a memo and a stack of documents. She'd told him she was taking a few days of vacation.

"Where're you going? Did I hear you say West Texas?" he said.

"Rob, don't start," she said, sighing. "I don't want to talk about my time off. Please, just try to get this stuff done while I'm gone, okay?"

He raised his eyebrows, but didn't probe further.

"Okay, Price. I'll see you next week."

She arrived at Midland International Airport at mid-morning the next day and found Tom waiting with a sheaf of pink roses. He hugged her and kissed her lightly on the lips. Soon she was ensconced in the passenger seat of his pickup for the two-hour drive to his ranch.

"I'm so glad you're here, girl. It seems so long since we had dinner together in Houston. Betsy can't wait to see you."

"I can't wait to see her."

"Would you mind if we stopped at her elementary school on the way down? The principal asked me a while back to give an anti-drug speech. It shouldn't take long."

"Sure, that sounds like fun. I'd love to see her school."

"Since it's Friday, I thought we'd take care of things like the speech, then spend the evening with Betsy. She wants you to sleep in the other bed in her room tonight, since we'll be leaving her tomorrow for Big Bend."

"Oh, that's so sweet. A slumber party!"

He cleared his throat and glanced at her quickly as they sped away along the desert plains on the empty highway.

"I made a reservation for us at the Chisos Mountain Lodge in the Big Bend Basin. The Park Service runs it, so it's not fancy. But we'll be alone together and can take our time getting to know each other."

"I'm looking forward to it."

She could feel herself blushing, but also felt a frisson of excitement. He obviously wanted their time together to be romantic and special. She wondered what he would be like as a lover. Get back to reality, Annie, she told herself. She quickly changed the subject.

"Didn't I read in one of the recent profiles that you like giving anti-drug talks?"

"I guess I do. I smoked pot in college, as most people my age did. But since I've gotten older and seen how all the drug-related violence plays out on the border, I've decided I should do what I can to change our culture.

"Kids don't realize that when they smoke a joint, they're supporting murder, kidnapping and all kinds of bad stuff," he added. "If they thought about what it means for Texas, they might look at drugs differently."

"I like that you're living your philosophy."

They arrived at Marfa Elementary School just before the assembly was scheduled to begin. They saw Betsy filing into the auditorium with her class. She broke from the line to embrace her father, then Annie. Dressed in jeans and a lavender shirt, she was tall for a ten-year-old and already had Tom's look of Viking royalty.

"Annie, you came back to see us. I'm so excited! Did Dad tell you we're going to have a sleepover party? That is, do you want to sleep in my room tonight? I have two beds and one is made up for you."

"Yes, Betsy, I'd love that. It's so good to see you. But you better catch up with your class. We'll see you later."

She sat on a side row in the auditorium and watched Betsy beam proudly as the principal introduced her father as "a candidate for governor and Betsy Marr's dad, who lives on a ranch right outside of town."

"Hi, Shorthorns," he said, addressing them by the name of the school's mascot. He launched into a child-friendly version of his anti-drug speech. First, the students appeared to listen intently. Then some of the older boys began whispering and cutting up. Annie thought it wasn't surprising that they would regard Tom as a fuddy-duddy who could be ignored. Most anyone who talked against drugs or drinking would probably have a mixed reception with that age group.

It didn't seem to faze Tom, but he struck her as someone who didn't worry particularly about being popular. It was one thing she liked about him, she told herself. Her mind inescapably wandered to Jake. Tom and Jake were so different. She doubted that Jake, who seemed effortlessly cool, would talk to kids about drugs this way. He'd probably use his humor and funny stories about his own childhood. Pay attention and stop thinking about Jake, she told herself as Tom wound up his talk.

"So remember, if you see anyone with marijuana or other drugs, please tell them they're hurting themselves and the state we all love so much. We don't want to do anything to harm Texas ever, right?"

"Right," the younger ones chorused. The music teacher played "Texas Our Texas" while the students sang the state song in their sweet young voices. Annie remembered hearing it with Maddy just a couple of months ago, the day she met Tom in Kinston. She blinked back tears.

She was quiet as Tom drove away after promising Betsy they'd see her later in the afternoon.

"Would you like to see more of the ranch?"

"Yeah, show me everything," Annie smiled. "I didn't get the tour the last time I was here."

They drove to some of the fenced cattle-grazing areas and Tom told her about breeding, raising and slaughtering cattle. He went down a side road with a large bunkhouse on the right. Beyond was an open field.

Annie was surprised to see three lines of soldiers, dressed in camouflage and marching in formation. Beyond them, other knots of men gathered around a target range, armed with pistols. The scene seemed incongruous, since large herds of cattle grazed nearby.

"What's that, the National Guard?" she asked.

"No, these guys are training for a few weeks on this part of the ranch," Tom said. "They're supporters of the secessionist cause who're learning to be soldiers."

"Oh, really?"

"Yeah, they've volunteered to train as special border action leaders. They'll be ready to help us when our group is elected. They're a pretty special bunch," he said proudly.

As they drove closer, Annie saw the back of a pickup truck loaded with weapons – machine guns, large knives, handcuffs and other paraphernalia. The men on the field --she didn't see any women – mostly looked young and clean-cut and seemed intensely focused.

Tom parked his pickup at the side of the road and they got out. A young man quickly walked over and saluted Tom.

"Hello, Mr. Marr. I'm Roger Millsap, leader of this battalion. It's a pleasure to meet you and to train on your ranch."

Hi, Roger," Tom said, shaking his hand. "This is my friend, Annie Price. What're you guys doing this week?"

"We've gone to the border a few times to practice, get the lay of the land and see if we can stop any incursions," he said.

"See any problems down there?"

"We saw what looked like a coyote with some scruffy Mexicans trying to cross the border near Del Rio," he said. "We fired a few warning shots and they ran off. We lit out of there fast, to avoid the Border Patrol guys."

"Okay, son," Tom said. "Just be careful. Remember, you're just training right now. You have no authority to shoot at anyone yet."

"Yes, sir. Good to meet you, ma'am." Millsap saluted and turned to rejoin the soldiers.

Annie was aghast. She hated the thought of paramilitary activity – it seemed dangerous to organize a bunch of citizens, give them weapons and expect responsible behavior.

"I didn't know you were doing this," she said quietly. He looked at her in surprise, registering her disapproval.

"Yeah, Dan Riggins – you remember him, don't you? – worked for the CIA, as you probably guessed," Tom said. "He's been putting this all together, with classes at Middle Texas and military maneuvers out here on the ranch and a few other places."

"Are you paying those men?"

"Well, they're guaranteed a job with Dan's security company. He's set up a business called Republic Security where they can hone their skills. Then they'll be ready to shift over and be part of a new army when Texas becomes a nation."

Annie felt the tension in her shoulders ratchet up as she watched the self-styled soldiers. She should have guessed Riggins would be the perfect person to organize a paramilitary force.

"Tom, you told me you didn't have any connections with Middle Texas College except for the fact that Ed Gonzales is your campaign treasurer."

"We're just using their teaching services, like anyone else," he said. "That's not much of a connection."

"I don't think you were being straight with me," she said, her anger breaking through. "Let's get out of here. I shouldn't be seeing this – it's a confidential part of your campaign."

"Sorry, Annie," he said evenly. "I didn't mean to put you in an awkward position. We'll go find Betsy."

On the way back to the ranch, he changed the subject to Big Bend and how much he thought she would enjoy it there. The rest of the day was uneventful, as they swam and ate dinner by the pool with Betsy. She tried to push away concern about what she had seen and what it might mean.

Later on, when Betsy claimed her for their sleepover, Tom hugged her and kissed her much the way he said good night to his daughter, looking at them happily.

"I'll see you in the morning. Sweet dreams, darling girls."

CHAPTER 35

Annie woke to the sound of raised voices, wondering where she was for a second. She felt the warm weight of Betsy beside her and remembered that the ten-year-old had climbed into bed with her around midnight. She really misses her mother, Annie thought. No matter how devoted Tom is as a father, Betsy needs a mother.

She slipped out of bed, careful not to wake her, and tiptoed into the upstairs hall. She heard two men arguing in loud tones. After listening for a moment, she was surprised to realize it was Tom and Jake Satterfield.

She quickly pulled on jeans and a T-shirt and scraped her hair into a ponytail. She tiptoed out of the bedroom and closed the door quietly, hoping Betsy wouldn't wake. She walked into the den in her bare feet. The two men stared at her and stopped talking.

"What're you two doing? Why are you here, Jake?"

"I came to tell Tom that I'm resigning from any role in his campaign," Jake said. "And I came to get you and take you home."

"Are you crazy?"

"No, you know you shouldn't be here with him. You should be with me."

"I can't believe you came out here. You don't own me."

"No, but I'm pretty sure you still want me. At least you acted like you did, that night at the Driskill Hotel."

"You bastard. Go away and leave me alone."

"Jake, the issues between us shouldn't involve Annie," Tom said. "She can make her own decisions."

"She should know about some of the things that you and Riggins, that fascist buddy of yours, are talking about doing."

"I don't know what you're talking about," Tom said.

"I thought secession meant controlling our destiny and improving our lives. But no, the first thing you want to do is keep

Texans from voting," Jake shouted.

"What do you mean, Jake?" Annie said.

"You're exaggerating," Tom said. "Everyone would get to vote in the new republic."

"Yeah, except votes by people who own land would count twice as much as votes by anyone else," Jake said.

"Is that true?" Annie looked at Marr, shocked.

"Yes, but it makes perfect sense," he said quickly. "Landowners should get more say over decisions in any government. We're not talking about depriving anyone of a vote."

"I can't believe I was taken in by these people," Jake said. "Tell her about the way you would treat children whose parents have come from Mexico without papers."

"Children whose parents are illegal aliens wouldn't be able to go to public school in the new republic," Tom said. "But it's not because we want to punish children. We need a big stick to keep people from coming here illegally."

"That seems harsh," said Annie.

"It used to be that way before federal judges got involved," Tom said.

"Annie, he's an extremist," said Jake. "I'll grant you that he's handsome, acts real polite and looks good on paper. But he and his friends are heartless."

"I don't think you're being fair," Tom said. "You've looked at some of our confidential position papers and jumped to conclusions. Some things we've discussed in our documents are highly theoretical."

"What about training those paramilitary skinheads to lead patrols along the border?" Jake asked. "That's not only stupid – it's dangerous."

"You don't know what you're talking about. I accept your resignation from my campaign. Now get out of here." Tom's voice got louder and his face turned red.

Jake crossed the room to hug Annie. She slid away from his embrace.

"Don't touch me. I can't believe you're meddling in my life after I warned you not to. Go away."

"Annie, I'm sorry I embarrassed you," Jake said. "But I'd like to take you home. I'll be at the Hotel Paisano in Marfa until noon. Come by if you decide you're ready to leave."

He walked out the door, his head held high. Annie and Tom stared at each other, astonished, before he recovered his composure.

"I'll get Maria to make some coffee for us. We need to talk before Betsy wakes up."

Annie looked at the clock. It was only 9 a.m. Jake must have gotten to Marfa late last night and come by early to see Jake.

She walked through the hall feeling dazed, and saw Betsy sitting on the stairs. Her small face rested on her knees and her arms tightly wrapped around her legs in her pajamas. She looked anxious and close to tears. Annie wasn't surprised that the loud argument had awakened her. She hugged Betsy tightly and led her to the kitchen.

"Tom, Betsy's here," she called.

He picked up Betsy and carried her to the patio, telling her Maria would bring her breakfast while he and Annie talked for a while in his study.

He came back with two large cups of coffee and beckoned Annie into his study. He closed the door and sat down on the sofa beside her, putting his arm around her. She moved away slightly and he didn't object.

"I'm sorry Jake and I upset you and Betsy," he said. "We live such a quiet life here that the poor kid doesn't know what to make of it when adults argue."

"Yeah, I feel bad about that. That's Jake, I guess. You always know where he stands." She tried to smile.

"I didn't know you and he were lovers. How do you feel about him?"

His voice sounded reproachful and she could see disappointment in his gaze. I guess I've fallen off his pedestal, she thought.

"We got involved a few months ago, but since he lives in Kerrville, we've both been too busy to spend time together," Annie said.

"How did he know you were here?" Tom asked.

"He called just before I left yesterday and wanted to come to see me in Houston this weekend. I told him I was coming here for a few days. I thought I'd better, because he might hear it from you or someone in your campaign."

"Do you love him?"

"I don't know him well enough to know that, Tom. He's been tied up with the Legislature and getting a divorce. Since you and I seemed to click, I wanted to get to know you better to see if there was a chance for something deeper."

"What do you think now?"

"I think I made a mistake coming here. I came as your friend, but I'm hearing and seeing things that I'd write about if I was here as a reporter. And you're a lot more connected with the college than you wanted me to know. It's a huge conflict of interest for me and I need to go."

"Annie, please stay. I promise you we won't talk politics. Hell, up in Big Bend, we won't even think about politics. I want to show you the best part of Camelot."

She smiled at the mention of Camelot, but felt heartsick.

"I don't think I'm your Guinevere, Tom."

"You're the only woman I've been interested in for a long time, and Betsy adores you."

"Tom, I like you a lot, but it's impossible to have a relationship with you right now."

"Why? Surely even a reporter deserves a private life."

"If I were to stop working as a reporter for the *Times*, or stopped covering Middle Texas College, or if you're longer running for governor, we could reconsider," she said. "But right now, we shouldn't see each other."

She blinked back tears and looked at him with sadness.

"If we go to Big Bend and become lovers, it's eventually going to break three hearts -- yours, mine and Betsy's."

"All right, Annie. It's your decision, but I hope things change. I want you and I think you still want me."

CHAPTER 36

Annie walked into the large rectangular lobby of the Hotel Paisano in Marfa and used the house phone to call Jake in his second-floor room.

"Hey, it's Annie. I'm down in the lobby. I decided to take you up on your offer for a ride back to Houston."

"Great, honey. Want to come on up to my room?"

"Now, why would I want to do that?"

"We could have a quickie before we hit that long, lonesome highway."

"What planet are you living on? Don't you get that I'm really angry with you?"

"Sure, but making up would be great."

"Don't even think about it."

"I'll try not to, but it's going to be tough with you sitting next to me for ten hours." He sighed heavily. "Give me ten minutes to pack."

"Well, get a move on, would you? We've got a hell of a long trip ahead."

She slammed the phone and looked around the lobby, seeing it clearly for the first time. The floors featured beautiful old tile in an unusual orange, gold and green pattern. The decor included cowhide chairs, mounted steer and buffalo heads, Western art on the walls and the cozy feeling of a cattleman's hotel.

She walked from one end of the lobby to the other, seeing the memorabilia from the 1955 movie, "Giant." She remembered reading that the epic Western was filmed in Marfa. The Paisano had housed the crew and its actors, including James Dean and Elizabeth Taylor. She felt sorry that she hadn't gotten to see more of West Texas on this aborted vacation – she really did love it.

Her departure from Marr's ranch had been wrenching, with Betsy pleading with her to stay and Tom behaving like a gentleman, but unable to conceal his hurt. He'd called his driver to take her to Marfa after she decided to stop at the hotel and talk to Jake.

She didn't have to wait long for him to pack. Jake bounded down the hotel's stairway with his overnight bag and planted a kiss on her lips. His smoky blue eyes looked serious, but his trademark grin had returned – albeit restrained.

"Hi. I'm really glad you're riding back to Houston with me. I'd feel awfully lonely driving all the way back across the state by myself."

"Well, we need to talk. You've blundered into the middle of a mess and made it worse. The least you can do is help me sort it out."

"That's what friends are for. I am your friend, even though you're not acting very friendly."

He hefted her suitcase and they walked through the hotel's front patio with its gurgling fountain. His white SUV was parked on Marfa's small-town side street. She climbed in and he began driving away.

"Isn't that a great old hotel? I'd like to bring you back sometime when you're not mad at me."

"I'm not sure I ever want to come back here – with you or without you."

"Aw, Annie. Are you going to give me a hard time for the next ten hours?"

"No, I probably won't be awake for ten hours. I didn't get much sleep last night."

His jaw tightened and he drove his SUV faster, swinging into the open highway outside town. He gave her a quick, measuring glance.

"Did the amorous attentions of our future king of Texas keep you up all night?"

"No, I didn't sleep with Tom. I slept with his daughter in her room. She kept me up most of the night."

"I'm glad. You're too good for him." She was surprised to see how happy and relieved he looked. But she was still angry.

"Don't kid yourself. We were saving ourselves for the trip to Big Bend. Then you showed up. Why did you tell him about us being together at the Driskill Hotel? You made me feel like a slut."

"I was marking my territory – the way men do among themselves,

I'm afraid. He knows you're not a slut, but I wanted him to know that you're my girlfriend."

"Jake, we've spent two days and one night together. That's not enough for a solid relationship."

"I know. But I'm going to work on that. I'm attracted to you, Annie Price, because you're so different from most women I know. Jeannie's a good mother, but her life starts and ends with tennis and the country club set. I like your intelligence, your seriousness about your work and your independence. I want to get to know you better and see what happens."

"Well, that doesn't excuse your coming out here and acting like Conan the Barbarian. I knew what I was doing."

"I think you were hoping for King Arthur to sweep you off your feet. I know he's rich and eligible. But he's also more dangerous than you know."

"You're acting like I'm some kind of fortune hunter. I don't care about Tom's money or his ranch. I like him and Betsy. I wanted to give the relationship a shot."

"At the cost of your journalistic integrity?"

She was silent for a moment before answering. "I guess that's why I'm riding back to Houston with you. I realized when I saw Riggins's junior army patrolling on the ranch that I shouldn't be there. Even though I'm not covering Tom's race, he's too involved with the college."

"Yeah, those baby-faced soldiers are kind of scary, aren't they? They're mostly right-wing militia nuts and CIA dropouts recruited by Riggins."

"Is that what turned you off Tom and his campaign?"

"That was one thing. But when I read some of their secret position papers, I realized they don't want a democracy. Giving landowners a vote that counts twice as much as that of ordinary citizens reeks of elitism. So does depriving little kids of an education just because their parents crossed the border to work as gardeners and maids."

"I'm bothered by that too."

"Their right-wing agenda would affect just about everything in Texas. They want to speed up death-penalty cases. They don't want convicted criminals sitting on death row year after year – they want to execute right after they're convicted. We thought Rick Perry was tough on death row cases while he was governor. These folks would make him look like a softie."

"Hmmm. What else?"

"I'm hardly a flaming liberal, but I believe in justice and equality and a fair shake for everyone. The secessionists don't believe in those concepts. I don't think Tom is as bad as Riggins, but I sense that Riggins'll be the power behind the throne, once King Arthur's elected."

"But the position papers you read are theoretical. There's no guarantee that Tom would actually carry out those ideas, right?"

"No guarantee, which is why I'm giving Tom the benefit of the doubt. I'm leaving the campaign, but I'm not going to talk about what I know as an insider – yet. If Tom is as much a fascist as Riggins, he'll show his true colors before long."

"What about Gonzales? He's the biggest mystery of the Tres Amigos, or whatever they're calling themselves these days."

"I think he was once a decent man with good values, but he got seduced by soft living and money. Have you met his wife? I know you'll think I sound sexist, but she's a Mexican bimbo with almost no education and barely out of her teens. It was obviously a shotgun marriage."

"Yeah, I gathered that, too."

"I get the impression the college is hiding some big, bad secrets – mostly through their contracts. You found out they were bilking the state for retirement contributions for their out-of-state teachers. That's bad, but they were actually relieved that you didn't report something worse."

"Like what?" she said.

"I don't know, but you need to keep digging."

"Did you find anything about the contracts in the position papers?"

"No, except that Riggins and Gonzales definitely view the contracts as a big source of money for the secessionists."

They lapsed into silence until Jake stopped for coffee. Then he urged her to rest for a while, so she put the passenger seat into a reclining position and slept for a few hours. When she woke, he was pulling into a truck stop an hour from Houston for a quick dinner.

She got out of the SUV and noticed three vanloads of men in camouflage spilling out of the vehicles. The black vans had a Texas flag painted on their sides and signs identifying them as Republic Security.

"You see that?" Jake said in a low voice as they walked into the restaurant. "Those men are more of the secessionist military leaders. I'll bet they're heading back the way we came – to Tom's ranch for training."

"But the sign says they're a security company," Annie said.

"That's what they're doing right now," he said. "There will be more of them out there as the campaign revs up – providing security and muscle wherever needed."

Annie felt chilled. *If I were still in West Texas, I'd be with Tom in a motel room on top of a mountain,* she thought. Suddenly she felt glad she was back home. She needed to clear her head and get on with her work.

She remembered that Rob was working his usual Saturday night shift at the paper. She should stop by and check in with him on any new developments.

"Can you take me to the *Times* building?" she said. "I need to catch up with Rob Ryland, my reporting partner. I left my car in the parking garage."

"Did you say your reporting partner is Rob Ryland?" Suddenly, Jake's face had a stricken look.

"Yes, why? Do you know him?"

"He's Dan Riggins's nephew. He's been feeding information to Marr's campaign. I heard his name a few times in connection with the *Times*, but wasn't sure who he was."

"Oh my God!" Annie covered her face in her hands. Her voice

trembled.

"He's a news clerk who was assigned to drive me everywhere to make sure I was safe on trips to the college. Talk about irony! He's probably reported my every move to Riggins."

"Annie, I wish I had known sooner. I would have warned you. You said his name – and suddenly bits and pieces fit together."

"You know what this means, Jake? He probably tipped them off about Margaret Redmond, maybe even about Maddy. He likely did everything but sign their death warrants."

Jake looked worried. "What are you going to do about it?"

"I'm going to confront him – as soon as we get there."

"Do you think that's a smart thing to do?"

"It's the only thing to do. I've got to get him off this story immediately."

"Well, I'm coming back to your place. I'll sleep on the couch, but I'm not going to leave you alone tonight. Tomorrow morning, we can figure out what to do."

"All right, but I'm not going to sleep with you."

"Do you think I'm only interested in getting into your pants?" Jake looked angry. "I want to make sure you're safe tonight."

He drove into downtown Houston and parked on the street in front of the *Times* building. She had scribbled her address on a piece of paper. She handed him her house key.

"Thanks, Jake. You're a true friend."

"Be careful, Annie. If he's anything like his uncle, Rob Ryland is a monster."

CHAPTER 37

Annie shivered as she walked through the deserted lobby of the *Times* building. It wasn't cold outside, but her body felt cramped and shaky after the long car ride, and she was bracing herself for an unpleasant encounter. She felt stunned by Rob's betrayal, but she tried to smile and speak normally to the elderly security guard at the console.

"Hey, Ms. Price. Don't you know it's Saturday night in Houston?"

"Yeah, I really know how to have fun, don't I?" He waved her through.

Getting off the elevator, she saw Rob sitting at his desk in back of the room. He was watching local TV news to see if the stations had any new stories he would need to chase for the *Times*. He appeared to be the only Metro reporter on duty. The night editor and a few copy editors looked busy reading stories on their computer screens. No one paid any attention to her arrival.

She walked directly to Rob's desk. He smiled and waved when he saw her coming. But he looked puzzled as she approached, taking in her road-weary appearance and her grim expression.

"Hey, Price. Back from vacation already? What's the deal?"

"Hi, Rob. I wanted to come in and catch you because I knew you'd be working tonight."

"Yeah? You got another scoop for us?" He grinned, but it slid off his face quickly as she stared at him without smiling.

"No, but if I did, you'd be the last person I'd tell. You'd race to the phone to blab everything to Uncle Dan Riggins."

"Wait a minute. What're you talking about?"

"Let's just say that I've learned – pretty late in the game – that you're a lowdown snake, a despicable spy and a thoroughly dishonest human being."

"Hey, you're jumping to conclusions. I'm your partner, remember?"

NANCY STANCILL

"You were my partner and I thought you wanted to be a journalist. But you couldn't care less about being a reporter, could you? What are you? Who are you, Rob?"

"Hold on and listen to me," he said, standing to face her. "Yes, I'm Dan Riggins' nephew. He was the only one who gave a damn about me after my old man died drunk and broke in San Antonio. I was ten, and Uncle Dan's sister – my mother – was an alcoholic too. I told you about her. My uncle helped keep our family going. Is it any wonder I owe him?"

"Just what do you owe him?"

"I owe him a lot more than I owe this newspaper. He and his friends in the Republic of Texas paid for my mother's funeral and for me to go to college. They took care of all of our bills. And they helped me to see how great Texas could be."

He smiled and regarded her levelly.

"Don't you see, Annie? I'm your future. Uncle Dan and Tom Marr will get the Republic of Texas started. Then a few chosen people of my generation will shape Texas into the country it was meant to be. You could be part of it too, if you'd just open your mind."

"You sound like you've been thoroughly brainwashed."

"I'm just realistic. This country we're living in has gone to the dogs – anyone can see that. The United States doesn't work for the people who live here any more. It's hopelessly screwed up and morally bankrupt."

"You're the one who's morally bankrupt," Annie said. "How can you live with yourself? I'm guessing it was your information that got Margaret killed – maybe even Maddy."

"You don't know that, Annie – and I don't either," he said, shrugging his shoulders. "Don't go making wild accusations you can't prove. You'll get sued if you don't watch what you're saying.

"I don't know how Margaret or Maddy died – and to be honest, I don't really care. Any revolutionary movement has its collateral damage. Those two women put themselves in danger by going up against the Republic. Whatever happened to them was their own fault."

208

"How can you say such things?" Annie shook her head in disbelief. "You said you were Maddy's lover. Didn't you feel anything when she died?"

"She considered me her boy-toy. She cared only about her pleasures and her meaningless little life. She didn't take me seriously. She didn't care about Texas either."

"I can't believe your attitude. I guess you're setting me up as the next victim, right?"

"Annie, you don't have to be anything. Just stop working against the movement and you'll be fine. You could be Tom Marr's wife – the first lady of Texas. Wouldn't that be better than working for this dying rag? Think of what your future could be."

"You're crazy, Rob. I'm putting a stop to this. You can't work at the *Times* any more."

"Oh yeah? Try to stop me."

"You need to resign. Write a note to Greg – tonight. For your own good."

"You haven't proven anything. It's your word against mine – and you're an alcoholic, just like my mother," he taunted. "In fact, I'll tell Greg about how you sexually harassed me when you were drunk."

"Rob, I could hardly sexually harass you. I wasn't your supervisor. And what you did to me that night came close to rape."

"Yeah, you don't even remember half the things I did," he smiled.

Annie couldn't believe what she was hearing. She felt sick at her stomach, but she wasn't going to let him see any sign of weakness.

"Say whatever you want about me. Call me a drunk or a slut or anything else that might come out of your slimy, reptilian brain. Do you think I give a damn? We're talking about lives and deaths of good people. All I tried to do was to teach you how to be a good reporter. Obviously, I was wrong to think you were even interested in journalism."

He looked down for a moment. When he raised his head, she was surprised to see his wet eyes.

"Annie, I loved working with you. The weeks we spent together reporting were some of the greatest times I've ever had. Surely you can see that. But I pledged my allegiance to the Republic of Texas. My loyalty to Texas comes first."

"Rob, you do what you have to do. I'll do what I need to do."

She walked away, heading to her desk. She sat down, turned on her computer and started drafting a memo to Greg. She felt Rob's eyes on her, but she refused to look his way again.

She didn't spare herself in the memo, telling Greg the embarrassing details about her drunken night with Rob and everything she suspected he had done while spying for the Republic of Texas. Greg would read the memo at home tonight or tomorrow. She hoped that by Monday, Rob would be gone.

CHAPTER 38

Annie hurried to her car in the newspaper's gated parking garage, got inside and locked the door. She was trembling with stress and exhaustion, but she made herself sit still as she hit Mark Ingram's number on her cell phone. It was late, but she felt he needed to know about Rob immediately.

"Hey, Annie. I was just thinking about you. I'm coming to Houston tomorrow and want to see you."

"Great, Mark. I'm sorry to call so late, but I need you to know something right away. You remember Rob Ryland, my reporting partner?"

"Yeah, what about him?"

"He's Dan Riggins's nephew and he's been spying for the Marr campaign."

"That's incredible. But somehow it makes sense. The secessionists seemed to know too much about what we both were doing. And Rob seemed smarmy to me, too good to be true."

"You were a lot more perceptive than me. If you're correct in your suspicions that they plotted to kill Maddy and Margaret, Rob's information helped them accomplish their goals."

"I think you're probably right. Have you talked to Rob?"

"Yeah, I confronted him in the newsroom just now."

"How did that go?"

"It was pretty ugly. He all but admitted everything, but said no one could ever prove anything."

"Well, he may be wrong about that. That's why I need to see you tomorrow. I've uncovered some incriminating stuff."

"Yeah, what is it?"

"Let's just say it looks like enough to put Riggins and Gonzales in prison for a long time. I don't want to go into detail over the phone. Tomorrow, I want to show you some of the stuff I've got."

"Wow, that's exciting. Will I be able to report it?"

"Yeah, the parts that I can prove."

"Where would that leave Tom Marr?"

"Hmm, still worried about him? Don't tell me you're still involved with that guy."

"No, I broke it off. But I still care what happens to him and his little girl."

"Well, he won't be facing as much trouble as Riggins and Gonzales. But he's hardly innocent. Can I trust you not to have any contact with him?"

"I won't talk to him until I need comment for a story."

"Are you sure, Annie? I have to be absolutely certain which side you're on."

"Yes, I promise. Don't you trust me?"

"Yeah, now that I have your word. I have one loose end to tie up tomorrow. I'm supposed to interview the sole witness to Maddy's accident. You remember I told you someone had come forward?"

"Right."

"She'll only talk to me in person. She's Hispanic and will be staying with someone who lives on the East Side in Houston. I know you're pretty fluent in Spanish. Want to come with me?"

"Sure, I'd love to help."

"Since you've tipped your hand to Rob, I'm a little worried about your safety tonight."

"Don't be. You know Jake Satterfield, right?"

"The state senator from Kerrville?"

"Yeah. He brought me back from Marr's ranch in Marfa. He's staying at my house tonight."

"Hmmm. Well, okay, Annie. Have fun."

"He's staying there tonight to protect me, Mark."

"Sorry, I won't pry. I'm getting an early start tomorrow. Can I stop by about 10?"

"Sure, I'll be ready to go."

"Stay in your house until I get there and keep the doors and windows locked. Please don't do anything stupid."

"I won't. See you tomorrow."

She thought about her other secret source, Ben Weatherby. She called and reached him at home in Kinston. She explained quickly about Rob, reminding him that Rob had driven her to the clandestine meeting with him and Margaret.

"I'm so sorry, Ben. Rob was supposed to be protecting me. Instead, he put Margaret – and likely you – in danger with Riggins and his gang."

"Annie, don't beat yourself up over this. There's no way you could have known."

"I know, but you're in danger. You could be next."

"I don't think they'd dare touch me so soon after the death of Margaret. It would look bad to have two people from the same part of the college dying mysteriously."

"You don't know. They seem to be getting more reckless."

"Well, as it happens, I'm taking vacation next week. No one knows my plans. So I'll just slip out of town quietly tomorrow. I have a feeling this is going to unravel pretty fast."

"You may be right. Take care and stay in touch."

"You do the same, Annie."

Annie drove the two miles to her house in the Heights, seeing Jake's SUV parked in the driveway. Inside, the lights shone brightly. She felt relieved and happy knowing he was there.

Since she had given Jake her key, she knocked on the door.

Jake opened it quickly. She stepped inside and he enfolded her into his arms. She felt her last bit of anger with him dissolving. She hugged him back fiercely and locked the door.

He had laid a fire in her tiny fireplace and was cooling a bottle of California chardonnay in her ice bucket.

"Babe, just sit down, have a glass of wine and relax. Tell me what happened."

"It was pretty awful. But let's not talk about it right now. I already talked to two of my sources on the way home. I'm worn out."

"I know you are. Let me hold you."

He pulled her close on the sofa and she sighed with pleasure. He kissed her slowly and the problems of the day began to recede.

"I should stay mad at you, but I can't resist you tonight," she said. "I guess you already figured that out."

"Well, I was hoping you wouldn't make me sleep on the couch, since we're finally in the same city at the same time."

She laughed and the rest of the night was pure pleasure.

CHAPTER 39

She knew Jake needed to get back to Kerrville to see his kids, but he insisted on staying until Mark Ingram showed up. So she made love with him again, feeling happy to have him in her big antique bed. She fixed him eggs, toast and coffee. They sat in her living room sipping coffee and talking quietly.

She told Jake about her confrontation with Rob, but hadn't revealed anything about their personal relationship. It looked like she and Jake would get a second chance to build something good. She was determined not to sully the waters.

"I can't believe that jerk deceived you and the newspaper the way he did," Jake said. "I ought to go punch him in the nose."

"He did a terrible thing," Annie said. "But Riggins used him and tempted him with a chance to belong to something big after a pretty sad childhood."

"Don't make excuses for him. What he did was so wrong."

"You're right. But I think he really enjoyed working at the *Times* and he had the potential to be a great reporter."

"He was lucky to have an ace like you to teach him."

"I guess I refused to see what he was doing because I wanted him to be good," Annie said. "I put a lot into mentoring him. Hopefully, I've learned my lesson."

"Don't stop believing in people because one mixed-up kid let you down."

"You're right."

She sat comfortably with him until hearing a knock at her front door. Mark Ingram stood there, sweating in jeans and a light jacket. The day already was turning hot. She invited him in.

"Mark, you know Jake, don't you?"

"Hi, Jake. I remember you from testifying before your Senate Public Safety Committee last fall."

"Yeah, good to see you again, Mark."

The two men shook hands as Jake stood up to leave. She followed him out to the porch and kissed him quickly.

"Thanks for everything, Jake – for bringing me home and for making sure I was safe last night."

"I love being a bodyguard for a body like yours." His sexy grin made her feel deliciously weak. "I'll call you. Please be careful."

Mark had settled in with a thick file.

"Would you like a cup of coffee?"

"Yeah, great. We've got some time before we need to leave. I'll bring you up to speed on what I've found out. Just listen. Later you can interview me, and I'll decide what I can say on the record for your story."

"Great." She handed Mark a cup of coffee and sat in a chair across from him.

He opened his file and started talking.

"You remember that Maddy traced how Dan Riggins, Ed Gonzales and Tom Marr met at UT thirty years ago and called themselves the triumvirate. Even then, they believed that Texas should secede from the United States and become a republic. They agreed they'd join together and make it happen when they got enough power and money. They decided that at the right time in the future, they would make Marr a candidate for governor with an openly secessionist platform.

"They stayed in close touch over the years, and all did well. Marr flourished with his family's ranch, Riggins became wealthy and powerful at the CIA and Ed Gonzales gained money and prestige through his college's contracting business.

"Then, three years ago, something happened that speeded things up. Gonzales got a young woman named Cecilia Lopez pregnant. He learned – too late – that Cecilia was the daughter of Manny Lopez, a large-scale marijuana trafficker who operates out of Matamoros. Manny forced Gonzales to marry Cecilia. In the process, he found out about Gonzales' lucrative military contracts. He wanted in on that market.

216

"He learned that Gonzales and his sidekick, Will Ward, were already skimming money off the contracts for themselves. Manny coerced Gonzales into adding "enrollment assistants" to the biggest teaching contracts. The assistants actually were handpicked drug dealers – selling Manny's marijuana to soldiers and sailors on military bases, posts and ships around the world. Because the contract employees had broad military clearances, they were able to smuggle Manny's dope to the most far-flung places.

"The military never suspected a thing. Since Manny gave kickbacks to Gonzales, all of a sudden Gonzales and Riggins had plenty of money to fund a large-scale gubernatorial campaign for Tom Marr. They set up clandestine bank accounts in the Rio Grande Valley near Matamoros and started funneling money into the campaign. They also spent millions of dollars setting up Republic Security – the security business that would in time form the backbone of an army for the new republic."

"Wow, amazing stuff," Annie said. "Did Marr know about the drug money?"

"As far as I can tell, he didn't know his campaign funds were coming from illegal sales of Mexican marijuana around the world. One of the linchpins of his campaign is to oppose Mexican drug trafficking and its influence on Texas, so it's ironic – to say the least – that drug money was fueling his run for governor.

"But he did know – and enthusiastically support – the formation of Republic Security as the precursor to a Texas army. I guess Riggins told him he was using his own money to set up the business."

"How was Marr's campaign money handled?"

"It looks as if Riggins and Gonzales urged Marr to focus on his speeches and schedule while they controlled the financial side," Mark said. "As a candidate, he was terribly naïve and trusted his college friends entirely too much.

"Another thing we've uncovered through the secret bank accounts is that money was used to pay a hired killer. Mysterious withdrawals were made shortly after the deaths of Maddy and Margaret Redmond. That piece is still in the preliminary stages of investigation. But it appears that money went from Riggins to a secret associate in West Texas."

"Unbelievable," said Annie. "Was Tom a part of that?"

"I don't think so, but that piece is still unraveling," he said. "If it holds up, Riggins, Gonzales and possibly Will Ward could be charged with conspiring to distribute drugs – and to kill two people they thought were getting close to uncovering the plot."

"This will be a fascinating story," Annie said. "Can we sit down for a few hours after you talk to this witness and go over it piece by piece?"

"Definitely. I'll show you key evidence I've collected in this file. We can figure out what I can say on the record."

"Great. I'm getting the scoop, right?"

"Yes, Annie. You've earned it with your dedication to this story."

She locked her house and followed Mark to her car. Since she knew the East Side of Houston much better than him, she had offered to drive.

"Tell me about this witness," she said. "Why has it taken so long to interview her?"

"She called up the Highway Patrol a few days after the accident and talked to an officer there by phone. The investigators helped me get in touch with her. She knew some key details about the accident, but she said she'd give a complete statement only if I came to visit her in person. I got the feeling she's probably antsy because she's in Texas illegally."

"So this is the first time you've met her?" Annie said.

"Right. She said she'd be out of the country for a few weeks. We finally settled on meeting here in Houston. She said her name is Alicia Medina and she'd be staying with a friend here. She has a strong Spanish accent, so you're helping by going with me to the interview. My Spanish is a bit sketchy."

"What do you think she can tell you?"

"Not sure. Any details about the accident would help."

Annie drove around the East Loop and exited in an area that appeared more industrial than residential. She drove through streets that included ramshackle factory buildings, rundown commercial areas, vacant lots and houses and apartment buildings. Finally they came to the right street. She double-checked the address and Mark pointed to an old, brick two-story apartment building.

"This is it," he said. "I think her friend's apartment is on the second floor."

She parked her white Camry, locked it and walked upstairs with Mark. The second floor had outside walkways with red iron railings and numbered apartments. The place looked unkempt and mostly deserted. They found Apartment 211 and knocked.

CHAPTER 40

A slender woman with long dark hair that bore a strange white streak opened the door, smiling sweetly.

"Are you Mark Ingram, the Texas Ranger?" She said in heavily accented English. "Who is la bonita senorita?"

"Hello, I'm Mark Ingram. Alicia Medina, right? This is my friend Annie Price, who lives in Houston. She was a friend of Maddy Daniels, the woman whose accident you witnessed."

Annie looked at the slender woman dressed simply in jeans and a tank top. She thought she'd seen her before, but where? Suddenly it came to her.

"Didn't I see you at Margaret Redmond's memorial service in Kinston, sitting with Dan Riggins?"

"Oh no, I have never been to Kinston," she laughed. "You think we Hispanics all look alike, si?"

Annie felt flustered. Did she come across as a bigoted Anglo? She rushed to apologize.

"Of course not. I'm so sorry. I felt sure that you looked familiar."

"Come in, both of you and sit down," the woman smiled. "I'm sorry there is no air-conditioning at my friend's apartment. I know it's hot. Can I get you a cool glass of water?"

"Certainly, we'll both take one," said Mark. The airless apartment already felt suffocating.

Alicia went to the kitchen and returned shortly, bearing two amber goblets clinking with ice cubes. Annie sipped, and Mark gulped, the ice water. Hers tasted slightly metallic, so she put her glass aside. Alicia took a seat on the other end of a beat-up gold sofa beside Mark. Annie sat on a heavily used brown recliner across from them. The apartment was filled with shabby furniture and the kind of paintings and pillows you'd find at a low-end Mexican bazaar.

After exchanging a few pleasantries about their visit, Alicia seemed eager to launch into her story. She was animated and her dark eyes glittered with enthusiasm, which seemed out of place to Annie, considering they were about to discuss a fatal car crash.

"Now I tell you about the accident. I am driving up Interstate 45 to Dallas and I see your friend's little car run off the road. The car ahead of me follows her quickly and stops, and a fat blonde senora gets out. She goes quickly to your friend's car."

"What kind of car was it?"

"I think it was a black Suburban. The big SUV you see on many roads in Texas, si?"

"Yeah. Go on," said Mark.

"I say to myself the senora is going to get help for your friend. So I keep driving. Then I start to worry a little, and pull off at next exit. I turn around and get back on the highway, so I can go by the place again and make sure your friend is all right."

She nodded and smiled brightly, looking pleased with herself.

"How long was it before you passed by again?" Mark said.

"Maybe eight or ten minutes. I go by the same place. The fat blonde senora is in the seat with your friend now. I see her hands around your friend's throat, so I call 911 and leave."

Alicia had punctuated her tale with dramatic hand gestures. Annie watched her closely, trying to visualize the scene. She looked at Mark to see what he thought and noticed that he was pale and sweating.

"Mark, what's wrong?"

"I feel sick."

"Let me get you more water," Alicia said, hurrying to the kitchen.

He stood up grimacing so that Annie could help remove his jacket, and quickly slumped down on the sofa. She sat down in the chair and began searching in her purse for stomach remedies. She was still digging through its contents when Alicia rushed back into the room. Annie looked up and froze.

Alicia brandished a large butcher knife. With a triumphant smile, she stood over Mark and quickly plunged it into his upper body, somewhere between his shoulder and his chest. He groaned and fell back into the couch. Then Alicia turned toward Annie.

Annie jumped up from her chair. Shocked and horror-stricken, she nevertheless acted instinctively. She grabbed Alicia's arms and pushed her back until she pinned her against the living room wall. She banged Alicia's head and shoulders as hard as she could against a large framed picture of bullfighters. Alicia winced with pain and struggled against Annie's grip, but Annie was taller, heavier and almost as strong. Annie sensed her advantage wouldn't last, so she started screaming -- loudly.

Mark lay bleeding on the sofa, but still conscious. With a huge effort, he wrested the knife from his chest, pushed himself up to grab the doorknob and pulled open the door. He fell back on the couch, sighing heavily. Annie heard someone on the outside walkway running toward the apartment. She hoped it was help – and not an accomplice of Alicia's. She screamed even louder.

Alicia broke free from Annie's grip, cursing in Spanish. She ran to the kitchen and Annie heard her quickly opening the window and jumping out. At the same time, a tall, middle-aged African American man rushed through the apartment door.

Annie made a split-second decision to help Mark instead of trying to chase Alicia. She grabbed Mark's jacket and pressed it on his wound to stop the bleeding.

"Please call 911," said Annie to the man, who had knelt down to examine Mark. He rapidly punched the emergency number into a cell phone he carried in his pants pocket. Then he helped Annie to stanch Mark's bleeding. He looked like he knew what he was doing.

"Annie, my file is in your car. Take it and read..." Mark said weakly.

"Don't talk, Mark. You're going to be all right," said Annie with more confidence than she felt. The man kept applying pressure to the chest wound and she held Mark's hand.

"Hang on, guy," she said in a soothing voice. "Help's coming." He groaned, this time more weakly, she thought.

A few minutes later, which seemed like a century to Annie, an ambulance screamed to a stop outside in the apartment parking lot.

Medics rushed up the stairs and took over, examining Mark's wound and giving him a quick injection. Annie hurried to the kitchen, knowing that Alicia had gotten away, but wanting to see how. Some air whooshed in the window that she had left open. Annie looked out and saw the fire escape Alicia had used to climb down and make her getaway.

Annie looked around the kitchen and spotted a black purse. It must be Alicia's, she thought. She rifled through it, taking out a wallet. She found a driver's license, removed it quickly, slid it into her pocket and replaced the wallet.

She also noticed a vial of prescription medicine on the counter and took it with her, guessing that Alicia had crushed pills and put drugs into the water she had served them.

She rushed back into the living room, where paramedics were loading Mark onto a stretcher. His eyes were closed, but his wound now was neatly dressed with a large bandage.

"We're taking him to Ben Taub at the Medical Center," a worker said. Annie knew that Ben Taub Hospital specialized in trauma cases.

"Right, I'll follow you in my car," she said. She paused to speak to the man who had come down the hall to rescue them.

"Thanks so much for coming when you did. " She shook hands and introduced herself to Tony Little, a broad-shouldered man in his mid-40s. It turned out he was also a paramedic who lived a few doors down in the complex.

"Not a problem, miss. We get all kinds of scrapes here, but that was one bad-ass woman you were tangling with."

"Yeah, I was really lucky you heard us," she said. "She was trying to kill us both."

"I was leaving for work and heard you scream. You probably saved his life."

CHAPTER 41

Annie huddled at her desk in the newsroom, trying to warm up. Her nerves were rattled and her hands were cold and shaking, but she needed badly to calm herself. Soon, she'd have to start delving into Mark Ingram's file and summon the brainpower to write a complicated story.

She had spent enough time at the hospital to make sure Mark was properly checked in. She had called his mother in the Hill Country and as matter of factly as she could, told her of his serious injuries. Then she drove to the police station and later to the *Times* office, to retreat to the safety of her desk in the fifth floor newsroom. After the terrifying assault at the East Side apartment, she figured this was the place she needed to be. She feared that if she went home, Alicia or one of her accomplices would find her and try to kill her.

Since it was nearly 9 p.m. on a Sunday night, the newsroom was almost empty. She welcomed the solitude because she needed to think through what had happened and her next moves. First, she needed to background the woman who had come so close to killing Mark. She had written down the information on the driver's license she had found in the assailant's purse before surreptitiously putting it back for police to discover. Just as she thought, the woman had used an alias. The driver's license was registered to Alicia Perez, not Alicia Medina, the name she had used at the apartment. Her address was Marfa, on the same highway where Marr's ranch and Dan Riggins' second home were located, she noticed.

Annie did a quickie version of the computer checks reporters routinely made when trying to find information about the subject of a story. It took only a few minutes of looking before the name of Alicia Perez popped up in a government database – in a listing of companies incorporated by the state of Texas. Perez and Dan Riggins apparently co-owned a company called Peruvian Pottery Ltd., an import business based in San Antonio. Her early impression had been correct. Perez was the woman she had seen with Riggins at Margaret's memorial service. She suspected that Perez was Riggins's girlfriend, judging from the body language between the two she had noticed that day. The police also would discover her identity soon.

She felt consumed with worry about Mark Ingram. She had hated calling his mother, but felt she could break the news more gently than a doctor could. The physicians in the emergency department at Ben Taub Hospital said the deep chest wound was serious, but he could survive it with luck. If he rallied by morning, he would probably be all right. She had become so fond of him – surely he wouldn't die.

When she walked into the newsroom, she had checked quickly to see if Rob was there. His desk was empty and it looked bare, as if someone had cleaned it out. Of course, Rob didn't normally work Sunday night after working a Saturday shift. But she hoped he was gone for good.

She needed to call her editor to fill him in. She reached Greg at home immediately. He sounded worried.

"Annie, where are you?"

"I'm at work."

She explained briefly what had happened that afternoon, her role in it and what Mark had told her about Gonzales, Riggins and the Marr campaign. He knew a few details about the attack, because a short version had run on local TV.

"Holy Moly. You've got a huge story. Of course, you need to report it fully before you can write about the college and the campaign money. Do you have Mark Ingram on the record?"

"No, when we talked about it, he wanted me to listen to his findings before we agreed what he could say on the record. I was going to interview him formally once he had talked to Alicia Medina, I mean, Alicia Perez. I have his file, but I need to interview him or someone in the Rangers who knows about his investigation.

"Oh Greg, I just hope he survives." Her voice trembled.

"Me too. Have you talked about it with our weekend police

reporter yet?"

"No, I was going to do that next. Bill Joyner has gathered most of the information and is waiting to interview me." She dreaded being part of the police story, but knew Mark would be the focus.

Greg changed the subject, sounding a bit embarrassed.

"I read your long note about Rob Ryland. Annie, I'm so sorry I teamed you up with him. I should have suspected something from his eagerness to work with you. But he had good credentials and came across as a go-getter reporter."

"Well, he fooled me, too. I'm just sorry that I let him, um, get so close to me."

"Annie, don't castigate yourself. What he did was horrible. I talked to him last night and told him to pack up his stuff and get out."

"Did he make any threats?"

"No, he seemed subdued. He said he was moving back to San Antonio, anyway."

"Good riddance. Maybe that's the last I'll hear from him."

"Well, he could be in big legal trouble – or not. It depends how all of the stuff with Riggins and Gonzales plays out. Are we exclusive on this story?"

"Yeah, but we need to wrap it up before other media get wind of it. You know the attack on Mark will have reporters asking more questions."

"Shouldn't you go home and rest?"

"To be honest, Greg, I feel a lot safer here. We've got the security console downstairs and the police stationed someone in the lobby for tonight. I told them I was worried about another attack."

"Okay, try to do all your background work tonight. Tomorrow morning you can start calling the Rangers and others you need. And try to grab a few hours sleep on the sofa in the ladies' room. You're going to need it."

"Thanks, Greg. You're a great boss."

"You're a reporter with real courage and guts. I'll see you tomorrow."

She needed to make one more call. She punched in her parents' number in Virginia.

"Annie, is that you?"

"Yeah, Dad. Where's Mom?"

"She's babysitting the grandkids tonight while your sister and brother-in-law are in New Orleans."

"Great. I need to tell you something that's happened. It's upsetting, so maybe you can give Mom a version that won't send her into hysterics."

She told him quickly about Alicia's attack on Mark, their escape and the police involvement.

"Honey, that's incredibly scary. I'm so glad you're all right. Are you at the paper now?"

She couldn't say anything for a moment. It was such a relief to talk to him that she started crying. She gulped and tried again to speak.

"Annie, are you still there?"

"Yeah, Dad," she said in a choked voice. "I'm just so upset with myself."

"Why?"

"I knew there was something wrong when we got to the door of that apartment and saw her. If I had trusted my instincts, we never would have gone inside. Mark wouldn't have gotten hurt."

"Annie, Mark's a law enforcement officer. In most situations, things wouldn't have turned violent. You two were expecting a witness, not a homicidal maniac."

"I know. But if he dies, I'll never forgive myself."

"Listen to me. You were just a little girl, but do you remember when Lindsey Mann died?"

"Kind of. Wasn't he the older man who worked in the composing room at the paper?"

"Yes. The Ku Klux Klan was trying to reorganize in the mountains. I found out and wrote stories and an editorial. They threatened us, but I didn't take it seriously enough. Then one night they firebombed the newspaper building. Lindsey, who was working on a special ad section, was killed. I felt about as awful as a man can feel."

"I was only six, but I remember some of the arguments you and Mom had after that happened. She wanted you to leave the newspaper business."

"Yeah, she was afraid you and your sister and brother would be the next targets. I was too. But we saw it through."

"Well, didn't you feel good about the outcome? Wasn't someone convicted?"

"A Klan leader went to prison and the rest of those bastards disappeared into the mountains again, like the cowards they were."

"I guess I was too young to remember the trial, but I've seen your clippings about it."

"The right thing happened with the trial, but it didn't bring Lindsey back. Poor guy probably didn't care about the Klan one way or another. Actions have unexpected consequences, for you and for others who don't even have a stake in it."

"You couldn't have known."

"Yeah, like the situation you were in today. Bad things can happen when you're trying to do the right thing, especially in the reporting business. Maddy didn't let it stop her. You can't let it stop you."

"I know you're right. Funny, I thought you'd tell me that what I did was stupid and dangerous."

"Some people might say that, but I wouldn't. I'm proud of what you've done."

"Thanks, Dad."

"You are tougher than you know. Always remember that. And send me your story."

CHAPTER 42

Dan Riggins paced the hardwood floors in the stylish Marfa vacation home he and his wife had built, waiting for Alicia to show up. She had called him from the road to alert him of the disastrous problem in Houston.

It still could be salvaged, he thought. If Mark Ingram, the Texas Ranger who had teamed up with Annie Price to interview Alicia, would only die tonight from the knife wound, everything could be handled. There were ways of taking care of the reporter. His nephew, Rob Ryland, was still awaiting instructions in Houston. Riggins felt confident he could manage everything.

He didn't blame Alicia, because he could never blame her for anything. It would be like blaming himself, which he long ago decided was pointless. He thought of Alicia only with tenderness and concern. She was a warrior without peer. Generally, she found ways to succeed in the most dangerous of missions. It was sheer bad luck that Price had accompanied the Texas Ranger and changed the odds at the apartment in Houston.

He also wondered how Annie had unmasked Rob. He admired his smart nephew for being able to live a double life, working as a reporter and spying for the movement at the same time. His younger sister had made a mess of her life and escaped into the bottle a long time ago, but she had raised a son resourceful enough to be a potential leader of the republic. Rob had used his charm and great looks to worm his way into that reporter's confidence, and even into her bed. Good for him – Riggins felt a bit jealous. Rob's role was reminiscent of some of his escapades with the CIA. He unfortunately had taken it hard when the *Times* fired him. He sensed that Rob was close to crying when he told Riggins what had happened. Riggins felt impatient with human frailty – unless it was his or Alicia's. Never show weakness, he sternly told his nephew. Stay there until I contact you.

He thought he heard the sound of Alicia's powerful SUV out front. He looked out the window and saw her getting out of the vehicle, her head bowed. Her footsteps sounded slow and dejected, not like the usual quick, staccato gait of his beautiful lover. She usually sounded so confident you'd think she commanded the planets.

He flung open the door. She fell sobbing into his arms.

"Oh Dan, mi amor. You must be so ashamed of Alicia."

"No, no, mi vida. If we're lucky, that Ranger will die tonight!"

"But I left my purse in the apartment. How could I be so careless?"

"Darling Alicia, it will be all right."

They sank onto the expensive Turkish carpet in the massive hall, kissing passionately. Dan shushed her and held her in his arms a moment, brushing back her thick hair from her face. He felt so glad to be with her, but sensed that nothing would ever be quite the same again. Alicia had lost her confidence and they were in danger of being exposed.

Within a few minutes, they began serious and frenzied plotting. Riggins decided they'd better escape to Peru, since both kept passports and other papers that allowed them into Alicia's home country for their export business.

Alicia looked more cheerful and they talked about how an extended vacation might be just what they needed to regroup for bigger battles in Texas.

"I must get my passport and a few things to take with me," she said, jumping up from the floor with renewed energy.

"Si, mi amor," he said. "But hurry. We need to leave."

"I will go quickly, lock up the house and return before an hour has passed."

"I'll do the same here," he said. "We'll leave for El Paso to fly out when you get back. So be quick. We must get to El Paso before the morning light."

Dan kissed her again. He hated being separated for even an hour. He heard her accelerate in the SUV, too fast as usual, and drive away.

He called Tom Marr's cell phone. It was busy, so he left a quick message warning that bad news was coming. He was glad he didn't have to talk to Tom. Then he packed, throwing things into a small bag and getting all the cash he had out of a safe hidden under the floor of his bedroom.

He thought about the trip ahead. It would be messy, explaining to his wife why he was in Peru for an extended period. But he'd manage.

Nearly an hour later, he looked at his watch impatiently. Alicia should be back by now. Where was she? He began to pace again. He opened the door and stepped out into the dark West Texas night.

He saw a convoy of police cars go by on the narrow road not far from his house. He ducked back inside. He knew what had happened to Alicia. Damn!

He waited until the cars were out of sight and carefully got on the road to El Paso. He'd fly to Peru and direct their activity from a safe hideout. He thought about Alicia in custody – she was so volatile. He couldn't predict how she'd handle it, what she'd do.

But she'd be all right. She had no choice.

CHAPTER 43

Annie slept at her desk, her head cradled in her arms. Suddenly, she felt someone tap her gently on the shoulder. She woke with a start. Where was she?

"Good morning, Annie. Did you stay up most of the night?"

"Hi, Greg. What time is it?"

"Almost 7 a.m. I came in early to see how you were doing and what I could do to help."

"The first thing I need to do is to call the hospital to see how Mark's doing. His boss and his mother should be there by now."

She made a quick call. A few minutes later, she stopped by Mark's desk.

"Great news," she smiled. "Mark rallied during the night. He's conscious and asking for me. I'm going to head over to the hospital."

"That's wonderful. Get as much information as you can – without wearing him out, of course."

At the hospital, she found Mark's private room. She shook hands with his mother, a sweet, rounded woman with fluffy gray hair, and his supervisor, Captain Randy Spencer, who seemed friendly enough but looked stiffly pressed in his Texas Ranger uniform.

Mark looked much better. He had color in his face and enough strength to be propped up in his bed with pillows. Annie kissed him gently on the forehead.

"Hi, partner. You really gave me a scare yesterday."

"Thanks for saving my life, Annie. I'm still weak, so I'll let Randy do the talking for us."

"Great. I brought back your file, which you had left in my car. Randy, what can you tell me?"

"First of all, you'll likely be relieved to know that early this morning, we arrested a woman named Alicia Perez at her home in Marfa. We retrieved her wallet from the Houston apartment and discovered her true identity," Spencer said.

"Thank heavens."

"We believe she carried out the attack on you and Mark – and likely was responsible for the deaths of Maddy Daniels and Margaret Redmond."

"I'm not surprised. She acted like a one-woman killing machine." Annie shuddered.

"We picked up Will Ward in Kinston – he's in custody there. We also have issued federal warrants for the arrests of Dan Riggins and Ed Gonzales. However, we think both of them may have left the country."

"What about Tom Marr?"

"He probably will be charged at some point with campaign finance violations. So far, we don't think he had anything to do with the murders, or the conspiracy to distribute marijuana through the college's military contracts."

"Wow." Annie took a deep breath. "Are we still exclusive?"

"Mark insists that you get the exclusive. But it will end at 4 p.m. today when we hold a press conference at the governor's office in Austin. That's the best we can do. It'll give you time to get your first story posted on the *Times* website before your competition."

"That's fair. Let's begin."

An hour later, Annie came out of the hospital, her head spinning with details of the story she would write. Since Mark had briefed her yesterday, she used her time to ask new questions and get quotes from Spencer.

She walked to the fourth level of the parking garage, put the key in the lock of her Toyota and started to open the door.

Suddenly, someone grabbed her roughly from behind and clapped a hand over her mouth. She felt fear and the lack of air choking her.

"You thought you could get me fired and be rid of me. But I'm stronger and smarter than you. Now I'm calling the shots."

She recognized Rob's voice – and the Ivory-soap smell of his skin. She struggled to free herself.

He released his grip abruptly. She whirled around and saw he had a small but lethal-looking knife pointed at her.

"Rob, don't let your uncle take away your future," she said. "You're better than that."

"You don't know what you're talking about," he said. "Just get in the car. You're going to drive me to Marfa."

"No I'm not. Rob, don't hurt me. If you do, you'll be in worse trouble. Let me go."

She gazed at him steadily and held his hazel eyes. He still held the knife, but somehow she knew he wouldn't use it.

"Drop that knife."

Captain Randy Spencer stood behind Rob pointing a pistol.

Rob threw down the knife on the parking-garage floor and put up his hands. Spencer quickly cuffed him as she watched.

"Rob Ryland, you're under arrest for attempted assault and kidnapping."

He read Rob a Miranda warning as two other Rangers got off the parking-garage elevator and quickly joined Spencer. Rob's eyes dropped and his posture slumped. His clothes and his hair were disheveled and his appealing choirboy look was gone – perhaps forever.

"We followed you out, because I was afraid of something like this," Spencer told Annie. "We had a warrant for Ryland's arrest, too."

CHAPTER 44

After the Houston Police took Rob away, Annie hurried back to her office. She had phoned Greg and brought him quickly up to date. She had three key phone calls to make before she could start writing her story. She knew she'd have to hurry to get it done and posted on the website before the press conference. She felt calm and focused – Rob's arrest had helped.

She touched in the mobile number she had for Dan Riggins. She thought perhaps he might still be in the country. Would he answer his phone?

"What do you want, Annie Price?"

"Where are you, Dan?"

"Do you think I would tell you?"

She heard the animosity he no longer had to conceal in his voice. She sensed from the background noise that he might be at an airport.

"Do you care that Rob, your nephew, was just arrested after trying to kidnap me from a parking garage?"

"He must have let his emotions get in the way of his planning. A lesson he'll have to learn. What do you want?"

"I wanted to see if you have any comment about the charges against you. For fairness."

"Since when have you been fair?"

"Do you have anything to say?"

"Nothing on the record. But on a personal level, I want you to think about what you've done. You've helped to kill a dream for tens of thousands of people in this state. But secession will happen, whether you want it or not. All you've succeeded in doing is delaying it – maybe for a year, or maybe for a generation. But the forces propelling it are too strong. Just think about what you've lost."

"You could be right," she said, hoping to keep him on the phone. "Secession may be in our future."

"You could've been a big part of it. Marriage to Tom Marr would've made you one of the most powerful women in Texas."

"But at what cost?" She said tearfully. "Did two good, innocent women have to die?"

"You can't measure something that could change the future of the world against the pathetic lives of two flawed women."

"Yes, I can and I do, Dan. I'm fine with my part in exposing the wrongdoing that you're mostly responsible for. And you've destroyed the career of a good man, someone that I care about very much."

Click. The phone went dead. Either Dan Riggins didn't want to hear her any longer, or it was time for him to board his plane.

He'd land on his feet, no doubt about it. She just felt sorry for his nephew. Riggins would view Rob's troubles as collateral damage.

CHAPTER 45

Ed Gonzales stood in the parking area of his father-in-law's compound. He was preparing for a short ride into the countryside in his comfortable Cadillac.

His mobile phone rang. He checked who was calling. He saw with some surprise that it was Annie Price.

"Hello, my dear. Why are you calling?"

"Hello, Dr. Gonzales. I'm calling to see if you can comment on the charges filed against you in federal court. I'm assuming you know that you've been charged with conspiracy to distribute drugs and kill potential witnesses."

"I am innocent of these trumped-up charges. I believe that they represent government misconduct. The charges are designed to destroy the defenders of the Republic of Texas."

"Where are you?"

"I'm not going to tell you. But you should know that I've resigned as chancellor of Middle Texas College. I'm no longer living in Kinston."

"Will you continue to be active in the Republic of Texas movement?"

"No, I'm not going to be involved in Texas politics."

"Is it true that your father-in-law is a drug kingpin named Manny Lopez, as the indictment alleges?"

"No comment. The prosecutors apparently have fevered imaginations. I must go, Miss Price. Good luck with your story."

He hung up.

Time to go. He had put some papers for Cecilia on the bedside table of their room at Manny's house. He couldn't get Marla on the phone, but he had left a long voice-mail message for his ex-wife in Kinston.

He took his time, driving a few miles farther into Manny's

property, where the scrub land with its sparse vegetation and parched soil seemed endless. He knew he'd never get beyond Manny's guard gate into the outside world without his father-in-law's permission.

He parked his car beside a large Mesquite tree and got out. It was as good a place as any to leave this world, he thought. He got the small handgun he kept hidden under the passenger seat for emergencies. This was definitely an emergency. He would sooner die than become Manny Lopez's prisoner for life.

Still, he lingered, thinking about the best parts of his life, the lazy days when he was a handsome student in Austin, the wintry night when he became a father for the first time. Did he really have to leave? Was it possible to shoot his way out of the compound? He knew the answer.

He walked around the large tree in a wide, slow circle, noticing a fat black crow that had landed on its top. You won't have to wait long, he thought. He opened his mouth, pointed the gun inside and fired.

CHAPTER 46

Annie reached into the back of the newsroom refrigerator and found her last Diet Coke. She popped the top and walked back to her desk slowly, dreading the last phone call she needed to make before writing her story. She punched in Tom Marr's number, visualizing his slightly crooked smile and the light-filled acres of his ranch.

A sweet childish voice answered right away, sending a spasm of sadness into her throat that made it hard to talk.

"Annie? It's you! Are you coming back to see Dad and me? I've missed you so much."

"Hi, Betsy. I miss you too, honey. I'm calling for your dad. Is he around?" She gulped and a stray tear trickled through her mascara.

"He's out by the pool. Let me get him."

"Hi, Annie." She heard Tom Marr's voice, deep and serious.

"Hi. I guess you know why I'm calling."

"Yeah, I heard about the charges against Dan, Ed and Will. And just between us, I'm sickened by what Alicia did. I hope you know I'd never be involved in that."

"Okay. But I need to go on the record with you. Do you have any comment on the indictment?"

"I'm stunned by the charges against Dan Riggins and Ed Gonzales. They're lifelong friends and dedicated public servants. I hope and pray that the courts find them innocent of these terrible charges."

"These acts were supposedly aimed at helping to elect you governor, weren't they?"

"I'd never condone the despicable acts alleged in the indictment," he said, sounding as if he was reading from a bad press release. "In fact, I'm ending my campaign for governor today. I'm also resigning my seat in the Texas House. There's no way to continue a campaign with these serious allegations hanging over it."

"Investigators are alleging that you failed to properly account for campaign donations. Is that true?"

"I'm sure that I've made mistakes through ignorance and carelessness," he said in a slow, sad voice. "I won't shirk responsibility for those mistakes."

"What's the future of the Republic of Texas? Care to comment?"

"The Republic of Texas is more than just my dream. There are too many people who want Texas to be a country for that fire to go out. I can't carry the banner now, but I'm sure that others will."

"Who do you think will pick it up?"

"Annie, that's all I can say right now. You can probably guess that I'm heartbroken," he said in the same numb tone.

"What'll you do, Tom?"

"I'll do the same things that I've always done, tend my ranch and raise my little girl. Off the record?"

"Okay."

"I'll be here in West Texas if you ever decide to give us another try. I can't offer you the glamour of the governor's mansion, but you'd have a good life with Betsy and me. It could be our own Camelot."

She hung up the phone, put her face in her hands and sobbed quietly at her desk.

"Are you okay, Annie?" Greg messaged her from across the room.

"I'll be all right. Just give me a moment to cry."

CHAPTER 47

Annie posted her breaking story at 2:35 p.m. on the *Times* website, well before the Texas governor's 4 p.m. press conference.

TWO CHARGED, TWO SOUGHT
IN SECESSIONISTS' PLOT

By Annie Price
Times Reporter

A West Texas woman today was charged in two killings and three others face federal conspiracy charges in a wide-ranging drugs and murder-for-hire plot aimed at promoting the secessionist candidacy of gubernatorial contender Tom Marr.

As a result of the charges, Marr, a West Texas rancher and two-term House member, ended his controversial candidacy today and resigned his seat in the General Assembly. Marr, 48, was not charged in the indictment, but possibly faces campaign finance violations.

"There's no way to continue a campaign with these serious allegations hanging over it," Marr said in a phone interview from Marfa with the *Times*.

Alicia Perez, 50, a Peruvian native who lives in Marfa, was charged in the killings of *Houston Times* newspaper reporter Madeleine Daniels and Middle Texas College Dean of Students Margaret Redmond. According to the federal indictment, Perez ran Daniels's car off the road on I-45 North before strangling her in a January incident. Perez also allegedly tampered with Redmond's car in February, causing carbon monoxide poisoning that killed her and two neighbors in a Kinston condominium complex.

Daniels, 39, the *Times* reporter, was investigating the college's multi-million dollar military contracting empire. Redmond, 45, the college official, had questioned whether the college was skimping on programs for its Kinston-based students to pursue lucrative contracts with the military, according to court papers.

William Ward, 60, vice-president of Middle Texas, was charged and jailed on two counts of conspiracy detailed in the 58-page indictment. Edward Gonzales, 48, the college's president, and Daniel Riggins, 48, a former CIA officer who lives in San Antonio, have also been charged. Riggins and Gonzales, longtime friends of Marr, ran his gubernatorial campaign. They are believed to be fugitives.

The federal papers allege that Gonzales, Riggins and Ward plotted to sell marijuana to soldiers and sailors through the college's worldwide network of contracts for at least two years. Texas Rangers investigators allege that contract employees, posing as "enrollment assistants," sold thousands of pounds of marijuana worth millions of dollars to service men and women on military installations in the United States and abroad.

The marijuana was allegedly supplied through Mexican drug kingpin Manny Lopez, who operates a major marijuana ring out of Matamoros, according to the indictment. Lopez allegedly became involved in the plot after Gonzales married his daughter Cecilia more than two years ago.

The indictment alleges that the trio hired Perez to kill Daniels and Redmond after deciding both posed a threat to the conspiracy. Financial records indicated that Perez was paid through a secret Rio Grande Valley bank account.

Texas Ranger Captain Randy Spencer said his agency began investigating the college and its contracts in the wake of the death of Daniels three months ago. The Rangers routinely monitor the activities of the secessionist movement for threats of violence after a 1997 incident in which members of the Republic of Texas took hostages in West Texas.

He credited Ranger Mark Ingram for breakthroughs in the investigation. Ingram, 45, of Austin, was seriously injured Sunday in a Houston knife attack by Perez. Perez, Spencer said, was posing as a witness to the death of Daniels.

Ingram, accompanied by this *Houston Times* reporter, went to interview Perez in an apartment on Houston's East Side. The Marfa woman stabbed him in the chest, but did not injure the reporter. Ingram is recovering at Ben Taub Hospital. Perez is jailed without bond in a federal facility in San Antonio. A bond hearing is scheduled Tuesday in U.S. District Court in Houston.

After the indictments of its two top officials, the board of Middle Texas College appointed Ben Weatherby, who chairs the English Department, as interim chancellor. The board will conduct a nationwide search for new leaders.

"These shocking events have saddened faculty, staff and students at the college," Weatherby said today. "We will work together to try to restore the reputation and an atmosphere that promotes excellent teaching at Middle Texas College."

Further details were expected today at a press conference scheduled in Austin.

CHAPTER 48

Annie was banging out her third story of the day for the *Times'* website when Greg walked up to her desk smiling.

In her rumpled jeans with no makeup and her hair pulled into a dank ponytail, she felt almost as messy as her cluttered desk. She had worked almost nonstop in the two days since she had gotten the scoop on the federal indictment. She had written four page-one stories for the paper, ten stories for the website and had helped direct three other reporters working on related stories. The contracts scandal at Middle Texas College with its murder-for-hire plot and the implosion of Tom Marr's secessionist campaign was the biggest story the *Times* had broken for years. As the reporter who owned the story, Annie had come to work at 7 a.m. and hadn't left before midnight the last three days in a row.

Still, she smiled happily. "What's going on, boss? You need me to write another ten stories?"

"You're really tired, aren't you?" Greg said.

"Yeah, but I'll be fine. This is the most exciting week of my life."

"Well, I'm adding yet another layer of excitement. How would you like to be on WUHT-TV tonight?"

"For what?"

"Our TV news partner wants to do an hour-long special on the scandal. The centerpiece would be Jeb Taylor Cook interviewing you."

"Jeb Taylor Cook? I'm surprised he'd waste his precious time interviewing a lowly newspaper reporter."

"Au contraire. The dean of Houston's investigative reporters apparently can't wait to meet you."

"Well, I don't mind doing it, but I look like something my cat dragged in. What time is the interview?"

"You need to be at the station at 6:30. You're done with your story for tomorrow, right?

"I'll get it to you in 15 minutes. Then I need to run out and find someone to wash and blow out my hair. And figure out something decent to wear. Okay with you?"

"Sure."

Annie scrambled to get to the station on time. She had dressed carefully in a purple blazer, creamy blouse, gray skirt and pearls. She thought she looked fine, but she felt unaccountably nervous. She had appeared on TV before, but usually in a lesser role as one of three panelists talking about some issue of the day. Being interviewed one-on-one was different, especially by the perennially popular, much-feared Jeb Taylor Cook. Cook, in his mid-sixties, acted too confrontational for her taste. As a young reporter, he had become famous for helping to uncover a string of rural brothels not far from Houston. Legend had it that a popular stage play of the 1980s, "The Best Little Whorehouse in Texas," was loosely based on those exploits. Most of Cook's stories bordered on the sensational and Annie thought he showed little empathy with his subjects. What would he do with a serious print reporter?

She tried to sit still while a makeup artist piled on mascara and purple eye shadow. She felt as painted-up as a Saturday-night hooker, but she guessed they had to do that to make sure guests made an impact on the small screen. She heard a knock at the door and Jeb Taylor Cook sauntered in with a wide grin. His thick curly white hair was set off by a cowboy hat and his trademark fringed jacket and bolo tie. He was one of the last of a breed of local reporters who flaunted their Texas roots.

"Hi, Miss Annie," he said, squeezing her hand in a grip that made her wince. "I'm glad to make your acquaintance after hearing so much about you lately."

"It's nice to meet you, Jeb. I've watched you on TV ever since I moved to Texas six years ago. What should I expect tonight?"

"Just tell your story, girl. Let me do the heavy lifting. It'll be a cinch."

"Okay. Want to go over anything before the show starts?"

"We don't have time, dear. We go on in 20 minutes. I've got to get to makeup now!"

Annie felt annoyed at his quick exit. She didn't trust him entirely and she hated ad-libbing.

Soon she was sitting next to Cook on a sofa in the TV studio. A film giving background on the college and the secessionist movement played as the producer counted down from ten to one. They were on the air.

"And here she is, the reporter who broke the case – Annie Price." With the camera and hot lights pointed at her on the sofa, she felt uncomfortable, but tried to smile and remember to keep her legs crossed at the ankle.

"Annie, I hear that there's a big new development in the case."

"That's right. We just broke a story on our website that the men who ran Tom Marr's campaign planned at least three violent attacks along the border."

"Can you tell me anything about the attacks?"

"Yeah, the Rangers believe they include three incidents that got statewide publicity – armed robberies of elderly churchgoers in Laredo, shootings at a school bus stop in Brownsville and the wounding of a tourist rafting along the Rio Grande in Big Bend National Park."

"Oh yeah, I remember those incidents. What were they trying to accomplish?"

"They wanted to make Texans so afraid of border violence that they would welcome stricter border controls. The secessionists were sending employees from their own security company to the border to stir up problems."

"Wow. Will there be more indictments?"

"That's what we're hearing."

"How did you get involved in this story?"

"Jeb, you probably know that Maddy Daniels started working on it months ago. She was a great reporter and a close friend. When she died, The *Times* asked me to pick up her work."

"Did you originally suspect murder in the car crash that killed her?"

"Not at first. But I talked with Mark Ingram, the Texas Ranger who was investigating the secessionist movement. He felt there were things that didn't add up and I agreed."

"Did you know the alleged second murder victim?"

"Yeah, I had interviewed Margaret Redmond at Middle Texas College. Soon after, she and another employee asked me for a secret meeting to talk about the contracts business."

"Did they know the contracts were allegedly being used to sell marijuana to thousands of military personnel?"

"No, they suspected something was wrong, but they didn't know what. They only knew that the contracts were making big money, but the Kinston campus never saw a dime."

"Redmond died in a carbon monoxide poisoning accident. What did you make of it at the time?"

"I couldn't help thinking that her death wasn't accidental. But I didn't know anything about Alicia Perez, the woman charged in the case."

"You and Perez had a physical confrontation after she allegedly stabbed Mark Ingram at the East Side apartment. What was that like?"

"I can't say much because I'll be testifying in the court case against her. But I was lucky to escape unharmed."

"Were you afraid?"

"I didn't have time to be afraid. But it's pretty scary being in a fight with a violent person and it's hard to stop thinking about it."

Annie parried other questions from Cook for about 15 minutes, beginning to relax. This was easier than she had feared it would be. Then he began a new line of questioning she sensed might lead into more difficult territory.

"You wrote the first story and the first profile of Tom Marr in which he revealed he was a secessionist. What did you think of his belief that Texas should become a republic?"

"Obviously as a reporter, I thought it was an important story. I didn't know enough about it to have an opinion."

"What do you think now?"

"It doesn't really matter what I think. It matters what millions of Texans think. But it's a flawed idea."

"In what way?"

"The United States isn't a perfect union. We'll always have problems and big regional differences. But I think Texas would seriously harm the rest of the country if it tried to go it alone."

"You're not a native Texan. Many who are don't agree with you at all. Why should the rest of the states bring down Texas?"

"I don't see it that way, Jeb. I love Texas and I love being a Texan, but not at the expense of our country."

"Just a few more questions. My sources tell me that you became personally involved with Tom Marr, that you were lovers. How can you defend becoming involved with him?"

"I wasn't Tom Marr's lover, but I was his friend, and a friend of his daughter, Betsy. He's a good man and a good dad."

"Don't you feel responsible for bringing down a good man and his attempt to unite Texans to fight for our independence?"

"I just report the news. Whatever happens to Tom Marr is because of his decision to surround himself with people who allegedly were breaking the law."

"Does it bother you that many Texans will hate you for ruining their hope for a republic?"

"As you know, Jeb, you don't become a journalist to be loved. If people in Texas want a republic, they can fight for it honorably. Using drug money and murder to achieve your goal isn't acceptable."

She felt like dissolving into tears, but held her head high and looked at him steadily. She could see him sag a bit as he failed to rattle her with his ambush.

"Should Tom Marr go to jail for campaign violations, or worse?"

"It's not my job to mete out justice. Whatever Tom Marr has or hasn't done, the courts will have to decide."

"Thanks, Annie. And that ends this portion of our special. Stay tuned to WUHT after the break."

The camera lights went out, the show's theme music began playing and Jeb reached over to shake her hand.

"Great job, Annie. Good TV for both of us."

She was flushed with anger that she didn't try to hide. "Well, I didn't appreciate the cheap shots you were taking about my private life. You were trying your best to embarrass me."

"Annie, you're being too sensitive. You're pretty and intelligent and you've got to admit, I've given you great exposure. Your career will probably really take off now."

"I doubt that, just as I doubt that I'd ever come on your show again."

"Do you think I care? Reporters like you are a dime a dozen – they line up to be interviewed by me."

"Fine. Have at it." she said. "But you're a complete jerk."

She walked into the women's dressing room, where Rina Hinojosa, one of the station's reporters and a good friend, was waiting for her. Rina possessed a sultry, dark-haired attractiveness and bright intelligence, but her slight suggestion of a weight problem doomed her to reporting cops and court stories instead of getting the anchor's chair she coveted. She had bemoaned the station's unwritten but restrictive standards many times to Annie.

"Girl, you were great," Rina said. "You stood up against Jeb's bullying instead of rolling over, the way some of his interview subjects do."

"I didn't expect his pointed questions about Marr. And he sure sounded partial to the secessionists."

"I wouldn't be surprised. You know his shtick is being the biggest, baddest Texan in the state. I hope the blowhard will retire before too long."

"Yeah, I hate his ambush-style journalism, but it's over and not worth stewing about. What're you doing this week?"

"That's what I wanted to talk to you about. You know that Alicia Perez will be brought back to Houston in a couple of days?"

"Yeah, I'm trying to plan our coverage."

"Since the *Times* is our news partner, you could come with us to

San Antonio in the TV van. We'd be there when the deputies bring her out and follow them all the way to the federal courthouse in Houston."

"That sounds like a great idea. Let me talk to my editor about it."

"Good, Annie. Call me tomorrow."

CHAPTER 49

Annie called Captain Randy Spencer, hoping for some fresh information on Alicia Perez. Spencer, the Texas Ranger who was Mark's boss and her surprise rescuer from Rob Ryland, had become her best source on the case.

"Hey, Annie Girl. What can I do for you?"

"Hi, Randy. I wanted to pick your brain about Alicia Perez."

"Sure, but you know it'll have to be off the record for now."

"I understand. That's fine with me. You talked to her after she was arrested, right?

"Yeah, and I must say it was one of the spookiest interrogations I've ever done."

"In what way?"

"She came into the San Antonio jail as cool as a cucumber. She'd been riding all night in custody, but she didn't look ruffled or troubled. She waived her right to a lawyer and agreed we could question her."

"Yeah? What happened?"

"She calmly admitted to the murder of Maddy Daniels and seemed proud of her work. She gave us details about stalking her, getting into Daniels' car after running her off the road and strangling her."

"Okay, let's move on. I can't think about that right now."

"I know she was your good friend, girlie. Sorry. Perez acted different about Margaret Redmond. Kept talking about how nice Redmond was and how sorry she was to kill such a beautiful woman. I know this is hard to believe, but I think there may have been some, uh, lesbian activity before she killed Redmond. Of course, that's a theory that I wouldn't want to get into print."

"You know I agreed that all of this is off the record. Poor Margaret."

"Well, that's about the size of it. She seemed to be glad to talk about those two killings, almost as a relief, but wouldn't say anything about Dan Riggins or her life in Texas and Peru, before that."

"Do you think she's sane enough to be tried?"

"I've been thinking about that. It's obvious that she's very different than most human beings I've encountered. She says things straight out that a normal person wouldn't. But I don't think she's insane – I think she's probably, what a shrink might say, damaged in some key way."

"That's very interesting, Randy. Do you think there'll be a focus on her mental health?"

"I imagine she'll see a few psychiatrists before she gets to trial. Both sides will probably insist on it."

"Anything else that struck you about her?"

"Well, I thought she seemed fearless and not at all worried about the future. It was as though being arrested wasn't real to her. She didn't care what was coming, because she wouldn't be part of it. That led us to ask for a suicide watch."

"That was probably the right thing. I'm going to San Antonio tonight with a reporter from WUHT-TV. We'll be there when Perez leaves the jail tomorrow to be transferred to Houston."

"Are you going with that horse's ass, Jeb Taylor Cook? I saw part of your interview with him on CNN last night. We all thought that guy acted like a jerk and you behaved like a lady and a professional, Annie."

"Thanks. That means a lot. No, I'm traveling with Rina Hinojosa and our photographers. Do you know what time the deputies will leave from the San Antonio Jail?"

"Well, this didn't come from me, but 4 a.m. is the time we've been told. One of our young guys, Frank Bonner, is going to ride along. I'll tell him to be nice to you."

"I'd appreciate it, Randy. See you soon."

"Take care of yourself, girl."

Annie hung up her office phone, just in time to pick up a call from her cell phone. She saw that it was Jake.

"Hi there."

"Hey, Annie. I saw your interview with Jeb Taylor Cook on CNN. You did great, but it left me worrying about your feelings for Tom Marr."

"Jake, I'm at work right now. I don't want to argue about Marr again."

"Me neither. But if you're going to carry a torch for him, where does that leave me?"

"You know I love you. Now that your divorce is finally getting off the ground, things can be good for us. But I developed feelings for Tom and Betsy, too. You can't expect me to forget them overnight."

"Okay, but if you're going to be with me, you need to let them go."

"Are you going to get all jealous again?"

"If I need to, but I don't want to replay that bad scene at the ranch."

"I promise you, Jake, I don't intend to see Tom Marr again."

"Okay, honey. It won't be long before the legislature is done and we can make up for lost time."

"That sounds good to me. I'll talk to you after I get back from San Antonio."

CHAPTER 50

Annie and Rina waited outside the Bexar County Jail in downtown San Antonio in the early morning darkness. With them were Bill Langan, Annie's favorite photographer at the *Times*, and Bob Downing, a KUHT-TV cameraman. Downing would drive the station's news van to Houston, following a jail van that would transport the jail's number one high-profile prisoner, Alicia Perez.

The four had gotten to San Antonio the night before and headed to the River Walk. They walked around to stretch their legs, stopped for a quick Tex-Mex dinner and checked into nearby hotel rooms for a short night's sleep.

At 4 a.m., Frank Bonner, the Texas Ranger mentioned by Randy Spencer, showed up outside the jail where they waited. He would accompany the jail van to Houston in his Rangers' car.

"Glad to meet you," he told Annie and her colleagues. Tall, thin, with close-cropped brown hair and the exuberance of a puppy, Bonner seemed so young. Is he even thirty, she wondered?

"You guys are welcome to drive along Interstate 10 with us, but don't get too close, for security reasons," he said.

Just then, a white van backed out of the jail parking area and two deputies led Alicia Perez out of the jail's back entrance. She wore the customary orange jumpsuit and her long dark hair was pulled back into a ponytail. She was handcuffed and her ankles were chained above her flip-flops.

She apparently recognized Annie, and stared at her in a way Annie found hard to interpret. Part anger and part curiosity, she decided. Langan quickly snapped photos and Downing shot film. Perez was placed in the back of the white van and the two deputies, a young man and a middle-aged woman, got inside the front. Annie and her colleagues raced to the news van. They followed Bonner's car and the white van onto the freeway, staying as close as they could without tailgating.

"Wow, I'm glad that went okay," Annie said to Langan. "Did you get some decent shots?"

"Yeah, but since it's still dark, they probably won't be as good as the ones we'll get when we get to Houston," he said.

Annie was glad that they had beaten the rest of the media scrum out of San Antonio. The local media probably expected a departure at 7 or 8 since the hearing was scheduled for 1 p.m. at the Bob Casey Courthouse in Houston.

The trip from San Antonio to Houston would take four hours along Interstate 10, a mostly flat, well-traveled road that stretched from Jacksonville, Florida in the east to Santa Monica, California in the west. Annie had driven the Houston to San Antonio stretch many times on weekend getaways. She loved the River Walk and the Hispanic cultural vibe of San Antonio.

"How's Mark Ingram, your cute Texas Ranger friend?" Rina asked.

"Much better," Annie smiled. "He'll probably be released from the hospital this week to recuperate in the Hill Country."

"Is he single?"

"Yeah, but he was madly in love with Maddy Daniels," Annie said. "I'm not sure he's ready to date again."

"Well, could you keep me posted?" Rina asked. "I could use a good man in my life. How's your love life, by the way?"

"I'm dating Jake Satterfield, the state senator from Kerrville, but it's kind of early. He's going through a divorce, so we'll see."

"Wow, another handsome, smart guy," Rina said. "You're a lucky girl."

Annie realized it was the first time she'd told anyone other than Maddy about Jake. Now that his divorce was moving along and she felt more secure about him, she could mention their relationship. It felt strange – but good – to say they were seeing each other.

The van became quiet and Annie fell asleep for a while. It had been such a hard week and she still was working long hours. She woke abruptly to the sound of shouting.

"Oh my God. What's going on?" Bob Downing said.

She sat up abruptly and looked out the van's front window. Her field of vision was limited, since she and Langan were sitting in the back. Downing was driving and Rina was in the passenger seat. She could make out, hundreds of yards ahead, the white van and the Texas Rangers car stopped on the right highway shoulder.

The two law-enforcement vehicles appeared to be boxed in by two black armored vans parked in front of them and two others behind them.

"Pull over, Bob," Rina screamed. "Something bad is happening. Stay back."

Downing slowed and coasted carefully to the shoulder, still far behind the stopped vehicles. He stopped the news van quietly.

Annie watched in horror as more than a dozen uniformed men jumped out of the sides of the black vans, carrying what looked like submachine guns. Two men opened the back of the sheriff's van and one picked up and ran with a woman she guessed must be Alicia. She could see the man heading with Alicia to the first black van on the shoulder.

"They're firing on the deputies and Frank Bonner," she shouted. "Everyone duck. They'll be shooting as us next."

Everyone tried to stay down, but they took turns sneaking looks at the action ahead. She could feel the thumping of her heart and the acid in her stomach. Were they going to die on the side of the road? She heard several shots fired in their direction. One hit their windshield and she heard Rina scream. She closed her eyes to pray.

Suddenly, she heard what sounded like one of the vans streaking up the freeway, followed quickly by two others. The shooting had stopped. The black vans had gotten away.

She inched up in her seat along with Rina and the two men. She could see several bodies sprawled along the shoulder.

"Jesus Christ," Rina said. "I think the Texas Ranger and the two deputies are dead."

CHAPTER 51

Alicia Perez sat stiffly in the back of the sheriff's van, her legs shackled and her hands cuffed behind her. The van stank of prisoners' sweat and the bad coffee the two deputies were swilling like pigs from a big thermos. Alicia didn't want their disgusting gringo coffee, but she resented them for enjoying it while she tried to find a comfortable position on the hard, worn-down back seat.

How did she end up in such a horrible place? Why did she have to listen to the fat senora in her too-tight blue uniform in the front of the van, talking, talking, talking to her skinny deputy partner who drove down the long highway at the pace of a snail. For two long days and nights, she had been locked up like an animal, reminding her of the bad times in Peru. She had been taken captive before, but she hadn't blamed herself until now for her troubles. When the police had rushed into her little yellow house and took her away to San Antonio, she had known it was her fault. She had left her purse in that Houston apartment and they had tracked her down easily. She should have run quickly with Dan. She was losing her touch, her skill and her luck that had made her an assassin to be reckoned with.

Inside the jail, the television had blared at all hours and the women on the cellblock had heightened the noise with cursing and yelling. Her head had throbbed like thunder in her brain, making it hard for her to think about her next move. When she could focus, she couldn't see a way out.

What would happen to her? After a while, she looked out the window to her left and saw, to her surprise, two black vans moving quickly and passing the ugly jail van. She thought she recognized those vans, the soldiers in fatigues inside. Were they men she had trained? Hope coursed through her veins like fresh blood, but she was careful to sit quietly.

Two more vans were approaching, and she knew without a doubt they were staging her rescue, just as she had taught them. How could she have doubted Dan Riggins, her man, her savior? Now there were four black vans, forcing the skinny deputy to pull over to the right shoulder and stop. She could hear the alarm in the raised voices from the front seat.

She was elated. Her soldiers tore out of the black vans and rushed to the shoulder of the road with guns. She ducked down in the back seat as they shot out the windshield and killed the senora and deputy. Her brave men forced open the doors and the dead gringos fell out like trash spilling from a garbage can. They scooped her up from the back seat, carried her tenderly out of the ugly van and deposited her gently in the black van that awaited her arrival. The driver sped away from the bloody scene and she knew she was safe, and saved.

CHAPTER 52

A week later, Greg hosted a Saturday party at his Galveston beach house to celebrate Annie's permanent assignment to the *Times* investigative team.

"You guys are the best," said Annie, as newsroom friends toasted her promotion with champagne and Shiner beers. Cilla Gage, her former editor, cheered with the group of about 20 newsroom friends gathered on the deck. A special guest, Jake Satterfield, raised his glass of champagne. Annie sipped a Diet Coke.

She was determined – for a few hours, at least – not to think about the shootings a week earlier on the freeway that had resulted in a statewide manhunt. Three shooters had been arrested and the state had launched multiple investigations.

Other developments kept dribbling out. The desiccated body of Dr. Gonzales had been found in the Mexican desert, a probable suicide. His former colleague, Will Ward, was rumored to be working with his lawyer on a plea deal.

Annie suspected that Alicia Perez and Dan Riggins were tucked away safely inside Central America or Mexico. His CIA training and their contacts would keep them hidden for as long as necessary, she thought.

She didn't know what made her look at her cell phone, but she noticed that someone had texted her. She read it and showed it quietly to Greg, then Jake. She put a finger to her lips and they nodded. They'd deal with it after the party ended. The message was halfway between a promise and a threat.

"We'll be back. Texas will be a republic. Soon. Riggins."

ACKNOWLEDGEMENTS

Stand-off in Texas (Mike Cox, Eakin Press, 1998) for its comprehensive account of the 1997 Republic of Texas stand-off in Jeff Davis County, Texas.

With great respect and deep appreciation:

For the support of my siblings:

Diane Hall, Melinda Poe, Steve Stancill and Jane Stancill and their families.

For the support of my early readers and mentors:

Claudia Feldman, Dannye Romine Powell, Judy Tell, Leslie and Eric Gerber, Jon Buchan and Tony Zeiss.

For the support of special editors and mentors:

Don Mason, Kenneth Ashworth and Ian Graham Leask.

For cover design:

Christine Long

For the support of my husband, Len Norman, and son, Jeffrey Stancill Norman.

CPSIA information can be obtained at www.ICGtesting.com
Printed in the USA
BVOW04s1421250515

401554BV00003B/6/P